"Just try to take Malcolm away from me."

Rebecca said the words low and furiously.

A muscle twitched in Daniel's jaw. "Do you really think I'd do that?"

"I..." She was shaking and had to hide her hands on her lap. "I don't know. I don't know you!"

Now he leaned forward, his eyes vivid with intense emotion. "Then why were you so sure I'd make a lousy father?"

She stared down at the place settings, her heartbeat drumming in her ears. *Stupid. Stupid, stupid, stupid.* They'd gotten past this. She should have kept trying to...to soften him. Not confront him. She'd once heard him icily tell someone on the phone "Don't try to take me on. You'll lose."

I can't *lose.*

Dear Reader,

I was delighted to be asked to celebrate Harlequin's 60th anniversary. Thoughts of anniversaries sent me digging through my files, where I found that I sold my first book to Harlequin exactly twenty-five years ago. I'd already published some books. My first four were coauthored with my mother (no, they weren't sexy romances: that might have been pushing it!). I then wrote a number of young adult novels. But I still vividly remember the thrill when I got the call telling me that the Temptation line wanted my book. I was in a daze. I had sold to Harlequin! I felt like I'd finally made it to the big leagues.

Harlequin Books was and is romance fiction, unmatched by any other publisher, which is why I'm still thrilled to see that logo on my books twenty-five years later.

Harlequin romances have changed in the past sixty years, just as the stories I've written for Harlequin have changed since that first Temptation book. Readers have cheered me on as I grew as a writer, have let me write books that are suspenseful or sweet, sexy or emotionally wrenching, without ever asking me to repeat myself.

It isn't just Harlequin celebrating this anniversary. Nope, I figure that it should be the readers and writers who ought to pop the cork on the champagne. I think of all the amazing Harlequin books I've read, while feeling extraordinarily lucky to have written some that have moved readers. So here I am, lifting my glass to Harlequin, to you, the reader, and to me, too. Happy anniversary!

Janice Kay Johnson

P.S. If you want to write, please do so c/o Harlequin Books, 225 Duncan Mill Road, Don Mills, ON M3B 3K9, Canada.

A Mother's Secret
Janice Kay Johnson

HARLEQUIN®

TORONTO • NEW YORK • LONDON
AMSTERDAM • PARIS • SYDNEY • HAMBURG
STOCKHOLM • ATHENS • TOKYO • MILAN • MADRID
PRAGUE • WARSAW • BUDAPEST • AUCKLAND

Recycling programs
for this product may
not exist in your area.

ISBN-13: 978-0-373-71602-9

A MOTHER'S SECRET

Copyright © 2009 by Janice Kay Johnson.

This edition published by arrangement with Harlequin Books S.A.

® and TM are trademarks of the publisher. Trademarks indicated with
® are registered in the United States Patent and Trademark Office, the
Canadian Trade Marks Office and in other countries.

www.eHarlequin.com

Printed in U.S.A.

ABOUT THE AUTHOR

The author of more than sixty books for children and adults, Janice Kay Johnson writes Harlequin Superromance novels about love and family—about the way generations connect and the power our earliest experiences have on us throughout life. Her 2007 novel, *Snowbound,* won a RITA® Award from Romance Writers of America for Best Contemporary Series Romance. A former librarian, Janice raised two daughters in a small, rural town north of Seattle, Washington. She loves to read and is an active volunteer and board member for Purrfect Pals, a no-kill cat shelter.

Books by Janice Kay Johnson

The Diamond Legacy Family Tree

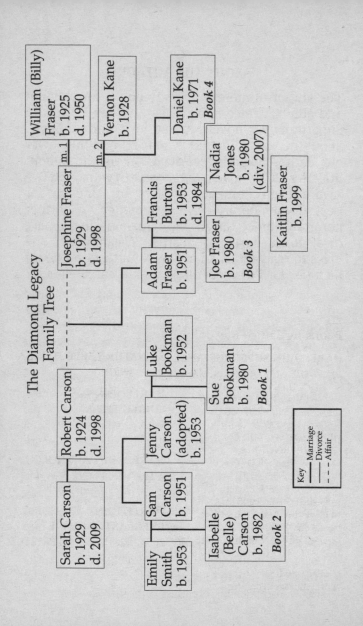

CHAPTER ONE

DANIEL KANE WAS GOING TO BE very, very glad when Christmas was over and done with for another year.

Gazing out the restaurant window at a spectacular view of rocky beach and Pacific Ocean, he sat sipping his coffee, digesting the damn good pan-roasted filet of halibut he'd just had for lunch and congratulating himself on getting through the permit process and pouring the first foundation in the new development of Craftsman-style homes Kane Construction was building here on the coast half an hour drive south of San Francisco.

He was also listening to Christmas carols. More annoying yet, they didn't sound like the Christmas carols the radio played when he was a kid and actually got excited about the season. These were rock versions of old standards, as well as new, not-so-catchy carols.

Hearing himself, he gave a grunt of amusement. He was thirty-eight years old, and thinking like a crotchety old man. *Tune the music out,* he told himself. Just because he wasn't a fan of the season was no reason to turn into Scrooge.

Losing his brother, though, mere weeks ago, did make it harder than usual to tolerate the excessive good spirits.

He swore under his breath. Damn it, he wouldn't let

himself feel blue. Today was about a beginning, one he had every reason to be pleased about.

More than most of his subdivisions, this one was a major victory. After more delays than he wanted to count, he'd lost financial backing and had to tap into his own investments for Cabrillo Heights. He'd believed from the beginning that it would pay off, but it was a bigger relief than he wanted to admit to actually see the houses start to rise.

The timing had stunk for his money to be so tight. His brother, Adam, twenty years older than he was, had spent at least a month in rehab this fall, in between his second and third strokes. The bills had to have been horrendous. Adam's son, Joe, had somehow taken care of them, but how?

Guilt assailed Daniel. *Damn it, I should have asked.*

Well, it wasn't too late to make amends. Once this development started paying off, he'd find out from Joe how much in the hole he'd had to go.

The foundations for not just the first house, but the first three, had been poured today. He had come down to watch even though he didn't have to be here. In his mind, Daniel was attending the birth of a major project. He expected these cottage-size houses to sell as quickly as they went up. New trends were for smaller homes, fine craftsmanship and green-built standards, all embodied in Cabrillo Heights, perched atop a hill with sweeping views of the marina, breakwater and the Pacific Ocean beyond.

Despite the ever-present undercurrent of grief for his brother, today, he had decided, was for celebrating. He'd been told the Moss Beach Distillery, built originally in the 1920s as a speakeasy, was the place to go. The restaurant clung to a cliff above the ocean. The best seats were on the patio, but the breeze held enough winter chill he had chosen to stay inside.

Mood restored, he took one last swallow of coffee, signed the credit-card slip and stood to leave.

As he strode through the room on his way out, already thinking about his afternoon, he glanced out the window at the patio. For some reason his eye was caught by two women and a kid sitting at a table, blankets wrapped around their shoulders. The Distillery staff provided the blankets if a diner got chilly, the hostess had told him earlier when offering to seat him outside. Huddling under a blanket hadn't appealed to him.

He dismissed the curly-haired redhead and the kid immediately. But something about the other woman, with sleek, mink-brown hair, reminded him of a former lover. The tilt of her head as she listened to the boy was familiar; even more so was the way she lifted her heavy fall of hair to push it back over her shoulder.

He was right by the doorway to the patio. His feet had already stopped moving when she turned, laughing, and looked right at him.

Her laugh died and they stared at each other. Rebecca Ballard. It really was her. He felt shock and a glint of excitement.

They'd seen each other for quite a while a few years back. She'd gotten to him more than most women did. Or maybe he couldn't forget her because she'd walked away so readily. He was the one to cool the relationship, just to make sure she realized a meeting at the altar wasn't in the forecast, but instead of clinging or getting angry, she'd seemingly shrugged and vanished from his life.

Yeah, that had bugged him. Sure, he'd planned to end

whatever they had going on so she didn't start having dreams he'd have to shatter. But it might have been nice if Rebecca had seemed regretful at parting ways.

Daniel had thought more than a few times about calling her. Her compassion and quick mind had intrigued him and made her good company. And physically, he'd never felt as if he could get enough of her.

But there was also a reason he'd put the brakes on their relationship, so Daniel had talked himself out of picking up the phone every time the impulse seized him. He was glad now he had, given the way she was staring at him as if he were the ghost that was reputed to inhabit the old speakeasy.

She said something to the other woman and stood, crossing the patio to him. In jeans, purple sneakers and a form-fitting tee, she was as slim and graceful as ever. A dancer when she was young, Rebecca had dreamed of a career in ballet until she grew too tall. The training had stuck, though. She *looked* like a ballerina, her carriage erect, every movement graceful, seeming to float instead of walk.

She studied him with wary eyes. "Daniel."

"Rebecca. I'm surprised to see you here."

"This isn't your territory, either."

"Now it is. I'm putting in a development in El Granada. The streets are in and we poured the first foundations today."

"Oh." She cast a glance over her shoulder, then said, "Are you arriving or leaving?"

"I've eaten."

An expression that might have been relief flickered over her face. She hadn't wanted to invite him to join her and her friend. "Why don't I walk you out?"

He raised his brows. "Fine."

They walked in silence until they were outside in the parking lot, surrounded by wind-shaped Monterey pines. The breeze carried the salty scent of the ocean. Ignoring a car backing out of a slot, she said, "How are you?"

"Good. You?"

"Fine."

How stilted could a conversation get? Why hadn't she just nodded in acknowledgment and turned back to her friend and the friend's kid?

"Business is booming."

"I'm glad to hear that." She paused. "I'm teaching these days."

"Really?" He vaguely recalled that she'd mentioned having a teaching certificate, but she had been with the Chamber of Commerce then, and had a real knack for marketing the city of San Rafael. She had a gift for reading people, knowing what they really wanted no matter what they said, and articulating those wants in the marketing materials. She knew when to talk, when to shut up. Maybe, he thought, those were gifts useful for a teacher, too.

Presumably anxious to get back to her friend, she stole another look over her shoulder. "Well, I won't keep you. I'm glad to have run into you, Daniel."

"I've thought about you," he admitted. "I almost called you a couple of times."

More like a dozen times, but he wasn't about to tell her that.

Her eyes widened. "That's flattering, but I don't think—"

"I'm getting real hungry," a young voice said from behind her. "When are you coming back?"

Eyebrows raised, Daniel looked past her to the young boy standing in the doorway, the other woman just behind him, flustered enough to make it obvious she'd had to hustle to catch up. What had she been doing—staring at the ocean while her son was making a getaway?

The boy gazed at him with blatant curiosity, ignoring the redheaded woman who'd captured his hand. His hair was a deep auburn close in color to Daniel's.

Rebecca had spun to face the kid, the flash of her eyes seeming alarmed. "I'll be back in in a minute, honey. Why don't you go sit down? You two can order, if you want."

The other woman was tugging the boy back toward the door. "We'll do that. Fish and chips for you? No rush."

The boy, maybe four or five years old, smiled beguilingly at Rebecca. He seemed to know her well. "Okay. But hurry. 'Cuz we're hungry. Aren't we, Aunt Nomi?"

Aunt? He'd assumed the woman was the boy's mother.

"We'll survive for a few minutes while—" she gave a little cough "—Rebecca talks to her friend." She steered him back inside, mouthing, "I'm sorry" over her shoulder.

Not until the boy and Rebecca's friend disappeared inside did Daniel look back at her. "You were saying you didn't think…?"

She stared at him so blankly, he could tell she didn't remember what they'd been talking about. "Think?"

Her face was dominated by her beautiful eyes, a warm brown flecked with yellow that seemed to brighten to gold when she was happy or excited. Her eyes had danced with gold when they made love. They were not dancing today.

His jaw muscles tightened. "Never mind. It was an idle thought, that's all."

"I…it really was good to see you, Daniel."

She was aching to get away from him, he could tell, stealing longing looks at the restaurant door. She might be cold. She was hugging herself. Or, hell, perhaps he was a walk down memory lane she'd rather not take.

"Glad things are going well for you." He nodded. "Maybe we'll run into each other again."

She gave him a tremulous smile. Were those tears shimmering in her eyes? But she said only, "Goodbye, Daniel," and hurried back into the restaurant.

He watched as the door swung closed behind her. At last he made himself walk to his pickup, get in and put the key in the ignition. Then he sat there, fighting the desire to follow her in and say, "I missed you. Please have dinner with me."

She had made her uninterest plain. More than that— she hadn't been happy to see him, whatever she had said to the contrary.

Live with it.

At last he made himself start the engine, back out and drive away.

REBECCA CLUNG TO THE BACK of her upholstered chair as if she'd be swept away should she let go. "Oh, God, Naomi," she pleaded. "What am I going to do?"

Her friend gazed at her in bemusement. "Why are you still in a panic? You dodged the bullet today. He must have thought Malcolm was mine. Why would it occur to him to wonder otherwise?"

"Gee, because Malcolm's the spitting image of Daniel at that age? I saw the photo album his mother put together. I can't believe he didn't know the minute he saw Mal!"

Her friend came around the chair and gave her a hug.

"We see what we expect to see. The guy wasn't interested in some kid who happened to be around. Now, if *I* hadn't been there…"

Rebecca whimpered.

"Yeah, that could have been bad," Naomi agreed. "But it didn't happen. And what are the odds you'll run into him again?"

Despite her near hysteria, she remained conscious that she had to keep her voice low. Malcolm was in his bedroom just down the hall.

"With him in the area half the week?"

"So don't eat out." Naomi was ever-practical. "Daniel won't be visiting the elementary school, or the preschool. In fact, why would he come to Half Moon Bay at all?"

"To check out the restaurants or the golf courses? Talk to real estate agents?"

"Stay close to home…"

"Naomi, he talked about calling me. He said he's thought about it a few times. I think he would have asked me out today if Malcolm hadn't interrupted."

Her friend stared at her. "What do you mean, *would have?* You stayed out there with him after we went in!"

"He…dropped it. He could probably tell I was horrified at the idea, even though he didn't know why. But what if he does decide to call? Now that he knows I live around here, all he has to do is phone information."

"Change your number to unlisted."

"It's in phone books!"

"Say no if he calls."

"But he could show up…" She closed her eyes, combating the swell of fear. "I should move. Just pack up. Today! No, I should have left the state in the first place. Why didn't I move to Arkansas or Maine?" she moaned. "Why did I stay so close to San Francisco?"

"Why did you?" her friend asked.

"Because it's home." Stupid, stupid. "It feels so remote here, so small town. He's never done any building in San Mateo County. He liked Sausolito, the East Bay. And what were the odds if he did happen to drive down here to play golf or something that we'd run into him?"

Plus, it hadn't occurred to her, even after Malcolm was born with his father's coloring, that he would end up looking so much like Daniel. She'd been increasingly worried as Mal grew into a toddler and the resemblance became more obvious.

The awful thing was, she couldn't wish for a single thing about her son to be any different than it was.

She took a deep breath. Of course she couldn't throw everything in the car and flee. She had a job, a classroom of kids expecting her to show up Monday morning. Without a recommendation from the Cabrillo Unified School District, she'd never work as a teacher again.

And, darn it, she'd made a good life for herself and her son right here. They had friends, a home. Naomi was right. *I'm overreacting.*

Daniel *had* seen Malcolm and not suspected. She wasn't likely to encounter him again by chance; with a four-year-old, she ate at McDonald's more often than she did an upscale place like the Moss Beach Distillery. She hung out at playgrounds.

Rebecca couldn't imagine Daniel Kane running to make a merry-go-round twirl. And fast food was definitely not his style.

She let out a long breath. "Okay. I'm over it. You're

right. I did dodge the bullet. The worst has happened, and I got lucky."

"I'm not even sure it was luck," Naomi said. "I meant it. People see what they expect to see. That's all he did. Although if Mal had said Mommy…"

Another whimper escaped Rebecca.

Naomi scrunched up her face in apology. "*I* almost said 'your mother.' Did you notice?"

"Are you kidding? I thought my knees were going to give out!"

Her friend was the first to giggle. She clapped a hand over her mouth. "I'm sorry! It's just… You should have seen your expression!"

Just like that, they were both laughing so hard, their eyes were watering. Malcolm came out to see why, and Rebecca couldn't stop long enough to reassure him.

Okay, so she was hysterical. But she thought she had a darned good excuse.

Later, after Naomi had gone and Malcolm was placated enough to go back to his plastic action figures, Rebecca made herself remember the moment she'd first met Daniel Kane's eyes.

Why, oh, why, had she felt a spurt of such pleasure when she saw him, despite everything? Why had she wanted him to smile at her, to say, "I've missed you"? Why had her heart nearly stopped when he told her he'd thought about her, that he had almost called?

Because she was an idiot, that's why. Because she was in love with him the entire time she'd dated him, and had somehow failed in the intervening years to fall *out* of love with him.

How could she, Rebecca thought wretchedly, when she

saw so much of him in Malcolm, the person she loved most in the world? How could she forget Daniel, when she was forced to think of him with guilt and gratitude and fear every single day?

How she wished she hadn't turned her head today just at the moment Daniel was glancing out at the patio. If she hadn't seen him, the pain of losing him wouldn't feel raw again. And she wouldn't have to agonize yet again over whether, in not telling him he had a son, she'd done something terrible.

DANIEL COULDN'T HELP HIMSELF. He kept replaying the whole scene, looking for clues he might have missed. What he didn't understand was why he'd become obsessed. Rebecca had severed their relationship five years ago with no apparent regrets, and clearly she hadn't felt any since. *Let it go,* he told himself, and had to keep repeating it every time he caught himself trying to remember exactly what she'd said.

Maybe it was an ego thing. He didn't like admitting she just plain wasn't interested.

Yeah, but he met women all the time who weren't interested. He didn't expect to be irresistible to every woman who caught his eye. So why was he so bugged by Rebecca Ballard's reaction to him?

Because he had missed her. Whether he liked it or not, she had wounded more than his pride.

He was in his office, looking at his computer monitor where cost projections for the Cabrillo Heights subdivision were laid out on a spreadsheet. Daniel couldn't make himself concentrate on them. His mind kept doubling back to that first sight of Rebecca, laughing.

He sat back in his chair and quit bothering to pretend he was scrutinizing the damn spreadsheet.

It was that first moment, he thought, when she recognized him midlaugh. A moment when something else had bloomed on her face. Pleasure. Awareness. Joy. His eyes narrowed as he remembered. He didn't think he was wrong in believing she had been happy to see him, until…what? A blink of the eye later, she had looked aghast.

From then on, she'd been civil, but the strain was easy to see. She ached for him to depart. All she wanted was to rejoin her friend and the little boy.

Daniel frowned. The friend wasn't anyone she had introduced him to, back when he and Rebecca were damn near living together for over a year. So "Aunt Nomi" was someone she'd met in the past five years. Well, Rebecca had always been good at making friends. Maybe this Nomi was another teacher.

Adults and kids alike had been drawn to Rebecca. It wasn't surprising the boy had seemed so comfortable with her.

Daniel's brows drew together again. More than comfortable, he thought.

I'm getting real hungry. When are you coming back?

Did children talk like that to friends of their parents? He sure as hell wouldn't have, when he was that age.

Forget the kid, he told himself, shaking his head. Figure out why Rebecca had been so shocked to see him. If she was truly indifferent to him, she wouldn't have been so uncomfortable.

Something else was going on. He wished he knew what that was.

HE'D SPENT WORSE Christmas Eves, although Daniel wouldn't have chosen the holiday for his own wedding.

In the unlikely event he ever got married, that was.

But for his nephew, Joe, and the pretty young teacher he'd evidently fallen for, it seemed to work. Joe had decided to propose in a big way, boldly doing so on stage after the Nativity play at the elementary school where Pip taught. Since he'd also flown in Pip's family all the way from New Zealand, it made sense to get married right away, while her family was still here in San Francisco.

They'd likely envisioned a small wedding, but had ended up with a nearly full church. Even though Pip hadn't been in the U.S. that long, she'd made plenty of friends. Between her family and half the staff of the school, she came close to filling her side of the church. Joe had friends and coworkers, too, and family.

Family that neither he nor Daniel had known about not so long ago. Daniel's mother, Josephine Fraser, had died ten years ago, leaving only Daniel himself, his much older brother, Adam, Adam's son, Joe, and Joe's daughter from his first—failed—marriage, Kaitlin. With Adam having died this fall, this Christmas their family group should have been small: Joe, Daniel and cute, ten-year-old Kaitlin.

But, no.

This wasn't the time to think about it.

Joe waited at the altar, a big, dark, often grim man in a tux. Daniel, as best man, stood at his elbow, glad he had an excuse not to be sitting with the half sister and her daughter and assorted others who made up this new family that so entranced Joe.

Joe's little girl, Kaitlin, solemn with a flower circlet on her head, came first, sprinkling rose petals. Her dark hair, usually confined in tiny braids, was a wavy cloud. She looked so cute in a pretty peach-colored dress, Daniel grinned in pride and affection from her first step at the back of the church. Mostly she concentrated on her task, her brown eyes serious, but she smiled as she acknowledged her dad and her beloved uncle Daniel before she found her place in the front pew.

And then came the maid of honor, another school-teacher, and at last Pip, glowing for the man she loved. Her pregnancy wasn't yet obvious, and she was lovely in beaded white satin.

Joe watched her walk down the aisle, an expression on his hard face that was new to Daniel. There was no doubt at all, and something that might have been wonder, in Joe's eyes. Daniel might have felt cynical if Pip hadn't looked as amazed and awed and…soft…when she smiled at this American she'd unexpectedly come to love.

The ceremony was simple, elegant and heartfelt. The kiss was passionate enough to send a stir through the crowd.

In the wake of the bride and groom, Daniel ushered both the maid of honor and Kaitlin out. And after breaking free of the crowd, Kaitlin drove with him to the hall rented for the reception.

"That was perfect," she declared. "Did you see Dad? And Ms. Browne?"

"I saw." Not naturally comfortable with children, Daniel made an exception for Kaitlin. He reached out and squeezed her thin shoulder. "You're happy about this, aren't you?"

"It's perfect!" The ten-year-old gave a shiver of delight. "I knew it would be."

The young were capable of such faith and hope, but Daniel found that, for once, he wanted to believe. Joe deserved a kind of happiness he'd never known.

He and Daniel had been raised more like brothers than uncle and nephew. Joe's father, Adam, was twenty years older than Daniel. They'd been too far apart in age to be close, although Adam had tried, when Daniel was young, to stand in for the father who wasn't very interested in his son.

The reception hall wasn't anything fancy; given how quickly this wedding had been put together, they'd been lucky to find anywhere large enough for the purpose. But white tablecloths, white gardenias, a band already warming up and a buffet table laden with food made the hall plenty festive.

Daniel was glad to be insulated from the new family again, this time by Pip's, sharing the bride and groom's table. They were flying home to New Zealand the day after Christmas, and savoring every moment with her in the meantime.

Pip's father offered the first toast, Daniel the second.

"To my nephew, who is really my brother and my best friend, and to the woman he loves as he's never loved before…" Daniel had trouble finishing. Couldn't remember what he'd meant to say. Joe pulled him into a rough embrace, slopping his champagne. Afterward, he went with what he saw on their faces, even though it was sappy as hell. Holding up his glass, he concluded, "To a lifetime of joy."

Everyone smiled and drank. Pip's mother, he saw, wiped tears from her eyes, and her father looked to be battling them.

The petite dark-haired woman at the next table offered a warm toast to her nephew and the lovely woman who'd joined her life to his.

Daniel drank to that one, too, but he didn't turn his head to meet her gaze.

Incredibly enough, she was his half sister. His brother Adam's full sister. Daniel was still dazed by the revelations that made it so.

His mother had been married twice, first to a World War II war hero who had been killed by a drunk driver shortly after coming home. Adam had always believed he was the result of that brief marriage. Josephine Fraser had remarried nineteen years later. Daniel, born of that marriage, had been barely five when his parents split, and he had virtually no relationship with his father now beyond obligatory Christmas cards.

This past year, Daniel, Adam and Joe had been shocked to learn that Adam's father was actually another soldier named Robert Carson who had fought at William Fraser's side and apparently had felt obligated to take care of his buddy William's widow. This despite the fact that Carson was married.

Daniel couldn't help growling damn near every time he thought about Robert's notion of "taking care" of a woman. What he'd done was make her his mistress, and so quickly Adam had to have been conceived awfully soon after the funeral of his supposed father.

That wasn't the worst of the revelations, though. The part that had shocked Daniel was that the affair had continued. Two years later, Josephine had given birth to another baby, a girl, and given her up so that Robert Carson and his wife, Sarah, could raise her as their own. Adam, just a toddler when his sister was born, hadn't remembered her. It was this sister, Jenny Carson, who had just toasted Joe and his bride.

Daniel could no longer think of his mother without anger. It would seem he'd never really known her, a woman who would give away her own child.

Should he feel lucky that she'd kept him?

Since she'd died ten years back, Robert Carson almost as long ago, and Sarah Carson this past year, this all would have been ancient history except that the younger generations now had to deal with the fallout.

Adam hadn't been able to. Daniel believed to this day that the shock of the revelations had contributed to Adam having that second, deadly stroke.

The Carsons' son, Sam, who'd been raised to think he was their only biological child, wasn't happy. He was particularly pissed to find out his younger, supposedly adopted sister was actually Robert's child by blood, as well as law.

Daniel's half sister, Jenny, had taken the surprises better than most, even though she'd learned that her father had lied to her all her life, letting her think she was adopted when she was actually his. But, hey, she'd grown up in San Francisco during the sixties, so maybe she came by her attitude of peace and love naturally.

What Daniel knew was that she didn't feel like family to him. Neither did her daughter, Sue. Ties of blood didn't mean anything to him.

And he had no relationship at all to Sam Carson, the golden boy who had resented finding out Adam was also a Carson, and older by a few weeks besides. Or to Sam's daughter, Belle.

If not for Joe, Daniel would have shaken his head, been pleasant if any of the Carsons called, and left it at that.

Joe, though, had finally embraced the extended family.

Somehow they'd all ended up gathered at Adam's bedside at the rehab facility. Almost all of them had attended Adam's funeral, and now they were gathered here today to witness Joe's wedding.

Only Sam was missing. Even his wife, Emily, was here, and their daughter, Belle, neither of whom were related to Daniel.

Unfortunately, the Carsons et al were acting a hell of a lot like family, no matter how much Daniel wished they weren't.

Yeah, but this was Joe's wedding, and he'd wanted them here. That was what counted, Daniel reminded himself. For Joe's sake, he'd be civil. Even friendly. He might even dance with Jenny, because he couldn't think of a way *not* to, short of rudeness.

Love wasn't a word much in Daniel's vocabulary, but he'd loved Adam, he loved doe-eyed Kaitlin…and he loved Joe. Who deserved whatever Daniel had to give tonight to make this Christmas Eve perfect.

PIP AND JOE HAD DECIDED to celebrate Christmas day at home. Tomorrow they would begin their honeymoon—a short one because she had to be back in the classroom right after New Year's. Daniel was one of the few people to know they were going only as far as Sausalito, the charming hillside town across the bay, where Joe had made reservations at an elegant waterfront hotel. They'd be taking her family to the airport before crossing the Golden Gate Bridge. Pip, he imagined, would still be teary at that point. She'd be unlikely to see her family more than once a year, considering they lived a half a world away.

Today, though, she brimmed with happiness at still having them here. Besides her family, Daniel and Kaitlin were the only additions. Joe's ex-wife, Nadia, had been generous, giving up her daughter for Christmas Eve and Day both, since this year they were so special to Joe.

Pip and her mom went all out on dinner, an amazing feat given that they'd also just planned and executed a wedding. Daniel, Joe and Pip's father did the cleanup. Content, they settled in the living room with coffee and admired the Christmas tree, bare of packages now but still bright and festive.

Christmas carols played softly in the background. Daniel was feeling mellow enough to mildly enjoy them. There was a time and a place, and this was it. Joe's happiness, he realized, was contagious. Kaitlin was the only person who'd been able to lighten Joe's face in the past. But his expression when he smiled at his pretty New Zealand–bred schoolteacher wasn't anything Daniel had ever seen before.

Joe might have gotten really lucky this time around.

Ten-year-old Kaitlin with her serious brown eyes sat on the arm of Daniel's chair and whispered, "They're being all gooey, aren't they?"

"I don't think they can help it," Daniel murmured, bemused by how hard his tough-guy nephew had fallen.

"Nope." Joe's daughter sounded remarkably satisfied. "Usually the school won't let kids be in their mom or dad's class. But since we're halfway through the year, they decided it was okay if I stayed in Ms. Browne's class."

"Mrs. Fraser's class, now."

"Yeah!" She wriggled in delight.

Watching his nephew, Daniel was struck anew by how much he looked like the young Robert Carson in photos. Once you were aware of the relationship, you couldn't miss it. According to the letter Sarah Carson had left to be opened after her death, she had always known about her husband's other child with Jo Fraser. She might have seen this grandson, since Joe and Sue had gone to high school together. That would have hurt. Even though he was dark-haired rather than blond, Joe took after her husband—square jawed and big shouldered—far more than her own son or granddaughters did.

The doorbell chimed, interrupting his reflections.

"Sue said she and Rick would try to stop by later." Joe stood. "I hope that's them."

He returned with not only Sue and her husband but Belle and her fiancée. Daniel looked warily behind them, but thank God the rest of the family hadn't descended, as well.

Belle was in front, her dark-haired fiancé's hand on her back. Daniel had met Sam Carson's daughter, Isabelle, only in passing. Belle, as she liked to be called, was definitely the golden girl, with a mass of wavy blond hair and vivid blue eyes. Her smile was warm as she greeted everyone. Daniel had been surprised that she didn't seem to share her father's arrogance. She and Sue were apparently close friends, and she seemed willing to like Daniel, the son of the woman who'd had an affair with her grandfather. Go figure.

It was Sue who unsettled him. He couldn't help thinking about his mother and the decision she'd made. Had she steeled her heart to the baby girl she obviously hadn't wanted, Sue's mother? Had she ever caught glimpses of Jenny as the years passed?

Maybe not. The Sunset District, where Josephine Fraser had raised Adam and then Daniel, had been for the working class, with modest tract houses that were now, of course, worth a small fortune given the proximity to the ocean beaches. The Carsons, far more prosperous, had lived in the hilly neighborhood of Twin Peaks, newly developed after the war for San Franciscans with money and craving a view. He almost hoped, for his mom's sake, that she hadn't seen Jenny.

Or, later, Jenny's daughter, Sue—God, her grandchild, as much as Joe was.

As if aware of his scrutiny, Sue returned his gaze, her brown eyes speculative. "I'm glad to see you, Daniel. I've hoped to get to know you better."

Everyone else was talking. Kaitlin had gone to lean against her dad. Since no one else was listening, Daniel chose to be blunt. "The fact that we're related seems academic to me at this point."

Her curved brows rose. "Too little, too late?"

Ostensibly relaxed, he smiled and inclined his head. Interesting that she'd echoed his own thoughts. "Something like that. And—" he moved his shoulders in an easy shrug "—since your mother is only my half sister, that makes you...what? A quarter related to me?"

He could see his mother in her, disconcerting given that, aside from the auburn hair, he didn't see her when he looked at himself in the mirror every morning when he shaved. He didn't see his father in himself, either, which was fine by him; his father had given up on the marriage to Jo before Daniel started kindergarten, and hadn't been much of a parent thereafter, either.

It was an irony that, despite blond hair, this Sue Bookman—no, Kraynick now, since her marriage— looked more like his mother than he did.

She conceded Daniel's point with a mild, "Still, we're

related. All of this has been amazing. Strange as it is to find out my grandfather had, well…"

"A lover?"

"Another woman he loved," she corrected. "I was going to say, strange as it is, I appreciate knowing who Mom's parents really were. With Grandma gone…" Her voice briefly faltered, before she finished more quietly, "I like the idea that I have actual biological relatives besides Mom."

Daniel could see that. Her mother had grown up believing she was adopted. Robert had never told her that he was really her father. And Joe had said that Sue was especially close to her grandmother, whose death had precipitated all these revelations.

"So…I'd like to know who you are," she finished. "Is that so bad?"

"No," he conceded. "Maybe I'm having a harder time because I'm not one generation removed. It was my mother who had an affair with a married man and gave up her own baby."

"That makes sense." She smiled at him. "No pressure, I promise."

They tuned in to the general conversation to find that Belle was explaining how their mothers were caring for Sue and Rick's babies—two fosters, as well as a toddler who was their own, in a manner of speaking. They had adopted Rick's niece after her troubled mother had died.

"Mom and Aunt Jenny will stay busy changing diapers and cooing." Belle smiled. "Leaving them in charge was a good excuse. We didn't want to overwhelm you with family."

It seemed to Daniel she was looking at him when she said that, but maybe he was imagining things.

He slipped away to use the restroom, coming out to find

Belle waiting her turn in the short hallway. "With a baby on the way, Joe and Pip are going to have to find a bigger place to live," she said, "preferably with two bathrooms." Starting past him, she brushed against his shoulder, then stopped, her hand going to her earlobe. "Shoot. Did I just lose my earring?"

She was undeniably wearing only one, long and dangly with freshwater pearls strung on gold. He looked to see whether she'd snagged it on his shirt, but then she cried, "Oh, there it is," and bent to pick it up. As she did, the filmy shirt she wore over a camisole rode up, leaving a gap of pale flesh between the hem and the waistband of her low-cut black slacks.

He was already turning away when his brain processed what his eyes had just seen. He swung back, gripping her arm as she straightened with the earring in her hand. "Wait," he said, his voice guttural.

Her eyes widened. "What?"

"I saw something on your back."

"On my back?" Comprehension cleared the alarm from her expression. "Oh. You mean, my birthmark? It's shaped like Italy, and some people think it's a tattoo until they look closely."

He cut her off. "Show me."

"I…" She stopped, studied his face for a moment, then dipped her head in acknowledgment and turned, lifting her shirt.

God. How could this be? Stunned, he stared at the brown mark, no more than an inch tall, shaped, as she'd said, like a map of Italy.

He'd seen one just like it. Saw it any time he caught a glimpse of his backside in a mirror.

CHAPTER TWO

DANIEL KNEW HE WAS GAPING.

Could birthmarks be familial? But…he and Belle weren't related. Her father was Sarah and Robert Carson's biological child. This made no sense.

He turned, lifted the hem of his shirt and pushed down the waistband of his slacks. She stared in equal shock at his matching birthmark.

"I don't understand," she whispered.

The birthmark, something Daniel normally never thought about, felt at this moment like a brand, burned into his flank. His gaze kept creeping down toward her hip. She stared at him with equal fascination.

After a moment, she shook her head. "It can't be coincidence."

Behind him, Joe said jovially, "You two blocking the bathroom for a reason?"

Wordless, Belle lifted her shirt again and angled herself so that Joe could see the birthmark.

"Goddamn," Joe breathed, turning to stare, stunned, at Daniel. "Isn't that exactly like…?"

"My grandfather…" Earring still in her hand, Belle was obviously grappling with the obvious. "He was your father, too, wasn't he?"

In a burst of fury, Daniel slapped a hand against the wall. Framed pictures hung on it jumped and rattled. "Why the…" He swallowed the obscenity that had been about to slip out. "Why would Mom have gone back to that bastard?"

What Daniel would have given to be able to call Adam and say, *What do you remember?* But Adam was gone, and there was no one else to ask.

Dad. Suddenly, sickeningly, Daniel knew; there was an excellent reason Vernon Kane had never been very interested in his supposed son by Josephine. He must have suspected.

Had Jo married Vern only to provide a father and a name for the child she already knew she carried? Had she used him that ruthlessly? No wonder their marriage hadn't lasted.

"It can't be." Daniel realized he was shaking his head in denial. Denial he knew was false. Still, he argued, "We're jumping to conclusions. There might be another explanation. Something they did to us in the hospital when we were babies. A treatment given on the same spot…"

"Weak."

Daniel glared at his nephew. "I'm trying to be logical here."

"We need to give samples for DNA testing," Belle said. "Then we'll know, one way or the other."

Daniel looked only to Belle. "You'll do it?"

"Well, of course I will!" she said indignantly. "Although it's really weird to think of Grandad and your mom getting back together so many years later…."

So many years. She wasn't kidding. Daniel had been born twenty years after his big brother.

"Or continuing their affair all those years," Joe put in.

Daniel shook his head. "Adam would have known,

I think. And Mom sure wasn't seeing anyone when I was a kid."

"But maybe marrying Vern was her way of ending the relationship with Robert."

"God." Daniel rubbed the back of his neck. "Maybe."

"You want to know, right?" Belle asked.

Did he? Would it make any real difference in his life?

No, he thought. Of course not. His mother was dead, Robert Carson was dead. There would be no heart-warming chance to get to know his real father, if indeed Carson *was* his biological father. The results of a DNA test might raise more questions than it answered. If Robert Carson had been the love of Jo Fraser's life, and Daniel, too, was Robert's son, why had she so clearly favored Adam?

Maybe it was just me, he thought bleakly, then reminded himself that how his mother had felt about him was history. He was all grown-up and no longer seeking his mommy's love.

"Yeah," he said. "Yeah. I want to know."

She nodded in satisfaction, and he felt a shift inside him. There was a link between them, unexpected and even unsettling. Maybe this was what Joe had felt earlier, discovering family.

Jenny Carson would be his full—not half—sister, Daniel realized. Arrogant Sam would be his half brother, and the pretty blonde smiling at him would be his niece. Half niece.

Hell, what difference did that make? She'd be related.

Adam and Joe had been enough for Daniel. Not since he was a child had he craved extended family. But the truth did matter to him. He'd spent a lifetime wondering why his mother had been able to give Adam affection she hadn't given him, why his father hadn't cared enough to spend time with him after the divorce. He had to *know.*

"Let's do it," he said. "But...can we not tell everyone today?"

They agreed, saving him from an hour of public speculation.

The two cousins left shortly thereafter, taking the husband and fiancé with them. Daniel pretended to enjoy his coffee a little longer before saying, "Merry Christmas," a last time and making his getaway.

Driving home, he was struck by the fact that, assuming all this was true, Robert Carson should have guessed Daniel was his kid. Guessed, and apparently had no trouble staying away.

So it appeared he had two fathers, the one on his birth certificate and his actual biological father, neither of whom had wanted to claim him.

Objectively, he knew Carson's reasons had nothing to do with Daniel himself. Why would they? He'd probably never even seen him. Vernon Kane had, but it wasn't as if, in photos, Daniel had been an ugly kid. Adam had insisted Daniel was born cheerful and ready to like everyone. His reserve and cynicism were learned, not innate. But at some point Vern had begun to suspect Daniel wasn't his son.

It was also true that, for whatever reason, Daniel's own mother had been less than enthusiastic about motherhood when he was born.

Occasionally, like now, the knowledge still hurt. Maybe the hurt had a sharper edge today, given this new revelation. Shrugging it off, it occurred to him that now, at last, he might be able to understand why she'd been ambivalent about him. Think of the stress, having to wonder whether he'd been fathered by her husband or her lover.

Daniel had turned down a street that was gaudily lit with Christmas lights on every house, where Santas and elves and crèches were wedged into small front yards. The sight raised his spirits.

Hallelujah, he thought. Christmas was officially over.

REBECCA BEGAN TO RELAX as Christmas came and went. If Daniel had been going to call, he would have done it by now. Clearly, he'd taken the hint.

She'd blown her worries out of proportion. Okay, he'd given her a passing thought now and again. Nonetheless, in five years, he hadn't mustered enough interest to come after her. So then they'd run into each other unexpectedly, and on impulse he'd been about to ask her out. He'd likely been thinking—as she unwillingly was, as well—about how good the sex they'd shared was.

She rolled her eyes. Not good—fabulous. Extraordinary. They had been hungry for each other until the very end.

That is, when they were together. Those last couple of months, he'd called less and less often. Conversation became superficial. His expression was often brooding when he thought he was watching her unobserved. She had guessed he'd met another woman, someone whose conversation did inspire him where hers had begun to bore him. What other explanation was there?

And then—oh, God, then—she had realized she was pregnant.

Don't think about it, she told herself now. What was the point? Daniel had made it clear marriage and family were not in their future. She, in turn, had had to make a decision.

Abortion wasn't an option for her. Neither was bringing a child into the world only to hand him off every other weekend—or, God forbid, for half of every week—to a man who hadn't wanted to have children in the first place. She, of all people, knew the costs of that kind of childhood. She and her sister had paid them.

No, thank you.

She would be enough for this baby, she had decided fiercely. And she had been. She was.

Malcolm was a happy, confident child.

Rebecca was proud of him at Christmas. He'd ripped into his gifts with glee but he had been just as excited to watch her open his present to her, a pencil jar made of ceramic coils that wobbled and listed their way upward and were glazed a peculiar shade of purplish-brown. He and his preschool classmates had all made them, he told her excitedly.

"Mine's really great, isn't it, Mom?"

She had laughed and hugged him. Rebecca intended to give this gift a prominent spot on her desk at school. It made her smile every time she saw it.

Really, none of her doubts had to do with Malcolm. It was only sometimes, when he gave a belly laugh or flushed with pride at how well he was reading or said something peculiar and smart and funny, that she was painfully aware of how much Daniel was missing out on.

She never let those moments last long. She believed with all her heart that she'd made the right choice for all of them. Even when things had been at their best between them, Daniel was emotionally remote. Imagining his expression if she'd announced that she was pregnant was enough to make Rebecca shudder. She felt fairly certain he would have seen her pregnancy as a ploy to seize hold of him, just when he was easing away.

Someday Malcolm might really want to meet his father. It wasn't as though she intended to carry the secret of his parentage to the grave. But she would not let him be pulled two ways as he was growing up, not the way she and her sister had been, with their parents at constant war.

Much as she loved living and working in Half Moon Bay, the time might have come to move. It would be smart to avoid any other chance meetings. She could start sending out résumés now, and she and Mal could move this summer. They'd start afresh this coming fall when the school year began, when she wouldn't be deserting a classroom of children who depended on her, when Malcolm would be leaving preschool behind to enter kindergarten anyway.

She wouldn't even have to go that far away, perhaps just down the coast to Monterey or farther south to Santa Barbara. Or somewhere around Tahoe. The winters would be cold, but Malcolm would enjoy learning to ski.

Yes, Rebecca decided, turning out lights that night and pausing at her son's bedroom door to see his tousled head on the pillow and his arm firmly clutching Mister, his beloved stuffed lion, a move might be smart.

Even though Daniel had made no effort to track her down.

"HAVE YOU GIVEN THAT DNA sample yet?" Joe asked.

Cell phone to his ear, Daniel set down his wineglass and propped his stockinged feet on his coffee table. The phone had rung before he could start cooking dinner. "What's the hurry? You know it'll be weeks, maybe months before we get results."

"You're not anxious?"

"I'd like to know," he admitted. "But it's not going to change anything."

Actually, he had gone to the clinic, but didn't want to admit he'd been so eager.

Not eager, he told himself; he just believed that there was no point in putting off facing what had to be faced. Dealing with it, and moving on. Why procrastinate?

"This means you have another brother."

He'd have liked one when he was younger, an ally closer in age to him. Now, the idea of acknowledging another man as his brother felt too much like replacing Adam, who'd screwed up his own life later but had done his best when Daniel was young to make up for his father's neglect. Sam Carson was no substitute.

Daniel shrugged before realizing Joe wouldn't be able to see him. "Do you remember Rebecca Ballard?" he asked abruptly.

There was a moment's silence as his nephew changed gears. "The one who looked like a dancer and worked for the Chamber? Sure. Why?"

"I ran into her the other day. I was down in El Granada, had lunch at this place in Moss Beach. She happened to be there."

"Yeah?" Joe sounded cautious. "And?"

Daniel realized he was on his feet for no reason. "No 'and.' She just caught me by surprise."

"There was something about her," Joe said thoughtfully.

"What's that supposed to mean?" He walked over to stare unseeing out the window.

"Nothing. Just strikes me that I don't remember a single

woman you dated that long ago except her." He paused. "You wouldn't have mentioned seeing her if you weren't bothered."

"No," he said brusquely. "Just a blast from the past."

"Ah."

Joe let him change the subject, and they hung up shortly thereafter. Daniel carried his glass of wine into the kitchen and took some ravioli out of the freezer. He'd toss it with pesto sauce.

As he sliced French bread and waited for the water to boil, he cursed himself for mentioning her at all to Joe. Why had he?

Maybe the idea of getting back together with her appealed to him because she was familiar. All this family crap had him on edge. He kept thinking back to his childhood and seeing scenes as if they were double exposed. Who was the mother he'd taken for granted, as kids did? Clearly, she'd had an inner life he had never imagined. He'd always known she battled depression. Given Adam's problems later in life, Daniel had suspected it might run in their family. Now he knew, or guessed, that grief rather than clinical depression had cast the shadow he'd felt like an aura. Grief for the child she gave up, grief for the man she must have loved for much of her life.

He drained the ravioli and dished it up along with some asparagus and the French bread, then went to the table to eat. He distracted himself with the front page of the newspaper, but was still moody even after he'd cleaned up the kitchen.

Daniel had to think to remember where he'd put the photo album his mother had kept for him. There had been one for Adam, too, and later for Joe, who must also have his father's now. For each of them, the annual school pictures were included, as well as occasional snapshots from family vacations or momentous occasions.

He found it in a bookcase in his bedroom after having a flash of memory: Rebecca sitting cross-legged on his bed, the album open in front of her. She'd asked him about pictures, the people in them, why that trophy had meant something and whether he and his mother had just quarreled before a picture was snapped. Daniel suspected his answers hadn't been particularly revealing.

Now he carried the album downstairs, poured himself some coffee, and went back to the living room. He flipped it open on his lap, to the first picture, in the hospital within a day of his birth. Vern had probably taken it, or else, presumably, he'd have been in it. Mom wore a hospital gown, but had brushed her hair as though in preparation for having the moment recorded. The tenderness as she looked down at him, a standard-issue newborn cradled against her breast, surprised him. *Tender* wasn't a word he associated with her.

He got a little better-looking in the pages that followed. There he was, grinning at the camera, chubby still and sitting in a playpen. A couple of pages later, he was just learning to walk—maybe Vern or his mother had captured his first step, or close enough. A few pictures included Vern, a solidly built man who was considerably shorter than Daniel had ended up. Daniel couldn't see a trace of himself in Vernon Kane's round face, not even in the shape of their eyes or noses, the line of their brows. Maybe he should have wondered sooner. Presumably, Vern had studied him and come to the same conclusion.

Most of those early pictures were of marginal quality. People in them were squinting at the sun, or were slightly out of focus. Hazy memories made scenes clearer in his mind, but this album wasn't exactly an award-winning photographic record of his childhood.

And then he turned the page and found himself looking at his kindergarten picture, professionally taken and as bright as the day he'd carried the packet home in his book bag. His face was freckled, and his hair had already darkened from the bright copper tufts he was born with to something closer to his current color. He was smiling, but…warily. Not with the open gaze Daniel expected to see.

He stared at the picture, but it wasn't his face he saw. Superimposed was another boy's, one who had gazed speculatively at him while asking Rebecca when she was coming back into the restaurant.

A boy who looked so much like Daniel at this age, they could have been mirror images except for the eyes. Unlike Daniel's, the boy's were brown, a warm chocolate brown.

Just like his mother's.

The kid had come out boldly because he didn't understand why his mother had gone off to talk to that strange man.

"Son of a bitch," Daniel murmured.

The puzzle pieces slotted into place so damn effortlessly, he couldn't understand how he'd failed to fit them together sooner.

She'd been pregnant when she left him, and she'd never told him. No wonder she was shocked to see him! No wonder she'd hustled him out of the restaurant before he could get a good look at the boy—at his son. No wonder she'd been dying to get rid of him.

I have a son.

A son who, thanks to Rebecca Ballard, must think his father didn't give a damn.

"MOM, THE PHONE'S RINGING!" Malcolm bellowed from his bedroom.

Rebecca laughed and rolled her eyes as she reached for the handset. "I hear it," she yelled back, then hit Talk. "Hello?"

Daniel's voice was deep and distinctive. "Was I going to be invited to his high-school graduation?"

The kitchen floor seemed to drop and roll beneath her feet, a sensation terrifyingly familiar to a lifetime resident of a city famous for earthquakes. She had that disoriented, queasy feeling that lodged her stomach and heart somewhere they didn't belong and made her want to run. She backed against the refrigerator, needing its solid bulk to anchor her.

"Daniel," she whispered.

"A father, it seems."

"I thought…you hadn't realized."

His voice was taut. "The sight of him…niggled. I finally got to thinking enough to take out the photo album my mother kept."

She squeezed her eyes shut. The pent-up need to flee pressed harder and harder at her chest wall. Unwillingly, she said, "He looks just like you did."

"Except for his eyes."

"Yes."

Rage roughened the timbre of his voice. "Why didn't you tell me?"

"You didn't want to be a father." She knew she sounded desperate. She was pressing so hard against the refrigerator, the pointed corners of the magnets hurt. "We didn't have any future."

"What does that have to do with it?" He spaced the words coldly. "Not all parents live together."

"That's not what I wanted for him."

"He's my son, too."

Her face contorted. It was at least a minute before she could whisper, "Yes."

"I'm coming over tomorrow night."

At that her eyes popped open. "You know where I live?"

"People aren't hard to find."

"Malcolm…"

This pause had a different quality. "Is that his name?"

Malcolm Daniel. She could not tell him right now that she had acknowledged him.

"Find someplace for him to go if you prefer," he said, his voice hard. "We're going to talk about this either way. Seven o'clock."

He was gone, only the dead quality of the silence telling her that protest was useless.

Her hand, when she took the phone from her ear, was shaking.

"He came, he saw, he knows," Naomi said, her tone brisk even though her hug when she arrived had been sympathetic. "Now you have to deal with it."

"You're a big help."

"I'm a big help, too," her son said right behind her.

Rebecca had been so wrapped in apprehension and misery, she hadn't heard Malcolm come down the hall pulling his small blue suitcase, a miniature of the kind adults hauled through airports.

Steadying herself, she bent to hug him. "I know you can be." Wrinkling her nose, she said, "Do you really need that much stuff?"

"Last time I went, Aunt Nomi got tired of Chutes 'N Ladders. So I brought *lots* of games this time," he explained.

Behind Rebecca, Naomi choked, then recovered herself quickly. "Gee, that's great. You ready to hit the road, kiddo?"

"I don't wanna hit the road." He scrutinized her anxiously. "Mom says you have to drive extra careful when I'm with you. Right, Mom?"

"Right." She pretended to skewer Naomi with a stare. "Five miles below the speed limit the entire way."

Since her friend lived no more than a mile away and the drive didn't require her to get onto the Cabrillo Highway at all, Naomi wouldn't be driving over thirty-five miles per hour. But Rebecca wasn't about to stint when Malcolm needed reassurance. Tonight, she guessed he'd picked up on her tension.

"Cross my heart." Naomi grinned at Malcolm, her freckled face alight. "Whatd'ya say? Shall we go have fun?"

"Yeah!" He hugged his mother hard, but hesitated on the threshold. "Unless Mom'll miss me too much."

"I have a grown-up thing I have to do tonight," she told him. "But I promise I'll pick you up by nine."

Comforted, he was willing to go. Rebecca followed them to the door and watched them walk to the car. Malcolm, voice high and excited, told Naomi how his bedtime was usually eight. But Mom was letting him stay up real late tonight.

If only he knew, she thought, heart aching.

He will know. Soon, I'll have to tell him.

She made herself shut the front door and leaned back against it. Wonderful. Now she was left alone to pace and imagine the worst until Daniel showed up.

The worst? Hadn't it already happened? He'd seen Malcolm. He was a man who would want what was his, and no judge would need DNA testing to confirm Malcolm was Daniel's son.

A firm knock on the door she leaned against made her gasp and spring away from it. Hand pressed to her mouth, she fought for composure.

Had he been parked down the street, watching as Naomi took Malcolm away?

Probably. She had to get a grip. She made herself close her eyes and take several slow, deep breaths. There, that was better. She could handle this. Him. She didn't know how, but she wasn't letting him steal her son.

A second, louder knock vibrated the door. She opened it and said, "Hello, Daniel."

The anger she had expected made his face hard. For just a second, she let herself assess him as she hadn't been able to that day at the restaurant. His hair was shorter than she remembered it, his shoulders broader, more heavily muscled. He was dressed as if he might have gone out to dinner with friends, in slacks and a long-sleeved blue shirt that she guessed was silk. He always had dressed well when he wasn't on a work site. He carried those clothes well, too. Rebecca had become used to other women looking whenever she was out with him.

Without saying anything, Daniel stepped past her into the small living room, immediately shrinking it with his mere presence and making her self-conscious.

She crossed her arms in self-defense, seeing her home through his eyes. No, the cottage wasn't fancy. The furnishings were quirky and personal, assembled over the years as she had need and saw something that appealed to her. In fact, she'd had the same sofa for ages. She had a flash of memory, Daniel pressing her back on it, yanking her clothes off with hungry urgency. *Please don't let* him *remember.*

But he wasn't looking at the sofa. He was turning slowly, taking in the scuffed, scratched hardwood floor that desperately needed refinishing, the old-fashioned sash windows that required all of her muscle to open them even a foot to let in air, the cracked vinyl floor through the arched entry into the kitchen.

Well, so what? she thought defiantly. Not everyone was rich. She and Malcolm had wonderful neighbors here in Old Town Half Moon Bay. They could get to the beach within minutes. He'd taken pony rides at a ranch just outside town. Not half a mile away were fields of pumpkins and cut flowers. Malcolm had a swing set in the tiny backyard. He had everything he needed.

"So this is where you've been hiding out."

She stiffened. "This is where I *live.* If I'd wanted to hide out, I would have left the state."

Tension radiated from him, and, as if he couldn't help himself, he took a few steps away, then swung back to face her.

"Why didn't you get an abortion?"

Her chin snapped up at that. "Why would I? I wanted

to have children. I'm perfectly capable of supporting us. I was thrilled."

"But not so thrilled you told me. When did you find out, Rebecca?"

Find out? Not until the end of their relationship. Suspect? Sooner, but she already knew Daniel Kane wasn't cut out to be a family man. She should have run then, but she hadn't. For another month she had let herself hope.

"I was three months along the last time I saw you."

"Three months." He shook his head, his gray eyes dark with bitterness. "We were still spending a couple of nights a week at each other's places. Sleeping together. Talking over dinner." He paused. "Making love."

"Was it making love, Daniel? Or just having sex?"

He shrugged contemptuously. "Either way, you lied to me every day. Did you despise me so much?"

"No." She took a quick step toward him, her heart wrung by the flicker of pain she would swear she had seen. "Oh, no. I thought…I suppose I thought I was protecting you from having to make decisions you wouldn't have liked."

He snorted. "How noble of you. You were protecting me from the knowledge that I was having a son."

"I didn't know…" Rebecca stopped.

He stared at her.

"I mean, whether I was having a girl or a boy."

He made an impatient motion. "Girl or boy, most kids have a father."

"What would you have done if I'd told you I was pregnant?" She flung the question at him, as if it would sting, and yet she hoped he'd answer honestly. She'd wondered so often.

A strange expression crossed his face. Rebecca had no idea how to read it, and had little chance anyway, he hid his emotions so quickly.

"Does it matter now?"

"Yes." In the face of his looming size, she plopped down on the sofa. "Yes, it does. You're angry at me for misinterpreting how you would have reacted back then, but you can't tell me how you *would* have reacted."

"All right. I would have been shocked. I assumed you were using birth control."

"I *was* using birth control!" she snapped.

As if she hadn't spoken, he said, "Once I thought it over, I would have taken responsibility. Asked you to marry me."

If he had, even if she knew he didn't love her, that he was only asking because it was the right thing to do, she would have said yes. Then think how miserable they both would have been.

She crossed her arms as if that would hold in the pain. One of the main reasons she hadn't told him, she realized now, was her fear that he *would* ask her to marry him for all the wrong reasons and that she would be weak enough to accept.

"I would have said no," she lied. "You were making it pretty plain you'd lost interest in me. To my mind, love's definitely a requirement for marriage."

"Then we would have shared custody. I'd have helped you out financially."

"But you see," Rebecca said quietly, "I didn't need your financial help. And shared custody may be equitable for the parents, but it sucks for the kids."

His eyes narrowed. "Your parents were divorced."

Gee, he remembered a tidbit about her background. How nice to know.

"Yes, they were. Which meant Lea and I might as well have been tied to the end of a bungee cord. Plummeting down one day, yanked up the next, completely powerless. One year at Mom's, the next year at Dad's. Sometimes a month here, a month there, depending on what some judge decreed. It was horrible! I refuse to do that to my child."

There was a long silence. She was shaking, aware of how passionately she'd spoken, how much she'd given away. But if she'd hoped to soften him, to make him listen, she had failed.

"Got news for you." His jaw muscles spasmed. "From here on out, you'll be sharing him, whether you like it or not."

CHAPTER THREE

SOMEHOW SHE'D PULLED her knees up without realizing it and was huddled in the corner of the sofa while Daniel still stood, staring at her with such contempt.

"You don't know him!" she cried. "You don't love him. Why are you doing this?"

"Tell me. What does he know about his father?"

She hesitated. "He hasn't asked much."

"Much?"

One day after his friend Evan's father had spent an afternoon patiently teaching the two boys how to hit a ball off the batting tee, Malcolm had asked on the way home how come he didn't have a dad. She had explained that his father was someone who hadn't been in her life for very long, and that they'd chosen not to get married and be a family together. He had seemed satisfied, if rather quiet for the rest of the drive.

"It's not something four-year-olds think about."

"What did you intend to say when he was ten? Fifteen? Eighteen? Were you going to admit that you'd never told his dad he existed? Or did you plan to tell him, 'I'm sorry, he's not interested in you'?"

She'd lain awake nights worrying about just that. Should she be honest and tell her son she hadn't wanted his dad involved in his life? Would he come to resent her for making that decision? She hadn't found an answer. Like Scarlett O'Hara, she'd thought tomorrow was soon enough. It was hard right now to imagine him feeling she'd somehow deprived him by ensuring he had a stable home.

"I wouldn't have said that." Her voice came out thin, hopeless. "I would have been honest."

Past tense, she realized in despair. However much she might fight Daniel over this, she would lose. Legally, Malcolm was his, too. If he took her to court, she'd look bad for having deprived him of his son.

"Are you married?" Daniel jerked his head toward the short hall that led to the bedrooms, as if she had a man stowed in one of them. "Is there someone he considers a dad?"

Oh, she wanted to lie! She certainly wasn't going to admit that there had been no man since him.

Nor did she want him to suspect that she'd been breathless since she opened the front door because he was still the single sexiest man she'd ever met. She didn't even know why she reacted this way to him and no one else. She hated finding out that was still true. Yes, he was big and well-built and his eyes, a stormy dark gray, had sometimes seemed to reveal a vulnerability that had made her weak-kneed.

Or weak in the head, she scolded herself, to think for a minute that a softening of his usually closed expression meant anything deep.

"No. There's no one right now." Rebecca chose her words carefully. "I…haven't wanted him to get attached to anyone I wasn't serious about."

He considered her for a moment, frowning. At last he gave a stiff nod. "All right. How are we going to do this?"

This. Rebecca felt sick. Daniel Kane wanted to talk about the mechanics of her giving up half her child's life.

She sought to calm herself. He had a right to be angry. And honestly…giving Daniel visitation rights to their son wasn't the end of the world. It might feel like it right this minute, but surely, surely, he would help her make this easy for Malcolm. He wouldn't be like her own father, who was more interested in waging war with his ex-wife than he was in the welfare of his two daughters.

She clasped her hands tightly together and said quietly, "Would you please sit down? So I don't feel as if you're trying to intimidate me?"

For a long moment he didn't move. But at last he gave a choppy nod and sat in an easy chair facing the sofa. Only an old wooden trunk she used as a coffee table separated them.

"Thank you."

"Is this the beginning of another plea for me to stay the hell out of my son's life?"

"No. I'm going to ask if…if maybe you can get to know Malcolm before we tell him. He'd be so scared…" She stopped before her voice could break. He would think she was trying to manipulate him.

Again those eyes narrowed for a flicker. "He didn't look shy to me."

"He's not. But he is only four and a half years old."

"When's his birthday?"

"June. June 6." She drew a breath. "The longest he's ever away from me is at preschool, and I often walk over to have lunch with him. He's a little boy, Daniel. If you insisted on suddenly taking him for the weekend…"

He scowled at her. "You've made your point. So what's the alternative?"

"Can I just introduce you as an old friend of mine? Maybe you could come to dinner some night, or we could all do something together like go to the beach. Once he knows you, it'll be different."

It was the best she could do. There would still come that first time, when she stood in the driveway waving as Daniel took Malcolm away for the night, or the weekend, and her heart cracked. But she could bear it if Malcolm went happily, if she was the only one suffering. If Malcolm was crying, or had his face pressed to the glass as the car disappeared down the road, she was afraid she'd go running after it until she collapsed in tears and some neighbor had to lead her, shattered, home again.

Not once had the furrows between Daniel's dark brows smoothed. They gave his face a brooding cast as he seemed to weigh every word she spoke, examining each suspiciously.

Which, she supposed, was fair. After all, she *had* kept her pregnancy from him, kept his son from him. He didn't have any reason to trust her intentions now.

But he did finally sigh and scrub a hand over his face. "You win. That seems reasonable. Why don't I take you both out for pizza? Tomorrow? No." He shook his head. "Saturday?"

"I'm afraid I have plans." Would he insist she cancel them?

But all he did was give her a skeptical look. "Then Sunday night. Does he like pizza?"

She managed a small, twisted smile. "He likes pizza."

"Six o'clock?"

"Earlier, if you can make it. His bedtime is eight. We usually eat between five and five-thirty."

Another nod. She could see him calculating. "I can make it." He stood. "Sunday, then."

Rebecca scrambled to her feet, too. "Thank you."

"Thank you?" His laugh held no humor. "Come on, we both know what you really want is to tell me to go to hell."

"That's not true. This is my fault." And it was—she'd been foolish enough to stay in the Bay Area. "I appreciate you thinking of Malcolm."

"Instead of thinking only about myself, which was what you anticipated?" His dry tone made it plain he believed she was snowing him.

She pressed her lips together. "I was afraid you'd let your anger rule you."

"And, oh, how tempted I am."

The soft menace in his voice made her shiver.

"Fortunately for my son, I can pretend to like you for his sake." He raked her with one scathing look, then turned and walked out.

Rebecca was left standing in her living room, flushed with humiliation and anger. And dread.

"MOM SAYS YOU USED TO BE friends. Like me and Jenna." While his mom set his booster seat in the back of Daniel's car, Malcolm scrutinized Daniel. "So how come I never met you?"

Could he succeed in convincing anyone, even a kid, that the two of them were friends? Daniel wondered. Three days later, he was still furious that she had intended to let his son grow up thinking his dad didn't care, condemning the boy to the sense of inadequacy that had haunted Daniel for a lifetime.

She had one hell of a lot of excuses, but what it came down to was she didn't want to share.

No, he wouldn't be getting over this anger soon, but he had to hide it. Pretend, for Malcolm's sake.

"I didn't know your mom still lived around here," he said in an easy tone. "Not until that day I ran into you at the restaurant."

"You didn't run into us. You just *saw* us," the boy corrected him.

"That's a figure of speech," Rebecca said. "Come on. Hop in."

He grinned at her and, keeping both feet together, hopped to the car. "Like a rabbit. Huh, Mom?"

"That was *another* figure of speech."

Daniel couldn't imagine that any four-year-old knew what a figure of speech was. Many adults probably didn't. After all, what did a "figure" have to do with anything?

Rebecca had to lift Malcolm into his car seat, since he persisted in trying to jump instead of climbing in.

She closed the car door, obviously flustered. "I'm sorry. He's in a phase."

"A literal one?"

"Uh…you could say that."

He would have smiled if he hadn't been so tense. It had occurred to him, in the past twenty-four hours, that becoming known and trustworthy to his son might require skills he didn't possess. He saw kids squalling in the grocery store when their moms refused to buy the sugary cereal they wanted. Toddlers playing at the park where he ran. That was as close as he'd wanted to get. Outside of the sixteen-year-olds who worked the drive-through at fast-food joints, Kaitlin was the only child with whom he'd actually held a conversation. But Kaitlin was different. He'd been part of her life since she was born.

Charming this particular four-year-old might be a challenge. What made the attempt even more uncomfortable was having to do it under the critical eye of the boy's mother.

Realizing that she'd been worrying in turn that he might critique Malcolm's behavior and thus her parenting skills loosened that tension a little.

They got in the car and he backed out of the driveway.

"You didn't put on your seat belt," the boy piped up. "Don't you wear your seat belt? Mom, how come that man didn't put on his seat belt the way he's supposed to?"

Hastily, Daniel buckled it. "Sometimes I fasten it once I've started driving. But that's a bad habit."

"Mom always checks to be sure everyone in the car has their seat belt on before she starts the car. Don't you, Mom?"

She smiled brightly over her shoulder, although he glimpsed the whites of her eyes. "I'm sure Daniel usually wears his, Malcolm. And this is his car, so he doesn't have to follow my rules."

Daniel was beginning to enjoy himself. The pretense was her idea, and she was suffering way more than he was.

"Do you make everyone wear their seat belts, too, Mr. Daniel?" the boy persisted. "Or do you have a different rule?"

"You don't have to call me mister," he began. "Just Daniel is fine."

"But Mom makes me call grown-ups mister or missus. 'Cept for Aunt Nomi. She's not really my aunt," he confided. "But she's kinda *like* my aunt."

The kid didn't have a shy bone in his body, Daniel realized, as Malcolm continued to share his thoughts about Aunt Nomi and any number of other adults he knew. Daniel did manage to interject that his name was Daniel Kane, and that Malcolm could call him Mr. Kane if he preferred. Malcolm thought Kane was a great name.

"A really good name," he said with unmistakable satisfaction.

Rebecca winced.

Daniel was uncharitable enough to savor her discomfiture. The boy's name should have *been* Kane. Would have been Kane, if she hadn't decided to cut Daniel out.

"This place okay?" he asked, slowing by a pizza parlor he'd spotted the other day.

"Yes." She cleared her throat. "We like this place, don't we, Mal?"

"Yeah!" The boy bounced. "We like pizza!"

Once he'd parked and they were walking in, she said, "I'm not really quite as much of a prig as he makes me sound. I just figure if I can influence him into thinking seat belts are important at this age, it might stick."

"You're not a pig, Mom." Her son, clutching her hand, looked up at her in astonishment. "Why'd you say you're a pig?"

Amused, Daniel listened as she valiantly attempted to explain the difference between *pig* and *prig*. Clearly, she'd failed, because she was still trying when Malcolm interrupted her and said, "We won't get a pizza with mushrooms. Right?"

"He doesn't like mushrooms," she murmured to Daniel.

He felt an odd bump in his chest. Looking down at the boy, Daniel said, "He's not the only one who doesn't like mushrooms. There definitely won't be any on our pizza."

"I'd forgotten," Rebecca said in a funny voice. "You don't like Brussels sprouts, either, do you? Or spinach. He doesn't, either."

He smiled at Malcolm. "We must have the same tastes, buddy."

"Brussels sprouts are *gross*," he was assured. "They stink!"

"Yes, they do," Daniel agreed.

Rebecca rolled her eyes. "You're a big help."

"Well, he's right."

"Mom always says I'll like stuff like that when I'm growed up. But I'm never going to eat food that stinks!" Malcolm chortled.

They established that he would also prefer pizza without pepperoni, sausage, Canadian bacon, onion or green pepper. He kinda liked pineapple, though. Daniel suggested that they ask for one quarter of their pizza to be plain cheese with pineapple. Then he said, "Veggie with no mushroom?" to Rebecca, and she nodded, looked startled, then blushed.

Daniel was surprised himself to realize how many of her preferences he remembered. Not just tastes in food, he thought, watching as she led the four-year-old to the bathroom. How much about *her* he remembered.

Like her scent. The entire time he knew her, she'd used the same shampoo. An organic, not-tested-on-animals, hard-to-find one that smelled of apricots and green tea. Even now, four years later, a whiff of that distinctive scent would have stopped him dead in a crowd as he turned to look for her.

The tiny, choked sound she made when she was trying to suppress a laugh. He remembered that, too. Yeah, and the throaty purr when she was enjoying his touch.

And those flecks of gold in her eyes that seemed to brighten when she was mad or excited or aroused. He vividly remembered the moment when he'd thought, *I could spend the rest of my life looking into her eyes.*

They hadn't even been having sex. No, they'd been chatting over breakfast. She was laughing at him as she snatched the front page of the *Chronicle* out of his hand.

Back then, the thought had no sooner slipped into his mind than he had ridiculed it. She had pretty eyes; so what? No glint of gold in chocolate depths was going to seduce him into making promises he wouldn't want to keep. It wasn't long thereafter that he'd started letting days pass between calling her.

The rest of my life. For the first time, Daniel identified the tight sensation he'd felt in his chest at the idea.

Panic. He'd been scared to death.

He was still frowning when Rebecca and Malcolm emerged from the women's restroom. She turned until she spotted him at the table he'd chosen. She bent her head to smile and say something to Malcolm, after which they both started his way.

There it was again, the feeling that made him think of drowning.

He swore under his breath. What ridiculous, romantic *mush.* This was the woman who'd had the full intention of raising his son to believe his father didn't give a damn.

Don't forget that, he reminded himself as he slid out of the booth and asked what drinks they wanted. *Don't forget it for a second.*

DANIEL WAS DOING A LOT of pretending these days. At the moment, he was sipping a beer and theoretically watching the Golden State Warriors play the Portland Trail Blazers. He enjoyed taking in an occasional game; while in high school, he'd indulged in dreams of making the pros himself. Right now, the action on the court was no more than a blur of color to him—it might as well be hockey or, hell, curling.

Joe lounged beside him, ostensibly having come over to Daniel's to watch the game on Daniel's large-screen plasma TV. There was a time when they'd done this more often. Only nine years apart in age, Daniel and Joe had grown up more like brothers than uncle and nephew.

This afternoon, Joe had admitted when he called that Pip was abandoning him for the evening.

"She and a couple of friends from her school are going out to dinner and shopping. She's starting to have trouble getting her pants buttoned. I guess it's time for maternity clothes."

Daniel had pictured slender Pip swelling until she had to waddle. Of course, on the tail of that image came one of Rebecca pregnant. Carrying his son. Pip was—what?— a month further along than Rebecca had been when she walked away from him.

"Damn," Daniel said in a tone idle by design. "You a father again. It keeps hitting me."

Joe still looked faintly incredulous. "Apparently I have a gift."

That was one way to put it. This was the second time he'd unintentionally gotten a woman pregnant. He'd married the first one, too, and done his damnedest to make the marriage work, even though Daniel suspected he'd never really loved Nadia.

The divorce had, in Daniel's opinion, been inevitable. Nadia had since met a great guy and remarried, although the last time Daniel saw her there had still been something wistful in her eyes when she looked at Joe.

This marriage was different. In recent years Joe had become a grim man, as good at closing himself off as his uncle Daniel was. Falling in love had changed him.

Halftime in the game had come, and Daniel muted the television with the remote. "There's something I've been meaning to ask you."

Joe turned his head, his expression cautious. "So ask."

"Did Adam have insurance to cover the hospital or rehab?"

There was a long silence. "No," Joe finally said. "But I handled it." The subject was obviously closed, as far as he was concerned.

"By bankrupting yourself?"

"No bankruptcy."

"But that's why you sold your condo, isn't it?"

Joe's struggle was brief but intense. He didn't want to admit to having been desperate. "Yes."

"Why didn't you come to me?"

"Because I knew you were stretched to the max. The only way you could have helped was to ditch the Cabrillo Heights plans."

Daniel set down his beer. "Would you have asked for help otherwise?"

His nephew grimaced. "Hell, yeah. But I did manage."

"I want to know how much you put out."

Joe told him.

"You okay in the short haul?"

"Yeah. Business has turned around. Pip makes a decent salary."

Daniel nodded. "Give me an accounting. As soon as the houses at Cabrillo Heights start selling, I'll write you a check for half."

Predictably, Joe argued. Adam was his father. His responsibility. Daniel stayed resolute.

Joe finally slumped back in his chair and lifted his bottle of beer in a salute. "You win. And I have to admit, some bucks will be welcome. Pip and I are planning to buy a house."

Remembering what Belle had said, Daniel smiled. "With two bathrooms."

Joe's laugh rumbled out of him. "Definitely two bathrooms."

Halftime was over. Daniel reached for the remote control to restore the sound, but hesitated. This was as good a time as any to tell Joe about Malcolm. He suspected his nephew wasn't any more invested in the outcome of this game than he was.

"Uh…remember me mentioning Rebecca Ballard?"

"Sure I do. Did you call her?"

Damn it, maybe he shouldn't have started this. Eventually he'd have to tell everyone that he had a son. But he still hadn't figured out how to handle it. As furious as he was at Rebecca, she was Malcolm's mother. He didn't like the idea of his friends and Joe despising her. She might have reason to meet some of them when they were exchanging Malcolm. And he sure as hell didn't want the boy overhearing some snide remark about his mother.

But, since Adam's death, Joe and Daniel had become increasingly close. And he wanted to tell somebody. A man who usually kept a tight rein on emotions, he felt as if he'd been in free fall lately. God knows, if there was anybody who'd understand, it was Joe.

Not letting himself have second thoughts, Daniel said, "When we parted ways, Rebecca was pregnant."

"What the hell…?" Joe digested that. "You didn't know?"

"No. She'd, uh, gotten the vibe that I wasn't interested in marriage or family."

Joe grunted, as if that was a given. "You'd have paid child support."

"She didn't want my money. Or to give me any rights."

"Did she claim the kid was yours when you ran into her? Are you sure she isn't scamming you?"

"I'm sure. She had Malcolm with her. She was trying to hustle me out of the restaurant so I didn't see him, but he came looking for her." Daniel paused. "She was with a friend, and I thought he was the friend's kid. But, damn it, I couldn't get him out of my mind. He looks like me, Joe. I could show you his picture, and you'd think it was me at that age."

"How old is he?"

"Four and a half. He's a smart kid. Likes to talk."

"When do I meet him?" Joe asked promptly.

"I'm not sure." Daniel took a swallow of the now-warm imported beer he'd been nursing for the past hour. "We haven't told Malcolm I'm his father yet. Rebecca wants him to get to know me first."

"And you're going along with this?" Joe sounded incredulous. "Aren't you pissed?"

"Pissed? Yeah. You could say that." He frowned. "But I want to make it as easy on Malcolm as I can. I don't want to have to bring him home sobbing because he misses his mom."

"No. God forbid." Joe was quiet for a minute. "So what's the deal? You're just stopping by now and again?"

"I took them out for pizza Sunday. He's a funny kid. He has a lot more confidence than I ever had." Thanks to Rebecca. Daniel had to admit as much, if only to himself. She was a good mother.

He might have felt trapped back then, if she'd told him about her pregnancy, but his kid would still have had a good father, too. Daniel remembered too vividly his hurt and puzzlement when Vern canceled weekend visits or forgot to show up when he'd promised to. Maybe Vern had an excuse, if he'd found out Daniel wasn't his kid after all. Daniel had been too young to even guess the truth.

What he knew was he'd never let down any kid of his. Not then, not now.

"Believing you weren't a family man doesn't seem like adequate reason not to tell you."

"It was more complicated than that. Her parents got divorced when she was eight or nine. I guess they had a bitter custody battle. She and her sister got yanked back and forth and hated it. She wanted Malcolm to be confident about where home was."

It was a minute before Joe said anything. Then, his voice was constrained. "Nadia and I have tried not to make it like that for Kaitlin, but it's hard."

Daniel's hand tightened on the bottle. "You're saying Rebecca was right?"

"Of course not. Just…don't let your bitterness hurt Malcolm."

"I'm doing my best."

His best, he thought, not to wonder what it would have been like to be married to Rebecca, to see her body swell with pregnancy, to be present at his son's birth and there as he grew up.

As clearly as if she were there, Daniel heard Rebecca say, *You didn't want to be a father. We didn't have any future.* Had he been capable of trying as hard as Joe had to make a marriage work anyway?

Remembering that smothering sense of panic he'd felt at the idea of spending the rest of his life with Rebecca or any other woman, Daniel wasn't as sure as he wanted to be.

CHAPTER FOUR

REBECCA GLANCED AT THE MAN walking beside her down the trail before, in automatic mom-mode, checking to see how far ahead of them Malcolm had run. He'd been excited to go to the beach, even though, this being January, they had to bundle up in sweaters and jackets. The sun was out, but a chilly wind was blowing. A favorite of Rebecca's because it was little-known, this was one of the many pocket beaches that dotted the shore south of Half Moon Bay. There wasn't even a real parking lot, just enough room for three or four cars to pull off the Coast Highway.

Daniel was being more patient than she had expected with this business of getting to know Malcolm. It had been almost an entire week since the pizza outing.

Patient? Or was it that he'd been bored spending time with a four-year-old? She bristled at the thought. How could anyone, never mind Malcolm's father, not immediately appreciate what a smart, funny, lovable kid he was?

Oh, wait. She *wanted* Daniel to lose interest. Now. Before Malcolm could be hurt.

She stifled a sigh before Daniel could hear it. No, he wasn't bored yet. Patience was one of Daniel's gifts. In business or seduction, he was able to lie in wait as deceptively and lethally as a big cat on the hunt. When she first met him, he had pursued her slowly, relentlessly and skillfully.

No, either he'd thought his purpose would be served by letting her stew, or else he was just plain busy.

He'd called Monday and suggested a Saturday outing. He apparently wouldn't be down to El Granada all week, as he had another project in the planning stages and would be meeting with the architect and city officials in San Rafael.

Today, he'd come by for her and Malcolm, a picnic already packed in a wicker basket. She only hoped the contents weren't too gourmet. Preschoolers did not have eclectic tastes. Malcolm was suspicious even of jam that wasn't strawberry.

During the twenty-minute drive along the curving Coast Highway, they had made sporadic, falsely cheerful conversation. Daniel had, to his credit, been careful to fasten his seat belt before starting the car and had made a point of sticking well under the speed limit. He seemed to feel Malcolm's penetrating gaze pinned on the speedometer. Annoyingly enough, her son wasn't just learning to count to five, like most other kids his age. No, he had fixated on speed limit signs and seemed to have no trouble correlating those numbers with the numbers on the car speedometer.

They'd parked in a turnoff on the bluff, joining only a couple of other cars, and started down the trail to the beach. Malcolm raced ahead.

"Mal!" she called. "Wait up!"

"But you're going slow!" he yelled back.

Rebecca heard a huffing sound from the man beside her and realized he'd laughed. The sound was almost rusty, as if he didn't often. He was fully capable of smiling with devastating charm, but now that she thought about it she didn't remember much laughter when they were together. He'd been a very…contained man. By the time they went their separate ways, she had realized how little she really knew him. It had been particularly foolish of her to fall in love with a man so unwilling to share his innermost self.

All but dancing with impatience, Malcolm waited just until they caught up, then hurried ahead again. By the time Rebecca stepped off the hard-packed trail onto the gravelly beach, her son was already crouched and picking through the pebbles.

"Look at this one, Mom!" he said excitedly, holding up a dark red stone, worn smooth by the water.

Daniel inspected it. "I think that's jasper. You have a sharp eye."

"Mom always just says they're pretty. She doesn't tell me their names." Malcolm looked at him with respect.

"I took some geology classes in college," Daniel explained. "I like knowing how the earth was formed. Plus, I always wanted to be a builder, and it's smart to understand the ground you're excavating."

Her son looked crafty. "Do you have a bulldozer? I have a toy one, but I'd really like to ride on a real one."

Rebecca opened her mouth, but Daniel beat her to the punch. "We might be able to arrange that someday. With precautions. Heavy machinery isn't safe for children."

"That would be great!" Future plan finalized, he asked, "Can I go look at the tide pools now, Mom?"

"Yes, but remember…"

"I can't pick anything up," he said with exasperation. "I *know.*" He darted ahead.

There was that sound again. Rebecca turned to see the grin lingering on Daniel's mouth.

He caught her eye. "Easy to picture him as a teenager."

She huffed out a laugh of her own. "Some days, painfully easy."

They followed more slowly. With the tide well out, the rocky pools that interested Malcolm were a safe distance from the waves. Rebecca pointed to a sandy nook up against the cliff that would protect them from the cold wind and suggested they put down their blanket and lunch basket there before they continued toward the water.

Daniel surprised her again by squatting beside Malcolm and studying the starfish and urchins and crabs that lived in the tide pools with an intentness to equal her son's. She stood back watching them clamber over the rocks and discuss what they saw. Their camaraderie inspired an uncomfortable pang of jealousy. Malcolm didn't even seem to notice that she wasn't at his side. Daniel was apparently more knowledgeable and therefore captivating.

She joined them when they walked down to the water's edge, where Malcolm chased the fingers of foam until, inevitably, he got caught and shrieked as the water poured over his feet.

Rebecca sighed. "I should have made him take his shoes off."

"Some discomfort will teach him a lesson," Daniel said unsympathetically.

"Parents generally try to save their children from suffering unnecessarily," Rebecca pointed out tartly.

Malcolm squelched over, his face crumpling. "I don't want my shoes to be wet, Mom."

"I know, sweetie. But you'd have cut your feet on the rocks if we'd taken them off earlier."

In the volatile way of a child, a moment later he was over his unhappiness and went back to chasing the receding waves until another one caught him. This time, he shrieked with laughter.

"He's a good kid," Daniel said, surprising her.

He was watching Malcolm, not looking at her. In running shoes, jeans and a bulky cable-knit sweater, he seemed younger today, his face more relaxed. The wind had disheveled his hair and he stood rocking back on his heels, his hands in his pockets.

"I told you he was happy." The minute she said it, Rebecca realized how he would interpret that.

Daniel glanced at her, his expression cool. "Yes. You did."

"I didn't mean that the way it sounded."

"Didn't you?" he murmured.

"No. I didn't," she snapped. "I meant just what I said. He's a happy kid. Well-adjusted."

She couldn't tell what Daniel was thinking, which further annoyed her. He simply turned, as if dismissing her, and went back to watching their son.

Their son. She closed her eyes. Why couldn't Malcolm still be her son alone?

"Why did you take up teaching?" he asked, breaking the silence.

She lifted a hand to hold back the hair the wind had whipped from her braid. "Partly because of the time off. Malcolm doesn't have to be in day care nearly as much as he would if I didn't have such long holiday breaks. Plus, my schedule isn't erratic the way it would be if I were still with the Chamber. Remember how often I had to travel, or speak to groups in the evening."

"Yeah." He was frowning now. "I can see that."

"I really do love teaching." Well down the beach, a couple walked hand in hand at the water's edge. Malcolm had stopped to watch sandpipers darting after the waves just as he'd done, although quicker to make their retreat. "Now I can't imagine how I let myself get sidetracked after college. I think it's what I was meant to do."

"What grade do you teach?"

"This year, fifth. It's a great age. They're just starting to flirt with puberty—"

"And each other."

She laughed. "And each other. Oh, so ineptly. But they're also still children. They're good readers, the math is advanced enough to be interesting, they're open to exploring new stuff. This year I've extracted a video camera from the district and the kids are taking turns filming a news show. You wouldn't believe how much more passionate they are about reading the newspapers!"

"What about the shy ones?"

"They enjoy being behind the camera. The kids consider that as cool as being the newscaster."

He merely nodded.

After a minute, Rebecca asked, "What about you, Daniel? I gather business is strong?"

"Can hardly keep up with demand."

"Are you still a workaholic?"

"More so." He flicked a glance at her. "You moderated my tendency."

"Really? I didn't feel as if I had any influence on you whatsoever." She'd hated knowing how little impact she had on him. Sometimes, when he was on the phone talking business and she interrupted for some reason, he'd give her this blank stare, as if he didn't even remember who she was. Daniel Kane liked having a woman in his bed. He even enjoyed some stimulating discussion. Her best guess, there at the end, was that he was ready for a fresh viewpoint in those discussions, not to mention some new adventures in bed. Out with the old, in with the new. She had quite passionately *not* wanted to meet her replacement.

He was quiet for a moment. "You had more than you thought."

Tempted to ask when he had ever done anything differently to please her, Rebecca kept her mouth shut. He was probably five girlfriends along. Did he even remember her particular quirks or wants?

Instead she asked, "How's your brother and nephew?"

"Adam died just this winter. A stroke."

"But…he wasn't old enough!"

"Fifty-eight." His gaze had become brooding and Rebecca doubted he saw Malcolm anymore. "It was hard on Joe."

"I can imagine."

"He's remarried. His new wife is pregnant." Still, he wasn't looking at her. "I told Joe. I mean, about Malcolm."

She nodded. Now that his brother was gone, Joe was his only family. She hated to imagine what Joe had said about her.

"He married his first wife because he was pregnant."

Slowly Rebecca turned to face him. "But the marriage didn't last."

"No."

"Having a child together isn't enough."

Frowning, Daniel said, "It seems to me we had other things going for us."

She'd thought so, too, once upon a time, when she fell in love. Before he lost interest.

"Does it matter now?"

"Probably not." He shifted to watch Malcolm again, leaving her chilled. Had he dismissed her, just like that? But she saw that Malcolm was running toward them, and Daniel said, "Hey, buddy. What did you find?"

"See? This rock sparks." He frowned and sounded it out carefully. "Spark-el-s."

Daniel crouched again to look closely. "This one is quartz. The shiny bits look like stars, don't they?"

"Yeah!" Malcolm admired his find. He was soaked now to the knees.

Rebecca looked down at their heads, close together, and felt another wrench in the chest. Their hair was exactly the same color, exactly the same texture. Even after four years, she knew what running her fingers through Daniel's hair felt like, because of their son. Malcolm was so small next to his father, who was solidly build with those big shoulders. Right now, his jeans were stretched taut over the long muscles of his thighs. When he held something out to show Mal, all she saw was his hand, strong and competent. She remembered his touch, calloused but gentle.

"I'm hungry," Malcolm said.

"Then what say we eat lunch?" Her voice sounded only the slightest bit ragged.

They started up the beach, the four-year-old trudging rather than running ahead. His energy was winding down. Most days he did still take a nap.

"You want a ride?" Rebecca asked.

He stopped. "Yeah. I don't like squishing."

She was about to bend to hoist him to her back when she saw Daniel standing silent and watching them. It cost her, but she found it in herself to be generous. "Maybe Daniel would give you a lift. He's bigger and stronger than I am."

Malcolm turned and studied Daniel. "I guess that would be okay," he finally agreed.

Daniel squatted again, grabbed his son and swooped him up to ride on his shoulders. When he stood, Mal grabbed his dad's hair. "You're real tall!" he exclaimed in alarm.

"And right now, you're even taller."

"I *am* tall." He still sounded shaky, but possibly interested in enjoying this experience, too.

Daniel strode ahead, Rebecca trailing.

"Lots taller than Mom," she heard her son say with pleasure.

Gee, how many ways could he find her wanting? And it was silly to get her feelings hurt, but she was feeling a little…vulnerable right now. She'd been so sure Mal would be terrified if a stranger swept him away for an overnight stay, but he was certainly adapting to Daniel at lightning speed. She couldn't blame Daniel if he concluded after today that they could drop the pretense.

Once they reached their picnic basket, she spread the blanket and Daniel gently lowered Malcolm. She took off his soaking-wet shoes and socks and wrapped his feet in the old towel she'd brought just in case. Daniel laid out the food.

Fortunately, he'd brought sandwich makings rather than sandwiches already put together. "I wasn't sure what he'd like."

"Cheese," she said, examining the various choices. "And you'll like this French roll, won't you, Mal?"

"Cheese is my favorite," he agreed. "You won't put that green stuff on my roll, will you, Mom?"

The "green stuff" was a pesto aioli, she decided with a sniff test. "Nope. Although I bet it's yummy."

He didn't actually want anything but the cheese on his sandwich, although he assured Daniel that he did eat lettuce and tomatoes and sometimes onion. He just didn't want them *today*.

Rebecca rolled her eyes. Daniel hid a smile.

Daniel had also brought him a couple of boxes of apple juice and a selection of bottled water and various sodas for them. There were chips and luscious, fat, ginger cookies from a bakery. Rebecca heaped her own sandwich with vegetables, as well as turkey and cheese, the pesto aioli and a balsamic cream she drizzled on top.

"Yum," she said, showing it to Mal, who forced a smile. "That looks real good, Mom."

Daniel gave another rusty laugh. "Was that code for 'yuck'?"

Letting him see her amusement, she said gravely, "I'm afraid so. But I've convinced him it's much nicer to pretend you can see the appeal of things other people like than to tell them what they're eating or wearing is yucky."

"Aunt Nomi wears these real ugly pants," Malcolm informed him. "But I just pretend she's got on jeans like me."

"Yeah, they have flowers all over them," Rebecca murmured. "Big flowers."

"I can see the temptation to say yuck."

"*She* thinks they're pretty," Mal said around a mouthful of roll and cheese.

They discussed why people had different tastes and why some men wore turbans and some women covered their faces and how Malcolm wished he never had to put on shoes. It was obvious by the time he'd nibbled at a quarter of one of the giant cookies that he was getting sleepy.

"Time to get home?" Daniel asked.

He was lounging on his side on one edge of the blanket, his head braced on his hand as they'd talked, his gaze often lingering on Rebecca's face. Sometimes that gaze was unreadable, but a couple of times she'd seen him look from Malcolm to her, anger sparking. She hated knowing how difficult this pretense of friendship must be to him.

"Probably," she agreed.

She packed up the basket with Daniel's help, then wrapped Mal's wet shoes and socks and the towel in the blanket while Daniel lifted the boy to his shoulders again. Then they started up the path, turning at the top to see how far the tide had come in. Their car was the last one here.

The drive was far quieter than the outbound trip had been. Mal was asleep within minutes.

Rebecca groped desperately for something to talk about but came up lacking. She was just conscious enough of Daniel in the enclosed confines of the car for her thoughts to be scattered. She couldn't seem to resist sneaking glances at his big, tanned hands, wrapped around the steering wheel.

What popped out was, "You had freckles when you were a kid, didn't you?"

He shot her a look. "Uh…yeah. On my shoulders and my nose." He glanced at himself in the rearview mirror. "I guess they faded away at some point. I don't remember when."

"Malcolm has them."

"I noticed." His voice was uninflected.

She swallowed. "He looks so much like you."

"I noticed that, too." He was quiet for a moment. Then, with suppressed violence in his voice, he said, "God, Rebecca…!"

"I'm sorry," she whispered, her head bowed. "You're a natural with him."

"And of course you thought I wouldn't be."

"I…didn't know."

Several miles passed before he said, more calmly, "We're not gaining anything here."

"No. It just hit me today, watching you with him, that…" She closed her eyes but made herself say it. "That having his dad will matter to him."

"Should I be flattered?" he asked with less heat than she'd expected.

"I'm just trying to…"

"Say you're sorry. I get it." He slowed to turn into Half Moon Bay. "I've missed four and a half years of his life, Rebecca."

"I know." Four and a half years she'd clutched greedily to herself.

Daniel didn't say anything else until he pulled into her driveway and turned off the car. Then he asked, "Can we plan on dinner some night this week? I'll be down here at least a couple of days."

That was it? They'd just go on the same way?

Grateful that she'd have the chance, Rebecca nodded. "Any night…no. I have a parent open house at school Tuesday night. Any other night."

They settled on Wednesday. He let her carry Malcolm

inside while he followed with the car seat, which he set just inside the front door. Then he waited until she reappeared from her son's room.

"Wednesday works for me." His gaze rested on her face. "You got some sun today."

"Sun? Oh!" She pressed hands to her cheeks. "I should have put lotion on. I did put it on Mal. I just wasn't thinking. I burn so easily."

"I remember," he said, his voice husky and oddly intimate.

She couldn't seem to look away from him. His eyes were intent, darker than usual. The air seemed to have been sucked from the room although the front door stood wide-open.

He was the one to back away, his expression so closed she couldn't imagine what she'd thought she had seen.

"I'll aim for five, five-thirty."

"Yes. Okay."

He nodded and left. Rebecca closed the door behind him and wondered how much else he remembered.

CHAPTER FIVE

DANIEL DROVE BY THE TURNOFF to Cabrillo Heights without even slowing. He hadn't lied to Rebecca; he'd intended to come down today to check out the progress at the work site. But he'd gotten stuck in the office dealing with unexpected resistance to the San Rafael subdivision from neighbors, and it wasn't as if he was needed in El Granada. He could have called Rebecca and said, "Let's reschedule." She'd likely have been thrilled to be able to put him off for another week.

But he hadn't called. Had never even considered canceling. In fact, he was going to be early.

The truth was, he'd been mentally crossing off the days ever since Saturday. Damn it, he was living to see Malcolm again.

Malcolm, and Rebecca.

Going home at night these past two weeks, Daniel had been unusually conscious of how quiet his house was. He found himself remembering his satisfaction when Rebecca stayed over during their year together. Even when he'd had to work, he would look up, and there she'd be, sitting at the end of the sofa with her feet tucked under her, usually reading. Somehow she'd always sense his break in attention and lift her head to smile at him. Whatever she believed, Daniel had put in fewer hours when she was around. Bedtime had been a great motivator to shut down the laptop.

He wondered what the boy—his son—would think of his house. Daniel found himself relieved that Rebecca's delaying tactics had given him time to ease into his fatherhood thing. Spending a couple of hours with a kid that age was one thing, being responsible for him for an entire weekend was another. As bold as Malcolm had been, that was in the company of his mother. There, he felt supremely confident. Daniel had a really bad feeling that Malcolm wouldn't happily go off to bed upstairs in this strange house shared only with the near stranger who was his father.

The highway between El Granada and Half Moon Bay was congested with commuters on their way home from work. Being stuck in the line of traffic made Daniel irritable and impatient, even as he knew he had more than enough time. He didn't want to look too eager.

At last he turned off into Half Moon Bay and a minute later pulled up in front of Rebecca's cottage. It was a crappy little place that should probably be razed, but he couldn't deny that she'd made it feel homey. That was another thing she had a gift for. She'd pick up some odd piece of junk at a flea market she had dragged him to, and the next time he was in her condo he'd see that, yeah, it looked perfect on the kitchen counter with mugs hanging from it, or that it had a sculptural quality against a white wall in her hall. He had once suggested that she could have been an interior designer if she had wanted. Rebecca had only laughed.

"No, I know what *I* like. Seeing through someone else's eyes is a whole other skill."

He'd immediately thought she could do that. When she said, "That would look perfect in your bedroom," she was always right. Just as he'd enjoyed every one of the books she'd loaned or given him, every all-time favorite movie of hers she had absolutely insisted he would love, too. He hadn't said it, though, didn't want to admit how well she understood him.

It wasn't his insatiable physical hunger for her that had made him shy away, Daniel had long since realized. No, it was her ability to get under his skin that had bothered him. What did she see when she studied him with those disquietingly perceptive eyes? Sometimes he'd imagined her peeling away layer upon layer, until she had bared even the hurt little boy who didn't understand why his mommy sometimes flinched from him.

He gave himself a shake, sitting there in front of her house. Apparently he had a streak of paranoia. Of course she hadn't seen anything but the confident, successful man he'd made of himself.

No, but the fact that her very presence could shake that confidence had been enough reason for ending their relationship. He didn't like the way she made him feel emotionally naked, and that was yet another gift of hers.

It was just too bad that seeing her again had reminded him how unbeatable their lovemaking had been.

Daniel got out, locked the car and walked up to her front door. No doorbell. He glanced at his watch as he knocked—5:07 p.m. He might look eager, but at least he wasn't early. And why shouldn't he be eager to see his son, after having been cheated of the first years of Malcolm's life?

Daniel braced himself when he heard footsteps and the

door opened. Even so, he was stunned by the impact the mere sight of her had on him. Yeah, she was beautiful, but he saw beautiful women every day and wasn't interested. Joe was right: there *was* just something about her.

Over a spaghetti-strap camisole she wore a cream-colored, loose-weave sweater that came close to sliding off one shoulder, leaving bare her long graceful neck and the delicate line of her collarbone. Hiding his reaction, Daniel thought it was damn sad when a woman's collarbone was enough to turn him on.

She wore her rich, brown hair bundled at her nape, giving her more than ever the look of the ballerina she'd once been.

"Hi," she said. "Come on in. Mal's in the tub. He went to a friend's house after school and managed to get filthy. Evan's family has two sheepdogs, and when the dogs started digging in a flower bed the boys decided to help them." She grimaced. "On the upside, they had a really good time."

He laughed. "And the downside?"

She grinned, her initial caution apparently overcome. "None for them. But I'm betting Evan's mother won't step inside to answer the phone again and leave them unwatched for even a minute."

Put like that… Should preschoolers ever be left unattended? "She shouldn't have."

"The backyard is fully fenced, and the dogs are big sweeties with the kids. Besides, Mal and Evan both are responsible for their age." She cleared her throat. "Usually."

His lips quirked again.

Her gaze touched on his mouth, then shied away. "Um… Go stick your head in the bathroom if you want. I'd better check on dinner."

Daniel nodded and watched her walk away. Worn over

black leggings, her sweater came to midthigh but was so thin it clung. She was curvier than he remembered her. Maybe carrying a baby had done that. He felt a flash of…oh, hell, not anger this time, but regret, that he hadn't seen her ripe with child.

He turned down the short hall. The bathroom door stood open and he heard a strange sound. *Blub, blub, blub.*

Startled, he stopped for a minute before realizing that the kid was blowing bubbles.

He stepped into the doorway. "Hey, Malcolm."

The boy had been floating on his stomach. He rolled and sat up, skinny and pale. And, yeah, freckled. "Hi, Mr. Kane! Did'ya see? I can put my face in the water. Mom says I can take swim lessons real soon. I can already float and everything. You wanna see?"

Daniel had barely gotten a, "Sure," out before Malcolm rolled over again and indeed floated on his belly. The big, claw-foot tub looked a lot like the one in Daniel's own bathroom in his 19th-century "painted lady" house. Rebecca had really loved that tub, and the fact that they both fit in it. They'd soaked the floor a few times, pushing waves over the rim when she rode him.

The memory was enough to make him shift uncomfortably. The next moment, he frowned.

She must have gone hunting for her own deep, old-fashioned tub. It wouldn't have come with this dump of a house. Had she wanted a bathtub big enough to share with someone else? The idea pissed him off, even though he knew his anger was irrational.

"Good for you," he said, when Malcolm surfaced triumphantly. "Learning to swim will be easy for you. The hard part for most kids is sticking their face in the water."

"Evan is scared of getting water on his face. He won't take a shower." Malcolm took a moment to savor some memory. "His face was real dirty, though. I bet he didn't like it when his mom made him wash it, huh?"

"Probably not."

"Do I hafta hurry? Did Mom say?"

"No, I think I'm early. I doubt if your mom has dinner ready yet."

"Good, 'cuz I *like* taking baths," Daniel's son said happily.

"Uh… Does your mom leave you alone in here?"

"We have a system," Malcolm told him earnestly. "That's what Mom says. Mostly, I have to make lots of noise. Like, if you weren't here, I'd have to yell, 'I'm okay, Mom,' or sing or something. 'Cuz if I'm too quiet, she has to come and check on me lots. And then sometimes she burns dinner."

"Gotcha." Daniel smiled and straightened away from the door frame. "I think I'll go talk to your mom now, so you'd better start singing again."

"Okay. But I'm gonna float first, 'cuz now I have a minute—'cept I don't know how long a minute is, but that's what Mom says—before I have to sing." He happily flipped over, sloshing water.

Daniel was laughing when he left the bathroom. The laugh must have been lingering on his face when he got to the kitchen, because Rebecca looked startled and shy.

"He told me about your 'system.' He doesn't know how long a minute actually is, but he has to sing really often."

Her mouth curved, too, as she relaxed. "Loudly. And I have to tell you, Mal is a delight in most ways, but…"

"Twinkle, twinkle, little star," their son bellowed from the bathroom.

Daniel winced and finished her sentence. "But he can't carry a tune."

She turned back to the stove. "Well, I'm not what you'd call musical, so he probably got it from me, but even I have enough ear to know there's probably not a lot of point in wasting money on piano lessons."

Daniel leaned one hip against the counter. "Have you ever heard me sing?"

"Uh…no."

"There's a reason for that. Apparently he came by his tin ear naturally."

She might not be able to carry a tune, but her laugh was musical enough to make up for it. "Oh, dear! I didn't realize. Poor Malcolm!"

"Doomed," Daniel agreed.

She cocked her head and raised her voice. "Mal?"

"I'm getting out now, Mom!" he called back. "'Cuz I'm hungry!"

"Dinner's almost ready." She dumped spaghetti into a large pot and glanced apologetically at Daniel. "We have spaghetti a lot. Four-year-olds like their five or six favorite meals over and over…and over. I thought this was a better alternative than macaroni and cheese or cheeseburgers."

"Both of which I like, too."

Either the steam from the boiling water or renewed shyness had turned her cheeks pink. "You aren't picky, are you?"

"Only about some things," he murmured, then with the next breath thought, *Crap.* Flirting with her at this point was not a good idea. He was careful to remove all inflection from his voice when he added, "Is there anything I can do to help?"

As if nothing awkward had been said, she set him to slicing French bread. He had no doubt she was glad to leave the kitchen to check on her son. God. *Their* son.

Daniel felt an uncomfortable stirring at the reminder. Maybe it was natural that this knowledge they'd created a child together was somehow sexual to him. Most men got that primitive response out of the way while their wives were pregnant, but he hadn't had the chance. He was only discovering now that his seed had impregnated her, and, damn it, that made him feel…

His jaw spasmed. Things he shouldn't feel.

Remember, she stole your son. This is about reclaiming him. It's not about Rebecca.

Their voices drifted from the bathroom or maybe Malcolm's bedroom. A moment later she reappeared.

"He's getting dressed."

He nodded. "Do you want me to butter this, too?"

"If you don't mind." She handed him a tub of margarine from the refrigerator, then put a colander in the sink and dumped the spaghetti and boiling water into it. Then she set down the pan and faced him with an air of resolution. "Tell me, are you involved with someone right now?"

Time seemed to slow as, knife in hand, Daniel turned to face her. "Why do you want to know?"

"I thought she—whoever she is—must be wondering about all this. You coming down here." She lifted her brows in a challenge. "Or haven't you told her?"

"There isn't anyone right now," he said shortly. Hadn't been anyone serious since her, but he wasn't going to tell her that. He hadn't even been on a date in months. The mild interest he occasionally felt for a particular woman no

longer seemed to justify the elaborate effort courtship—
or even seduction—required.

"Oh." Rebecca seemed taken aback. "I assumed…" She
bit her lip, her brown eyes searching his. "I suppose I was
worried about whether there'd be someone else involved
in taking care of Malcolm."

"There's no one," he repeated.

"Oh," she said again.

Why the hell couldn't he seem to look away from her?
Why couldn't he think about anything but her lips and the
texture of her skin and the hollow at the base of her long,
slender throat? He wasn't even sure if he was breathing.
She was; her breasts rose and fell as if she had gasped for
air.

The knife in his hand clattered to the countertop. She
jerked, but still stared at him, eyes dilated with panic or
with the same desire that was choking him. Had it really
been five years since he'd had her?

A chill swept over him. She'd known she was pregnant
the last time they made love. No, not just the last time—
their entire last *month* together.

And he had been preparing to ditch her.

Very deliberately, he turned away and picked up the
knife.

In a flurry, she left the kitchen.

Daniel let his head drop and swore under his breath. So
he wanted her; big news there. Maybe at some point he
could let go of his anger enough to imagine them trying
the marriage road, if only for Malcolm's sake. Oh, hell, be
honest—the idea held some appeal.

It also scared the crap out of him.

He pulled himself together and resumed buttering the

French bread just as she came back into the kitchen with their son in tow.

Malcolm announced, "That smells *great!*"

As if nothing had passed between her and Daniel, Rebecca turned off the stove. "Once Daniel is done, we'll put the bread in the microwave for a minute or two, and then dish up."

"Did you make a vegetable?" the boy asked.

She smiled at him. "Peas."

"Yeah!" He gazed confidingly up at Daniel. "I like peas. But I don't like broccoli."

"I don't, either."

"It smells kinda like…"

"Brussels sprouts. Yeah, it does."

Rebecca snorted. Except for her pink cheeks, she looked so much like she usually did, Daniel wondered if he'd imagined that earlier moment.

Appearing beside him, Malcolm looked up at Daniel, his freckled face open and friendly. "I can butter, too, if you want."

Daniel had to swallow before he could speak. *My son.*

"I'm all done," he said. "It's ready to go in the microwave."

"Great!" the boy confessed. "'Cuz—"

"I know. Because you're hungry." Daniel grinned down at him, feeling the alien urge to squeeze his son's shoulder or ruffle his hair. But he kept his hands to himself, because he didn't know how to make a casual gesture like that.

"Yeah!"

In passing, Rebecca bent down and kissed the top of Malcolm's head, then whisked the loaf of French bread away and popped it into the microwave. Resentment stirred in Daniel at the ease of her relationship with their son. She'd denied him one hell of a lot.

She asked him to carry the bowl of spaghetti to the table and followed with the sauce and peas. The microwave dinged, and they all sat down.

While they ate, Rebecca centered the conversation around Malcolm's interests. Her glances at Daniel were brief, casual and utterly impersonal. He might have been the merest of acquaintances instead of the man she'd all but lived with at one point, the man who had fathered her child. On one level he enjoyed Malcolm's chatter; the kid was bright, funny and uninhibited. On another level, though, Daniel realized he wanted to talk to *her*. He wanted to know what she'd felt earlier, in the kitchen. What her family thought of her having a baby on her own. He wanted to know how tough it had been that first year, having to work through the pregnancy, go back to her job shortly after Malcolm's birth. Whether she'd ever had low moments when she considered calling him.

Whether she'd really thought she was protecting Malcolm, or whether she was thinking only of herself. Or, worse yet, of hurting him, Daniel. Taking satisfaction in what he'd lost out on.

The boy might have been hungry, but he filled up fast. His plate clean, he asked by rote, "May I be scused? Can I watch TV, Mom?"

Rebecca shot an apprehensive look at Daniel but said, "Yes, you may. Thank you for asking so politely."

He slid from his chair and hurried into the living room. The TV came on.

"I don't let him watch very much," she said. "But sometimes—"

"Why would you apologize because he watches television? Don't all kids?"

Her gaze fastened on his face. "Did you?"

"I could watch all evening." He shrugged. "Nobody cared."

"Oh." Rebecca twirled spaghetti on her fork without any seeming intent to lift it to her mouth. "Maybe all single parents rely on TV as a crutch more than we should." Her voice was tentative, as if she were asking a question without quite wanting to frame it that way.

"Maybe. My mother did raise both Adam and me on her own, except for the few years she and my dad were together." *The man I thought was my father.*

Small lines pleated her forehead. "You always sound…distant when you talk about her."

He shrugged. "Unlike you, she wasn't…maternal." Normally he would have left it at that, but all of this had been on his mind. "Maybe more with Joe when she took over raising him. Either she'd gotten to a more patient time of her life, or she was trying to make up for mistakes. Maybe she thought it was her fault that Adam took off the way he did."

"Was it?" she asked softly.

"I don't know. I wasn't around when he was a kid."

"Do you ever wish you knew more about her story?"

"I do now." He put the brakes on. What was he *thinking?* She was…if not the enemy…at least no one he should be confiding in.

Except, he realized, that his biological heritage was Malcolm's, too. So she did have a right to know.

She had set down her fork and studied him with those too-perceptive eyes. "What do you mean?"

Daniel wished he had a glass of wine instead of milk. He took a swallow anyway.

"This woman named Sarah Carson died last year. Adam was asked to the reading of her will. He took Joe with him." Bald words for the bizarre experience of being asked to the reading of a complete stranger's will. "She left a letter," he continued. "Seems she'd known about her husband's affair with my mother. She knew Adam was his son." He paused. There was no way to spit out the rest of the story without feeling at least an echo of his initial shock. "Robert Carson and my mother had a second child. A girl. Mom gave her up as a baby, and she was raised by Robert and Sarah Carson, believing her entire life that she was adopted, never knowing he was really her father."

After a small gasp, Rebecca pressed her fingers to her mouth. "She gave her *away?*"

He nodded and went back to eating as much to give himself a minute as because he was still hungry.

"But... How could she?" Rebecca whispered. Her gaze turned, as if involuntarily, toward the living room. "I can't imagine…"

"Adam and the little girl were pretty close together in age. Maybe she thought she couldn't cope. It would've been tough, having everyone know Jenny was illegitimate."

"But…she could have moved. Started over somewhere else and pretended to be a widow."

"Yeah," he said unemotionally. He'd thought the same. "She could have."

He could see the thoughts whirling in her head. "If she already felt overwhelmed raising your brother, maybe she just couldn't imagine managing with two children."

"Could be."

"What kind of mother was she?" Rebecca asked, straight-out.

The beginning of a headache thrummed in his temples. Funny how reluctant he was to say, *Middling to lousy.* "I didn't go without, if that's what you're asking. She wasn't abusive. There were times we were happy. Times she was there when I needed her." He hesitated. "We talked some, before she died. Mom was forty years old when she had me. Adam was twenty when I was born. She didn't want to start all over with another baby, but she didn't believe in abortion. I think she got married when she realized she was pregnant. It was a lousy marriage." Daniel looked down to see he was mutilating a piece of bread with his hand. He brushed his fingers off and met Rebecca's eyes again. "On some level, she probably held me responsible."

"That's…that's awful!" she burst out.

"I survived."

"Your father should have taken you with him."

"It wasn't done in those days. A teenage boy, maybe. I was only five. Little kids were presumed to need their mothers. Besides…" He moved his shoulders, trying to ease their rigidity. Then he dropped his bombshell. "I'm thinking he suspected even then that he wasn't really my father."

"What?" Rebecca leaned forward, her lips parting in shock. "Then who…?" She blinked. "Was it *him?*"

"We think so." He told her, then, about Christmas Day, and about spotting the birthmark on Bella Carson's hip when she bent to pick up the earring.

"I remember…" Her gaze flicked lower, before her teeth closed briefly on her lower lip. "It is unusual looking."

"Hers is in the same spot and identical. Apparently her great-grandmother had one just like it. Robert Carson's mother."

"That's why you're telling me all this, isn't it?" she said slowly. "Because that means…"

He nodded. "Malcolm needs to know where he comes from."

"And…" She was visibly fumbling with all this. "That means there are all sorts of relatives. Not just Joe."

"No. It's…bewildering," Daniel admitted. "This Jenny is my sister, her daughter my niece. Then there's the Carsons' only child, who's my half brother, and *his* daughter. I was trying to stay out of it, but it's harder now that I suspect…"

"Know."

"We won't *know* until the DNA results come back. But, yeah. I know."

Rebecca sat silent for a minute. The only background was the tinny music from the TV. "And I thought *my* family was a mess," she said finally.

Daniel laughed, some of the tension leaving him. "Yours is normal screwed-up. Mine could stand in for a soap opera plot."

She laughed, too, but without conviction. "I'm sorry, Daniel. This must have been such a shock." She thought about it. "Or maybe not so much."

It was like her to have read his mind. "Finding out Vern isn't my father…" He shifted in his seat. "No, that wasn't a shock. It made sense. Learning that my mother gave up her own child, though…that's the part I can't wrap my mind around."

"No," Rebecca agreed quietly, her expression soft, compassionate. "I can see why."

Daniel pushed back his chair. "I seem to be poor company tonight. I appreciate dinner, but I think I'd better be taking off. Can I help you clean up?"

"No, you don't need to." She stood, too. "Are you sure you wouldn't like a cup of coffee first?"

He was stunned by how tempted he was to stay. But he didn't like having awakened her pity, and he didn't like his awareness that talking to her had been too easy. Too natural.

"No. Thanks."

"Thank *you*," she said. "You're right. I did need to know."

"I'll keep you posted."

She walked him to the door, waiting while he said goodnight to Malcolm, who was polite but, right that minute, not very interested in this friend of his mother's. They stepped outside into a cool evening. She wrapped her arms around herself. "You'll call?"

He nodded.

"Malcolm really likes you. He was excited about you coming tonight."

That stung, but Daniel hid his reaction. She was being generous about helping him build a relationship with the boy. Not much recompense for what he'd lost, but some.

They stood silent for a moment, awkward. She'd half shut the door, isolating them out here on the porch under the light from the single bulb. He wasn't more than two feet from her, close enough he could have wrapped a hand around her nape and tugged her to him.

Instead, he curled his hands into fists and made himself retreat to the first step. "Good night."

She shivered, and her voice was thin as she said, "Good night, Daniel."

He backed down another step, onto the concrete walk-way. She looked so damn lonely standing there.

Or was he transferring his own feelings? Who was really the lonely one?

Daniel swore under his breath and walked away, from self-pity, from her—and from the pull she still seemed to exert on him.

By the time he backed his car out of her driveway, she'd gone inside and turned off the porch light.

CHAPTER SIX

REBECCA HAD NO IDEA WHETHER this was a good idea or a truly horrible one, but she was committed now. She'd left her car in a lot and walked the three blocks to Mirabelle's, the restaurant where Daniel had suggested they meet. It wasn't far from the offices of Kane Construction near Union Square in San Francisco.

She had e-mailed him:

I think we need to talk when Malcolm isn't around. There's a lot we haven't said, or settled for the future.

His response had been terse and typically Daniel:

Fine. I can meet for lunch Friday if you come into the city. Mirabelle's at 12:30. Reservations in my name.

Maybe she'd have been smart to go on the way they had been, with surface friendliness for Malcolm's sake. But she was scared sometimes, by Daniel's flashes of raw anger, by the emotional chill she saw even more often, and by her own idiotic response to him. And by how she had hated the idea of another woman in his home and bed when Malcolm was with him!

She heard his voice, a little scratchy. *There's no one.*

Rebecca was ashamed now of her momentary leap of…not just relief. Joy. Because she knew perfectly well that she was reacting not as a mother, but as a woman who hated the idea of *any* woman in Daniel Kane's bed. Her relief was foolish besides; even if he wasn't dating right now, he would eventually. No, probably a whole lot sooner than "eventually." He wasn't a man to live celibate.

She snorted. Not all the common sense in the world had kept her from aching for him when he told her so matter-of-factly about a mother who hadn't really wanted him and a father who hadn't acknowledged him.

The really frightening part, Rebecca thought, was that Daniel could sound so indifferent. Did he really believe he hadn't been scarred by the lack of genuine affection in his home? Or was he just plain unable to feel love himself? And if that was true, did he want Malcolm the way he'd reclaim a possession simply because it should have been *his?* She felt a clutch of genuine terror at the idea of him taking Malcolm for weekends and longer if he didn't, couldn't, really love her son.

She'd justified this talk by telling herself that it might be time for her to hire an attorney. Probably she should have done that at the beginning, when he'd come to her house and demanded parental rights. Instead she'd been conciliatory out of guilt and…oh, face it…the fact that, on some level, she'd never quit loving him. And by letting him into her home and life, she'd put not just Malcolm but her heart at peril. Yes, she had to give him parental rights. But she could have done that by keeping herself at a much safer distance and by defining from the beginning where his rights ended.

While she stood hesitating outside the restaurant door, a man with a long, gray beard shuffled up to her. "Spare a dollar, miss?"

Rebecca had been asked for money three or four times a block since she left her car. She shouldn't be surprised, as much time as she had spent in the city, but this area not far from Union Square was home to such contrasts: designer boutiques, luxury hotels and law firms, while the sidewalks were populated with the homeless. Even now, as she reached into her purse, a pair of men in expensive suits brushed by her, followed closely by a woman with wild hair and dazed eyes who wore a pink chenille bathrobe and fluffy slippers.

Rebecca gave the beggar a dollar and then went into the restaurant.

Wearing a charcoal-gray suit as elegant as the two she'd seen outside, Daniel waited for her.

"Sucker."

She made a face at him, embarrassed to realize he'd been watching through the glass while she froze in panic on the sidewalk. "I always have been."

"You know the guy probably clears more than you make, and he doesn't pay any tax on it."

"Maybe. But what if he really is hungry?"

"Or wants his next drink."

"You never succumb?"

"That guy looked able-bodied to me. He should get a job." With a glance, Daniel brought the maître d' hurrying to them.

"You're ready to be seated now? Certainly. This way."

Daniel waved for her to follow the maître d'.

She'd forgotten how effortlessly Daniel commanded

service. Waiters never neglected him; taxicabs had a way of whipping to the curb whenever he wanted one, as if the force of his personality drew them from blocks away. Back then, whenever he'd exasperated her, she would close her eyes and imagine him stuck at the curb like normal people, a cold, slanting rain soaking his beautiful suit while fleets of cabs passed, impervious to his raised hand.

Rebecca rolled her eyes as she was led to the table by the window. Of course it had been held for Daniel.

The waiter handed them menus and went to get their drinks. She scanned hers and looked up to find Daniel had already set his menu aside and was watching her, his expression inscrutable.

"Do you have a favorite here?" she asked.

"I thought I'd go for one of the specials on the board."

All she'd seen was him when she walked in. Forget a board with specials. She wasn't going to admit that.

"So what's this about?" he asked brusquely.

"Why don't we wait until we've ordered?"

He slanted a look at her, then summoned the waiter. "We're ready."

Giving their orders took about thirty seconds. The moment the waiter walked away, Daniel sat back, contemplating her. "Well?"

"I want to find out what you have in mind," she said.

"Are you asking whether I intend to contest custody? Or which weekends in the month will be mine to have Malcolm?"

Low and furious, she said, "Just try to take Malcolm away from me…"

A muscle twitched in his jaw. "Do you really think I'd do that?"

"I…" She was shaking and had to hide her hands on her lap. "I don't know. I don't know you!"

Now he leaned forward, his eyes vivid with some intense emotion. "Then why were you so sure I'd make a lousy father?"

She stared down at the place settings, her heartbeat drumming in her ears. Stupid. *Stupid, stupid, stupid.* They'd gotten past this. She should have kept trying to…to soften him. Not confront him. Once, she'd heard him icily tell someone on the phone, "Don't try to take me on. You'll lose."

I can't lose.

"It isn't that," she said, lifting her chin. "I told you. It's not healthy for a kid to have two homes. To be torn between them, always feeling conflicting senses of obligation. It wasn't that I thought you'd treat him badly. I never thought that."

The waiter brought their drinks. Both sat silent until he was gone, Daniel's gaze never leaving her face.

"Tell me." His voice was quiet but insistent. "Tell me what happened to your family."

She hated to remember, but he had a right to understand why she was afraid. "It didn't start with the divorce." She drew a deep breath. "My parents always fought, but I think they really loved each other." Her half laugh was bitter. "Well, of course they did. People who feel indifference don't wage quite so vicious a war, do they?"

"No. My parents just…parted ways."

"I'm sorry, I didn't mean…!"

He shook his head. "Just an observation."

Sure it was. She had been careless—cruel even—to remind him that his own parents hadn't cared enough to battle over him.

Which, Rebecca wondered, would be worse?

"I think," she said with difficulty, "that after me, my mother didn't want to have another baby. The pregnancy was really difficult, and she spent the last six weeks of it on bed rest. Maybe she was scared. But Dad really did want more children, and eventually she let herself get pregnant again."

"To hold on to him?"

Rebecca gave a small, painful shrug. "Maybe. Only then, when she was big and clumsy and probably scared to death, Dad had an affair."

Daniel swore. "That son of a bitch. And, no, I won't apologize, even if he is your father."

A faintly incredulous laugh released some of her tension. "You don't have to. Mom never forgave him. I never forgave him, and I didn't even know why they split up, not until years later when I overheard them screaming at each other."

"How old were you?"

She blinked. "Oh… Maybe twelve or thirteen? What difference does it make?"

"Not a great age to find out what a bastard your father was." He sounded thoughtful.

"No." Remembering, she repeated, "No. But I'm not sure there *is* a good age to learn something like that."

"Couldn't you have handled it better as an adult?"

She frowned. "Maybe. Yes. Of course I could."

"Did you decide then and there that no men were trustworthy?"

Jolted, Rebecca argued, "That's not what this is about."

"Isn't it?" He looked at her without pity. "You decided when you found out you were pregnant that your kid was better off without a father."

"No, I decided my kid was better off without a father

who'd never loved me! Who wasn't interested in commitment or family! That seems to me to be a reasonable decision."

They were once again silenced when their food arrived. Rebecca smoldered as Daniel thanked the waiter, gave the napkin a practiced flick and laid it across his lap. He picked up his fork. "The food is good here."

"I know. You brought me here once."

His face became even more expressionless, if that was possible. "Ah. I'd forgotten."

She, too, spread her napkin on her lap and picked up her own fork as if she was actually interested in her pasta.

"Does your sister know your mother didn't want to have a second baby?" Daniel asked.

"No. I don't think so. I mean, I can't be sure, but I never told her."

His expression was once more grave, the anger banked. "How old were you when your parents split up?"

"Eight." She gazed unseeing at her food. "They tried to patch things up. Lea was four when Mom finally took us and moved out."

"And then?"

"And then Dad filed suit claiming she was an unfit mother. She accused him of abuse. Lea and I had a *guardian ad litem*. Judges took us back to chambers to ask what happened when Daddy got mad at us, or whether Mommy went out sometimes at night and left us alone."

"What did happen when Daddy got mad?" Daniel's voice was quiet, lethal. "*Did* Mommy leave you alone at night?"

"Nothing happened. No, she didn't. It was all…all made up. They were both okay parents, when they remembered they loved us."

"And when they didn't?"

"Then…" Her shoulders rose and fell, as she remembered desolation as arid and jagged as a field of long-cooled lava. "Then we were weapons, or maybe the battlefield, I'm not sure. Neither of them ever stopped to think, Rebecca is doing great in school this year. Maybe this isn't the time to reclaim custody. Or, Lea is starving herself to death. Am I part of the problem?"

"Your sister's anorexic?"

Rebecca nodded. "She's okay now, but it'll be a lifelong battle. She's stayed close to Dad and won't even return Mom's phone calls. I'm not sure why. Maybe she senses that he wanted her and Mom didn't."

"Or maybe he told her."

Stricken, Rebecca stared at Daniel. "Oh, God. He would tell her that her own mother didn't want her. She never said, but I'll bet he did." Thinking back, she calculated. "She started dieting right after some judge returned custody to Mom. Lea was maybe fourteen. She didn't want to go. Well, neither did I. I was a senior in high school that year. I got to graduate from a new one with a class of strangers. So I suppose…"

Now she read pity in his eyes, although whether it was for her or for her sister, Rebecca didn't know. Very quietly, he said what she was thinking. "She was controlling what she could."

"I can't believe I didn't realize! Oh, it was obvious that getting yanked around one too many times was the trigger. But at least I knew Mom did want me." She made a sound in her throat. "But if Lea thought Mom didn't really love her, that she was just trying to hurt Dad…" Her teeth ground together. "I'll kill him!"

"The thought hasn't occurred to you before?"

"I try very hard not to think about my parents at all."

"Eat," Daniel ordered her.

She looked down numbly. Her food was getting cold. She took a bite, discovered how good the pasta was, and took another bite. Seemingly satisfied, Daniel ate, too.

Until he stopped with his fork halfway to his mouth. "Does Malcolm see much of them?"

She shook her head. "They know I have a son. I don't see either of them."

"I'm glad to hear that." He took the bite, swallowed, and asked, "Lea?"

She was able to smile. "Yeah, Aunt Lea is almost as popular as Aunt Nomi. And she has better taste in clothing."

His mouth twitched. "No flowered pants?"

"Definitely not. Flowers aren't slimming."

"Why didn't I see much of her? No, wait. She was abroad most of that year, wasn't she? Tokyo."

"Right. She works for Thurman International."

"I do remember that she doesn't look much like you. Model thin…" He stopped, grimaced. "Is she really a blonde?"

"More or less. She stayed blond through college. I suspect she helps it along these days."

"There was something…" His brows drew together. "Fey about her."

Fey. What an odd word for him to have chosen, and yet…accurate. She'd sometimes thought her sister lacked substance. There'd be moments when Rebecca would glance up and swear she could see right through Lea. As though there was a visible Lea, the one she had made of herself through the agonizing years of recovery, and then there was the ghostlike one inside, the child and woman who had tried to fade into nothingness.

Suddenly Daniel scowled. "I was just wondering how we'd gotten sidetracked onto the subject of your sister, but you meant her as an object lesson, didn't you?"

"No." Rebecca bit her lip. "I didn't plan… I didn't actually plan what I was going to say today. But it's true. I hated my childhood, even though it didn't destroy me the way it did Lea. I couldn't protect her, but Malcolm…" Her voice broke. "I can't let anything hurt him."

"I'm not your father."

"No, you're *his* father."

He shook his head. "So you really don't believe a divorced couple can provide stability and love without one of them giving up rights to the children."

Flushed, Rebecca said, "Of course I know it's possible to…well…at least do better than my parents did. But you have to admit, growing up while hopping between Mom's and Dad's isn't ideal."

"Growing up without a father isn't ideal, either," he said flatly.

Rebecca stared. "You do care, don't you?"

He carefully laid down his fork. "About Malcolm? And whether he grows up thinking I don't give a damn?" A muscle in his cheek jerked. "Yeah. I care."

"Oh," she said softly, her greatest fear yanked out from under her as if it had been a rug. The floor beneath was hard and unyielding. "I thought, maybe, you just wanted him because you were angry at me. And because he's yours."

"I'm not…" He stopped, briefly closed his eyes. "No.

I can't say I'm not angry. I am. But I suppose, uh, I can understand why you ran the way you did."

"Thank you," she whispered. Her heart felt squeezed in a vise.

"Anger won't help us cooperate for Malcolm's sake."

"No." Still, her voice came out as a thin thread. "It won't."

"Will it help if I promise never to use him to get at you?"

She bobbed her head.

"I won't criticize you to him. I can promise that much."

She barely hesitated. "I won't, either. I mean, you to him."

"Is he ready to find out I'm his father?"

She wanted, so desperately, to lie. "Maybe," she said, her voice low. "Yes."

He nodded, watching her. "I can be patient."

She did know, all too well. With difficulty, she said, "Maybe it's not Malcolm I've been waiting for."

"Maybe it's not."

"You have been nice," she admitted, almost inaudibly.

"I'm not the bastard you seem to think I am." He uttered a sound that might have been a laugh. "Funny, when it turns out I am a bastard after all."

"I'm sorry," Rebecca said, painfully aware of how inadequate the words were.

Daniel shook his head. "Doesn't matter. It's not as if Vern was a devoted dad."

"If he had been…well, then he would have been your father in every way that counted, wouldn't he? No matter what the DNA test says. And then this…well, maybe this really wouldn't have mattered to you."

He stared at her for a moment. "Yeah." He cleared his throat. "I suppose that's true."

"This Robert Carson might not have had any idea you were his. Unless…" She frowned. "Do you look like him?"

He shook his head. "Joe does. The jaw, the shape of his face… I have my mother's coloring, which muddied the waters."

"You passed it on to Malcolm."

"Except for the eyes. He has your eyes."

She nodded. "But every time I looked at him, I saw you."

"I didn't forget you," he said unexpectedly. "Every couple of months, I thought about calling you."

"But you never did, or you would have known I moved."

"No. I'd pick up the phone, but… No."

It wasn't any mystery why he hadn't called. He must have sensed that she had fallen in love with him. Perhaps he hadn't gotten bored with her at all; it might only be that since he didn't share her feelings, he thought it best to make sure she didn't expect something that wouldn't happen. But then…why had he considered calling her? He met other women all the time. With his powerful build, riveting light eyes and commanding presence, finding a new lover wouldn't be much of a challenge for him. So why had he ever given her another thought?

She wanted to know, and she didn't. It would hurt to find out that all he'd missed about her was the sex. Yes, the attraction between them had always been potent. It was still there, a tug he obviously felt, too. But later she'd realized that her helpless response wasn't just physical. Any slight tenderness in his eyes, the gentleness of his touch— or the sheer desperation she sometimes awakened in him— had wrenched her emotions and meant she had given herself to him utterly.

Consciously, he may never have known she was his, heart and soul, but on some level he must have been aware. She had given him more than most women would or could. Maybe that had just plain made the sex better.

Looking at him across the table, Rebecca thought, *I can't do that again. I can't. I have to remember how much it hurt when he started making excuses. When I made the choice to disappear.* And then, *No matter what, I can't let myself be tempted.*

And so, she didn't ask why. *Why didn't you call? Why did you keep thinking about me?* Wouldn't ask.

"You might start thinking about how often you'll want to see Malcolm. We should agree on a parenting plan to…to avoid trouble later."

"I can do that. Just remember, I'm prepared to take this slowly. I'm not going to push our son into anything he isn't ready for."

Our son. Her womb cramped at the acknowledgment that they had made a child together.

She managed to nod. "Okay. Thank you."

Lines deepening on his forehead, Daniel asked, "Did we accomplish anything here? Whatever you hoped for?"

"Yes." Rebecca offered him a smile that was still complicated, still crooked, but more genuine than any that had yet curved her mouth today. "I needed reassurance."

"I'm…not a jackass."

Why the hesitation? Because he didn't want to use the word *bastard* again, not in reference to himself?

But she didn't let herself wonder long.

By unspoken agreement, as they sipped their coffee neither mentioned Malcolm or family. Daniel talked about the economy and the impact fears of recession were having on the price of houses. She told him about a twin she had in her class, who kept almost entirely to himself.

"Putting Sean and Ian in separate classes hasn't helped. Sean might be slightly more social, but not much. I worry. They can't possibly be enough for each other."

"They're identical?"

She nodded.

"Somewhere I read about a set of identical twins who married identical twins. It was as if only people like them could truly understand them."

She shivered. "Or who didn't need real intimacy themselves, because they already had it with their own twin. Ugh. I'm not sure you've made me feel any better."

"But maybe they *are* content, unto themselves."

"Maybe."

What about him? Rebecca wondered a minute later as he ushered her out of the restaurant. Was *he* content, entirely unto himself?

Probably, she thought bleakly, he'd eventually meet the love of his life. Why should she assume he was solitary by nature or choice, just because he hadn't fallen in love with her?

Malcolm. Focus on Malcolm. It was her funny, smart son that mattered, not her own wounded ego.

"Where are you parked?" Daniel asked.

She gestured. "I'm just a couple of blocks—"

"I'll walk you." His tone made plain that argument wouldn't dissuade him.

She didn't say much as they traversed the city sidewalks, and neither did he. But the entire way, she was nerve-pricklingly aware of him beside her, strolling to match her shorter stride. Rebecca wished she knew what he'd been like as a little boy. Had he been as verbal as Malcolm? Quieter, more guarded? If he'd felt unloved, how had he acquired the confidence that was as much a part of him as the color of his eyes or the strength in his big hands? If only his brother Adam was still alive, she would have had someone she could ask, but now there was no one. Something told her that Vernon Kane, the man who'd given Daniel his name, knew him less than even she did.

They reached her car. Rebecca dug her keys out of her purse and faced Daniel.

"Thank you for making time for me today."

He frowned, but so briefly she thought she might have imagined it. Or as if he was annoyed at himself, not her. "It wasn't a problem."

"We haven't made any plans," she said awkwardly.

"No. I wasn't sure what to suggest next." He moved his shoulders in a shrug, or maybe just a gesture of discomfiture. "I have no idea what little boys enjoy doing."

She blinked. Daniel, unsure of himself? "But…*you* were a little boy."

He rubbed a hand over his jaw. "A long time ago. And I've got to tell you, I don't have many memories from before—"

He shut up so quickly, she guessed. "Your dad left?"

"*Vern* left," he corrected her.

"Oh. Well… Mal likes story times, and playgrounds, and the beach." Daniel already knew that. "The zoo. We should go to the zoo one of these times." Not *we,* she realized, her heart sinking. *He* should take Malcolm to the zoo. That was the kind of thing he would enjoy enough to make up for her absence. Then inspiration struck her. "Could you show us your job site in El Granada? He really is enamored of big trucks these days. And bulldozers. I'll bet he'd love to see it now, and then later once the houses are going up."

Daniel nodded, relaxing. "Sure. How about Saturday? We could have lunch down at Princeton-by-the-Sea. Maybe go for a walk on the breakwater."

She smiled. "Mal would love that."

They agreed on a time. Before she could become self-conscious, Daniel bent his head and kissed her cheek.

"Thanks," he murmured, voice gravelly and pitched for her ears only. Then he walked away, leaving her to stare after him and press her hand to her cheek.

Wondering—oh, no!—what he would have done if she'd happened to turn her head just then, and their mouths had met instead.

What a fool she was.

CHAPTER SEVEN

"THAT'S REAL BIG." Malcolm eyed the bulldozer with respect. The gaze he turned on Daniel was more calculating. "It's *your* bulldozer?"

With rueful amusement, Daniel felt his chest swell with pride. *Yes, my son, behold: all that you see is mine and will someday be yours.*

So to speak. Of course, the houses and the lots they sat on would have long since sold and these particular pieces of equipment would be rusting in a junkyard by the time he left his construction empire to his son. And, of course, there was an excellent chance Malcolm wouldn't be interested in his father's line of work. Hell, the kid might want to be a rock star or a marine biologist.

Or an attorney. He had the gift of the gab, and the broad, innocent smile calculated to get him his way.

"Can *I* drive it?"

Standing with her hands on his shoulders, Rebecca moved involuntarily but didn't say anything. She didn't have to, not with the narrow-eyed way she was pinning Daniel with her stare.

"I'm afraid not. You're way too small right now. But I'll tell you what." Daniel smiled back at the boy. "I can lift you up to the seat, and I'll show you what the levers and pedals do."

"Really?" The boy's eyes were wide with awe.

Daniel swung first Malcolm up, then himself. He explained that he couldn't start the engine because he didn't have the key with him, then gave simple instructions for operating the dozer. His son listened, asked questions and said, "Boy, I wish Chace could see me now. *His* dad drives a truck, and he's always bragging. But this is way better!"

Waiting patiently on the bare ground, Rebecca stifled a laugh. Daniel just grinned and ruffled the kid's hair, surprised at how easily the casual gesture came to him. "Glad I can give you bragging rights."

He jumped down, dirt puffing around his feet, and reached up for Malcolm, who was already asking, "What's 'rights'? Does that just mean something to brag about?"

"Something *better* to brag about," his mother said, her eyes still laughing even though her mouth was solemn enough.

Malcolm's feet had barely touched the ground when he said, "I don't see any houses. Mom says there's gonna be houses here."

The tour was every bit the success Rebecca had predicted. The four-year-old loved climbing up on the now-dry foundation of the first house and walking around inside. He insisted on Daniel showing them where the bathrooms and kitchen would be.

"And it's gonna have windows, right? And kids' bedrooms?"

Daniel explained that many of these houses would be owned by couples who didn't have children at home. "Mostly," he explained, "people whose kids have already grown up. And maybe some who are busy with their jobs and don't have any yet."

"Like Mom was, before me."

Daniel was careful not to look at Rebecca. "Uh…right. Like your Mom was."

Malcolm skipped a couple of steps, then turned back to Daniel. "Do you think these houses would be big enough for people with one kid? Like me?"

Daniel shrugged. Who needed a home office? "Yeah, sure. Why not?"

"Or maybe two? Sometimes," Malcolm confided, "I wish I had a brother or maybe a sister. My friend Josh has a new baby sister. She cries a lot, but you can tell she really likes him. Sometimes she'll quit crying just 'cuz he talks to her. I might like it if Mom's tummy would get big like Josh's mommy's did, and then she'd have another baby."

Daniel couldn't help it. His gaze went to Rebecca, leaning against the rough concrete of the foundation, and to her slender waist. He had a vivid, erotic memory of rubbing his cheek against her taut stomach, tickling her belly button with his tongue before moving his mouth lower, to the silky vee of brown hair. God help him, he imagined that belly swollen with child. *His* child. And this time, when he laid his cheek against her stomach, he might feel a mysterious ripple. Life created by them.

He had a hard-on, just like that. Worse, his chest felt as if it were being squeezed in a vise. He would have given anything to see her pregnant with his son.

He would give anything to see her pregnant again, with another child. His child.

He should have turned away, but he couldn't make himself. He lifted his gaze from her stomach to her face and saw that she was watching him, not Malcolm. He would have sworn she'd been remembering, just as he was.

Maybe imagining, too. It didn't help to see the turbulence in her brown eyes, the flush on her cheeks.

Gripping Daniel's hand, Malcolm was jumping, counting on this new friend to keep him steady. He kept talking, too, but Daniel didn't hear a word he said. He was unable to look away from Malcolm's mother, the one woman he'd never been able to forget. He wanted, with a grinding hunger, to see her naked, to find out what marks motherhood had left on her body, to cover that body with his, to claim her.

Rebecca finally bent her head until a curtain of thick brown hair hid her face. Daniel gritted his teeth and turned away, stunned to have been hit so hard by desire. Desire awakened by the idea of impregnating her. And he knew damn well that she'd seen on his face exactly what he was thinking.

Not the way to convince her that she could relax around him, trust him with her son. She'd made plain that she thought he was a son of a bitch, not someone she wanted influencing Malcolm. He might have blown all the progress he'd made, Daniel thought.

Assuming that progress had been real, given how low in general her regard for men was.

He couldn't remember ever feeling as violent toward anyone as he did toward her father, who by failing to keep his pants zipped had set in motion a miserable childhood for both his daughters. Daniel was glad she had no contact with her father, glad he wouldn't eventually have to be civil at some unintended meeting.

But, damn, it did piss him off to know she saw him as no better than the SOB.

His brows drew together as he let Malcolm tug him toward the concrete slab that would be the two-car garage.

Ironic, wasn't it, that his own biological father was another man who hadn't been able to keep his pants zipped. He, at least, had claimed to love Jo Fraser, as well as his own wife, or so Sarah Carson had believed. Sarah had been able to forgive her husband and hold on to their marriage, but Daniel wondered if she'd have changed her tune if she had known he hadn't severed ties with Jo, that in fact he'd fathered yet another child with her seventeen years later.

Goddamn it, Mom, why didn't you talk to us? Why didn't you tell us what you felt, what you thought? Why you loved him enough to give up all chance at a normal life? Enough to give up one of your children?

What would it be like to live in sunny confidence that other people meant well? He and Rebecca, damaged at an early age, would never be lucky enough to find out. Anyway, it made sense that Rebecca *wanted* to believe he was no better than her own father. How else could she justify her decision to keep his son from him?

Reluctantly, Daniel was coming to believe she really had been frightened, not selfish. Nature made mothers of any species fierce when protecting their young. Right now, it must be killing her to sit, looking at rough concrete as though she cared about the texture, when in reality every fiber of her being was focused on her son, and on monitoring how careful Daniel was with him.

She owes it to me.

He wasn't sure he believed that anymore. She'd been as screwed up by her parents' form of love as he'd been by the lack of love. Considering her fears, she'd raised an amazing kid.

Would he be doing them both a favor to walk away? It wasn't as if he had the slightest idea how to be a father.

The thought was agonizing enough to draw a hoarse sound from him.

Was that what Robert Carson had decided, when he found out Jo was pregnant again? Had he believed his son would be better off without him? Had Jo told him another man was courting her, wanted to marry her?

Daniel looked down at the boy's freckled face, so like his own at that age, and felt his resolve harden.

Guess what, Dad? I wasn't better off without you. Neither was Adam. You screwed up big-time.

No, he wouldn't be going anywhere. His son would know his father. Somehow, eventually, Daniel would convince Rebecca that he wouldn't hurt Malcolm. Which might be a tough sell, when he was beginning to wonder how much he'd hurt her.

Or was he flattering himself to believe she'd cared enough about him to be open to hurt?

"SUE CALLED TODAY," JOE SAID over dinner at his house. "She's pregnant."

Pip, smiling, had obviously heard the news. "I'm so glad for her and Rick."

Sue Bookman had been a friend of Joe's back in their high school days. Joe had admitted once to being in love with her. Daniel suspected they were both relieved they hadn't had sex, now that they'd found out they were first cousins. He pictured her face from Christmas, when she had told him she'd like to know him better. Pretty, in a straightforward way that didn't depend much on makeup. And she had the unusual combination of blond hair and deep brown eyes. Joe had assured him the blond part was natural.

"Given that she's the one who fosters all the babies,"

Daniel said, "at least she's not stumbling blindly into parenthood."

Pip laughed. "Unlike me." Her soft gaze found her husband. "Fortunately, I can depend on Joe's expertise."

Daniel took a bite while they exchanged a sappy look. He wanted to be cynical about it, but couldn't help hoping theirs was the love match it appeared. Joe wanted a wife and kids and a home. The failure of his first marriage had hit him hard.

"We have an announcement of our own," Joe said, reaching across the table to take his wife's hand.

Daniel raised his brows.

Pip's face glowed. "I had an ultrasound. We're having a boy."

Joe's voice deepened as he said, "We're going to name him Adam."

Daniel looked from their faces to their linked hands. His vision seemed to have blurred and he'd developed a lump in his throat. It was a long moment before he trusted himself to speak clearly. "Naming him after Adam… That's, uh, a really nice thing to do."

"I wish Dad could have known—" Joe's throat must have clogged, too, the way he stopped so suddenly.

"Yeah. Me, too," Daniel said, inarticulate but knowing he was understood. He stood and circled the table to squeeze Joe's shoulder and kiss Pip on the cheek.

Kaitlin might have wrinkled her nose and said they were being gooey. Daniel suspected she would be, too, when she heard the news. She had loved her Grandpa Adam.

Daniel resumed his seat and Joe said, "You've met Sue's fiancé a couple of times. Rick seems like a great guy. He had a daughter before who died, so having another child of his own has got to mean even more to him than usual. Sue was crying when she called me."

Pip, perhaps involuntarily, laid both hands over her stomach as if to protect the child.

Shocked, Daniel wondered what it would be like to have your child die. He was staggered by the horror when he pictured losing Malcolm, and he hadn't raised him from birth. He could only imagine how utterly Rebecca would be destroyed. And protecting your family was innate for most men. To not be able to save your own child… God.

The conversation had moved on while he brooded. Pip was grumbling because Sue apparently wasn't having any morning sickness. "Everyone should have to suffer," she declared, but with an impishness that told him she didn't really mean it.

Daniel had found himself sneaking peeks at her all evening. Her pregnancy wasn't blatant yet, but there was a gentle curve and her hands occasionally fluttered down to protect that small bulge. Pregnant women used to make him uncomfortable, for reasons he still hadn't quite identified. Since he found out Rebecca had carried his child, he'd become weirdly fascinated. Could Malcolm really have been so tiny, he was barely a bulge in Rebecca's stomach? Had she, too, laid her hands on the minute movements inside her while her eyes grew dreamy? Damn it, he was jealous of Joe, able to casually touch his pregnant wife. And now this Rick, who would be there from the beginning as Sue bore their baby.

The men helped Pip clear the table but, at her insistence, left her loading the dishwasher and sat down again with mugs of coffee.

"Since I'm not supposed to have any," she had said, inhaling the aroma of the cup she'd just poured for her husband. Apparently caffeine in any significant amount wasn't recommended for pregnant women.

Stirring cream into his, Daniel belatedly heard the question Joe had just asked him.

"Have I considered marrying her?" His teeth ground together and he set down his cup so hard the coffee splashed. "What the hell do you think?"

His big, dark-haired nephew watched him, narrow-eyed over his own cup. "It does make sense."

Flailing more against himself than Joe, Daniel said, "As much sense as your first marriage."

"You wouldn't have married Rebecca if she'd told you back then that she was pregnant?"

Daniel scowled, then scrubbed a hand over his face. "Yeah. I would have married her back then. And we'd probably be long divorced with all the bitter feelings that brings."

"At least I tried to do the right thing."

"Compared to what I'm doing?" Daniel asked in a dangerously polite voice.

"I didn't say that."

"Then what are you saying?"

Joe shrugged. "I'm just asking. That's all."

"If Rebecca had wanted to marry me, she would have stuck around back then. Maybe thought to mention that we were having a baby together. Instead, she went out of her way to make sure I didn't find out. I can pretty well guarantee that marrying me is not on her mind."

"But has it crossed your mind?"

"You know it has!" Daniel started to push back his

chair, then changed his mind and sank back down. "I've thought about every option. But, damn it, Joe! You seem to be cut out for family. I'm not."

"Are you so sure? You sound like you're enjoying Malcolm."

Daniel took a swallow of coffee in hopes it would sooth the burning sensation in his chest. "I'm…trying. But I feel so damned clumsy. Being a parent…that's one of those things you learn from your own parents. Mine called in absent."

"Mine weren't anything to brag about."

"You had Mom. For whatever reason, she did better by you than she did for me."

He'd believed then that it was because Joe was Adam's son. Even when she was disappointed in her oldest boy, Jo Carson had loved him and continued to have faith in him. She'd believed in Daniel, too, but the softness wasn't there for him, only starch and determination. As an adult, he'd come to realize how many forces had been at work. His birth had propelled her to make decisions she must have known were wrong. The disintegration of her marriage, the later need to penny-pinch, to squeeze in overtime when she could—it had all affected her ability to be the kind of mother she'd been twenty years earlier. Or ten years later, when her grandson needed her.

"Maybe she did," Joe said, "but I think you're wrong to see yourself as some kind of emotional cripple. No, you shouldn't marry Rebecca for Malcolm's sake and for no other reason." He paused. "You sure you aren't in love with her?"

Daniel wanted to issue an immediate denial, but he kept remembering how conflicted he had been, both driving her away and wanting to be with her. For the first time, it occurred to him to wonder whose feelings had really scared him. Hers? Or his own?

"What a bizarre triangle they had," Daniel said, maybe to change the subject, maybe not.

"You mean, the Carsons and Grandma?" Accepting the jump, probably even understanding the reason for it, Joe propped his elbows on the table. "No kidding. To agree to raise your husband's baby by another woman…" He shook his head. "She must have really loved him."

"You could look at it more cynically," Daniel suggested. "Life was harder for a divorced woman in those days. She took on the baby, she won. He was all hers. She didn't have to worry about joining the work force, raising Sam on her own. How Jenny's mother coped wasn't her problem."

"Maybe that was part of it," Joe conceded. "But from what Jenny says, Sarah adopted her wholeheartedly. She never felt resented or unwanted."

"She was a cute kid."

"She was a reminder of the other woman Robert loved."

Daniel couldn't argue with that. Finding Rebecca and Malcolm had taught him how intimately sharing a child bound a man and woman. It was tempting to see Robert Carson as a real son of a bitch—but according to Joe, neither Sam, Jenny or their daughters Belle and Sue had described him that way. Chances were, Carson had thought of Jo every time he looked at his daughter. If he'd genuinely loved her, that must have been hell.

Was it Jenny's presence in his life, the reminder of what he'd shared with her mother, that had worn him down, so that eventually he went to see Jo?

"What was she thinking, making the same mistake again?" Daniel asked.

"You mean, when she conceived you?" At Daniel's tight nod, Joe gazed unseeing at the buffet that held Jo Fraser's best china. "I made the same mistake again."

Pip was running water in the kitchen and wouldn't be able to hear them. "Not with the same woman."

Joe shook himself. "God, no."

"But then, you didn't love Nadia."

"No. I thought I could make myself, but…no."

What *had* Robert and Jo said to each other that night? Let's make love just once, for old time's sake? They hadn't had the excuse of youth anymore. When they conceived Daniel, Jo Fraser was thirty-nine years old and Robert Carson a couple of years older yet.

Old enough to know better.

Maybe that was explanation enough. He was in his forties, loved his wife, but they'd probably had their ups and downs after so many years together, and during all those years he'd lived with regrets. How could he ever forget Jo, seeing her in their daughter's face every single day?

And Jo was facing forty years old herself. Had she been afraid that she'd lost any chance of finding real, lasting love? She had a few pictures of her first husband, but in them he was only a boy. No, her powerful, adult love had been given to the married man who vowed to see that she was all right after her husband's death. The man who'd fathered her two kids. Living as near to each other as they did, maybe shopping at the same grocery store or pharmacy, chances were good that she saw him occasionally, along with the daughter she'd given up. And then, after Joe was born, she saw him again in her grandson's face.

It was surely understandable if, for one night, in the grip of powerful memories, they relived what might have been.

The bigger question was why she hadn't aborted the baby she must have soon discovered she was carrying. The Carsons, Daniel knew, had been Catholic. Robert would have abhorred the idea of abortion. An occasional Presbyterian, Daniel's mother was unlikely to have let religious scruples stop her.

His best guess was that she was also sleeping with Vern Kane and had never been certain which man was the father. Vern had stuck around until Daniel was five years old. Since Daniel had been a hefty eight pounds ten ounces at birth, only eight months after their wedding day, Vern would have had to know this kid wasn't his if he hadn't made love with his wife until their wedding night.

Maybe Jo had believed, however desperately, that she could learn to love Vernon Kane. Or maybe she had loved that baby she carried enough to want to give him the father Adam had never had.

Nice thought, Daniel told himself. Not very likely, but nice.

He stirred. "I'd better get going."

"Pip!" Joe called. "Daniel's trying to sneak out without saying good-night."

Laughing, his wife appeared from the kitchen. She let Daniel kiss her cheek again, gave him a hug and left Joe to walk him to the front door.

"Belle keeps asking about the DNA results."

"Yeah? Why's she so hot to find out?"

"She seems to think that birthmark—" Joe nodded toward Daniel's hip "—gives you two some kind of bond."

The idea made Daniel uneasy, but he shared her feelings. It was as if they'd been marked to be sure they would find each other. However much he scoffed at the fancy, he couldn't quite talk himself out of it, either. Seeing his birthmark on her lower back had been one of the more unsettling experiences of his life.

"I'll let her know. I promised."

"I'll tell her." Joe cuffed his shoulder. "We're looking forward to meeting Malcolm. And we'll all be nice to Rebecca if you want to bring her to some family thing."

God. He'd have to do that one of these days. He couldn't imagine Rebecca was big on "meet the family," especially under the circumstances. On the other hand, he thought she'd like Sue, Belle and Pip.

"I'll think about it."

Driving home, Daniel turned his mind back to the tangled relationship of Robert, Sarah and Jo. Why did their motives matter so much to him now? All three of them were dead. So why should he care how his mother had felt about the three men she'd loved, or at least slept with? What difference did it make whether Robert had known Daniel was his son?

He wished he didn't give a damn. Early on, when Joe was going through some of the same tumult about Sarah Carson's revelations, Daniel had asked him why the long-distant past had him so stirred up. He couldn't remember Joe's answer, but, blast it, now he was just as stirred up. And he didn't like living nonstop with a queasy sense that a fault line deep in the ground was beginning to shift.

His best guess was that, if it hadn't been for finding out about Malcolm, he wouldn't have been as deeply affected by the discovery that Vern wasn't his father. All of this was jumbled together for him now. How could he be a father himself without knowing who his own father was? Why Vern, despite doubts, had acknowledged him, when his biological father didn't. Why neither man in the end had loved him.

But most of all he wished he understood why his mother hadn't really loved him, either. If she had, he suspected he'd have asked Rebecca to marry him five years ago. They'd be raising their son together, maybe have another baby by now. He'd have known *how* to love a woman, what family meant, instead of always feeling as if a plate glass window separated him from other people.

A plate glass window that now seemed to be shivering with that oncoming seismic activity. Glass, he thought, tended to shatter under enough pressure.

Pulling into the garage at home, Daniel swore aloud. To hell with all this heartburn. He wanted his old life back.

But as the garage door glided shut and he turned off the car engine, he pictured Rebecca and Malcolm and knew he wouldn't go back, even if he could.

CHAPTER EIGHT

HOLDING HER SON'S HAND, Rebecca stood outside Daniel's house in the middle of a block of other late-nineteenth-century residences in exclusive Pacific Heights, all beautifully restored. Malcolm stared wide-eyed.

"Look, Mom! That house is purple!"

Purple, pink, dove-gray and teal, the Queen–Anne style home three doors down from Daniel's was indeed gaudy. Daniel, of course, would never paint a house purple. His was one of the more subdued on the block, while still boasting the spectacular array of colors that gave it and its neighbors the name Painted Ladies. Italianate in style, his house was painted sage-green, with brackets and cornices and trim in black, white, deeper green and rose. That pink had delighted her. When she'd teased him, he'd insisted the painter who had done the work had suggested it. Rebecca didn't believe him.

He had told her once that these houses had been colorful in their day, but in the early part of the twentieth century had mostly been painted white or gray. Not until the 1960s, when the hippies had painted houses in the Haight-Ashbury district bright, defiant colors, had the movement begun to dress San Francisco's historic ladies in glorious colors.

Why the heck couldn't Daniel have moved in the past five years? Was that too much to ask?

Rebecca dreaded walking into his house. It held such a host of memories, most of which she'd succeeded in blocking out until he'd reappeared in her life. She'd loved his house so much, tied in with her feelings for him as it was! The fact that he'd chosen to buy and restore one of the elaborately adorned Victorians that had survived the 1906 earthquake rather than live in a new house he'd built had initially surprised and then intrigued her. Wanting to live in a house with so much history meant connections must matter to him, she had decided. He was a businessman, yes; ruthless in getting his way, probably. But the house, built in 1864, was so romantic, it showed a softer side of him, suggested he would eventually want a wife and children to fill the bedrooms. Family and connections.

More fool her.

After their Cabrillo Heights tour last week, Daniel had suggested she and Malcolm come to his house for lunch the following Saturday. "Let him get familiar with my place, too," he'd said, and she had agreed, hiding her deep reluctance. Yes, when Malcolm came for his first visit without her, it would be easier for him if he'd already visited his dad's house, had seen it in the security of her company. Even so, every instinct in her had screamed, *Say no!* But how could she, if this casual lunch date would make the inevitable transition to overnight stays with his father less frightening for Malcolm?

Her stomach felt hollow as they started up the steps to the porch. She'd been so happy here, so much in love. An occasional overnight had expanded that year to Rebecca spending half the week here. She'd taken over several drawers and part of the medicine cabinet. She had believed, with all her heart, that Daniel would ask her to marry him.

Until she realized one day how many excuses he'd made that week alone. And then the next week, and the next. He didn't want her there as often, even though he made love to her with the same hunger and even tenderness as always. There was someone else, Rebecca began to believe. That, or his interest was waning. Was she boring him?

She remembered her stomach-clenching panic, because she had just begun to suspect that she was pregnant. She was already nervous, because he *hadn't* asked her to marry him or ever talked about having children someday. But if he loved her, she had tried to convince herself, it would be all right. Maybe he wouldn't have chosen to start a family yet, but he would come around to wanting this baby.

It took her six weeks of his cancellations and excuses to accept that he didn't love her at all, that he was not-so-subtly letting her know that he was winding this relationship down. And yet still he made love to her with single-minded intensity, as if she was the only woman in the world. The way he kissed her, and held her and said her name while he moved inside her had seemed to contradict all his hints. That last night, his voice had been raw when he said, "God, I want you." And yet afterward, he'd slipped out of bed as soon as he decently could and gone downstairs, no doubt to work.

She had lain alone in his bed, staring up at the high ceiling, and known she had two choices. Tell him, tie him to her forever whether he liked it or not. Or walk away now, dignity intact, and raise this child on her own.

For her, with her history, that had been no choice at all. So she'd pretended to be asleep when he got up in the morning, showered, kissed her cheek and left. As soon as she was sure he was gone, Rebecca had packed her few possessions left at his house, written him a breezy, glad-we-had-fun-but-I'm-moving-on note, and left it with her key to his house on a side table in the entry.

Some part of her persisted in clinging to the hope that he would call, or even show up angry at her apartment and say, "I love you. Damn it, marry me!" But of course he didn't do either. She'd read him right. He was probably relieved when he came home that day and found the note. He'd escaped the necessity of an ugly scene or hurt feelings. Why wouldn't he be glad?

And now here she was with their son, who was clearly entranced by this fairy-tale house. Soon he'd have his own bedroom here, and he would be in love with his amazing new father.

And I'm jealous.

How pathetic was that?

The door knocker in the shape of a mermaid was new. *The Little Mermaid* being one of his favorite movies, Mal was further delighted.

Within moments of her letting the mermaid knock on the shining brass plate, Daniel opened the door. "Rebecca. Malcolm. Come in."

Wearing faded jeans and a finely knit sweater in dark green, he took her breath away. Beyond a swift glance at her, he seemed to have eyes only for Malcolm.

For once, her son was rendered shy by the grandeur of the parquet-floored entry with an elaborate crystal chandelier above. He clung to his mother's hand.

"Smells good," she said. "Are you cooking?"

Daniel grinned at her. "Versus slapping peanut butter on bread? Yes, I am. Occasionally I get inspired."

She remembered. He was a creative cook when the mood came upon him, ordering out otherwise. His pasta dishes put her mundane spaghetti to shame. Creative, on the other hand, didn't go over well with Malcolm.

Reading her mind, Daniel said, "I'm making macaroni and cheese. Just slightly improved. If he doesn't like it…I do have peanut butter."

"Then all is well," she said lightly. "Have you made any major changes to the house? Do we get a tour?"

Oh, sure, torture myself, why don't I?

"Yep. The macaroni and cheese won't come out of the oven for another twenty minutes." He smiled at Mal. "What do you think? Do you want to see the house?"

Malcolm nodded eagerly. "Mom says it's old. She says there weren't any cars when it was built."

"That's right. Instead of a garage in back, there would have been a carriage house for horses."

The house was tall but narrow, rooms to each side of a central hall on each floor.

Mal loved the bay windows and the magnificent fireplace with a scrolled mantel in the living room. Upstairs in the front guest bedroom, he thought it would be a wonderful idea to climb out the window onto the balcony.

"Afraid not, buddy," Daniel said, shaking his head. "I sit out there once in a while on hot nights, but it was designed to be decorative, not to bear weight, so I'm nervous about really using it."

A smaller bedroom at the back of the house would be more suitable for Malcolm, Rebecca thought. She was grateful that Daniel didn't open the door to his own room, although he did show them the bathroom that he had enlarged vastly by stealing space from another small bedroom. The floor and lower walls were tiled in black-and-white checkerboard, above which the walls were papered in pale green with a repeating black filigree pattern. A huge, glass-walled shower violated the period look but managed to be fairly unobtrusive. Mal ignored it, happy to see the deep claw-foot tub.

Peering into it, he said, "It's even better than ours. Isn't it, Mom? I never knew anyone else who has a bathtub like ours. Aunt Nomi doesn't, and Chace doesn't, and..."

Rebecca stepped back into the hall, letting Daniel deal with the flood of information on people who *didn't* have an old-fashioned bathtub deep enough to float in. She didn't think she could bear to stand there in that bathroom, excruciatingly aware of Daniel, and talk about the bathtub where they'd made love. Perhaps even conceived Malcolm.

She was a masochist, agreeing to come here! Why hadn't she made an excuse, let him introduce Malcolm to his house on his own? This hurt, being a guest welcome here only to smooth the way for Mal to feel at home.

She supposed she was rather quiet when they went back downstairs. She felt Daniel's scrutiny and ignored it, pointing out handsome period details to Malcolm as if he'd care.

They ate at the round oak table in the bay at the back of the kitchen, looking out through French doors onto a brick patio and small garden confined by brick walls. They had eaten breakfast out there whenever the weather was warm enough. Rebecca couldn't look anywhere without the ache beneath her breastbone spreading, filling her until every breath hurt.

Mal nibbled politely at the macaroni, made with four

different cheeses, agreed that he might like a peanut butter sandwich, too, then happily ate the ice cream that followed. Somehow Rebecca participated in the conversation, although by the time lunch was over she couldn't remember a single thing they'd talked about.

"Can I go outside?" Malcolm asked, sliding off his chair.

Rebecca started to rise, but Daniel said, "I was just going to pour coffee. You can keep an eye on him from here. The gate's closed."

She hesitated, then sank back down. Malcolm slipped out the door, leaving it open. He crouched to concentrate on something in a flower bed—a bug maybe. Insects were one of his current interests.

Daniel set a cup of coffee in front of her. "This isn't a house for a kid, is it?" he said ruefully, going back to the refrigerator for cream.

"Are you kidding?" Rebecca laughed, hoping he couldn't hear the pain in it. "It's…magical. Any kid would love it. It's the kind of house where you think maybe you really could open a wardrobe and find a magical kingdom on the other side. It has attics and nooks and a stair banister that someday he'll want to slide down. If your furnishings were fussy, it might be a problem, but I didn't see much he could damage."

He sat down across from her and handed her a small pitcher of cream. "I thought…that bedroom at the back of the house. It's next to mine."

"And the window doesn't open onto the balcony."

Daniel nodded. She felt his gaze on her face, even as she watched Malcolm out the window. Her son was now trying out a glider, swinging his legs to try to persuade it to move.

Voice gravelly, Daniel said, "Seeing you here brings back memories."

Her throat closed. She made some incoherent agreement.

"I missed you."

Oh, God. Was he *trying* to torture her?

Mal had moved on to the detached garage. He was jumping to try to see in the window, well above his head. *Please get bored,* she begged silently. *Please come back in. Give me an excuse to say, "We have to go."* She sat mute. Honestly, what could she say? You broke my heart? She wouldn't have admitted that even if he were prying off her fingernails one by one.

Still quiet, still watching her, he said, "I've begun to regret that I couldn't be the man you needed me to be."

Rebecca was suddenly angry. The sear of heat was a welcome change from her desolation. For the first time, she met his eyes.

"What do you mean, you *couldn't* be? You're a man of great determination, Daniel. You could have been whatever you chose. So just knock it off, okay? We had fun together. You got tired of me. Don't…don't…" Abruptly, tears threatened. She willed them away. "Don't make more of it than it was, just because we have a son together."

His face went blank. He had a talent for that, hiding his emotions, leaving her endlessly guessing what he really felt.

There was a long silence. Neither of them drank their coffee. Rebecca wanted desperately to escape.

"I didn't get tired of you."

Her heart cramped, but she held on to her fury. "Then

what?" she fired back. "You met someone else? You were too busy? It doesn't really matter, Daniel. It was a long time ago."

"You're right," he said flatly. "Finding out about Malcolm has…made me think. That's all."

She pushed back her chair and stood. "We really should be going." She started toward the French door to call Malcolm in.

Daniel rose to his feet and blocked her. "Damn it," he said. "I keep wondering…"

His voice sounded strange. She froze, perilously close to him. "Wondering…?" she whispered.

"Whether this has changed." He reached out and tipped her chin up.

She should have wrenched herself away. But she'd wondered, too. How could she help it? Maybe she'd feel nothing when they kissed. And then she could get over this foolish crush that wasn't really love.

Their noses bumped, and his lips brushed softly over hers. Again. The tiniest touch, and she was melting, lost. He nipped her lower lip, then gently sucked it. She made a shaky sound and laid a hand on his shoulder. He growled something and then was kissing her, really kissing her, his tongue sliding into her mouth, and she was about to collapse—

"Mom!" her son exclaimed, pushing open the door. "You want to sit on the bench? I can't make it rock by myself."

Daniel reacted faster than she did, stepping back. She had one fleeting glimpse of his face, the skin taut over his cheekbones, his eyes glittering, before she faced her son.

"Just for a minute, and then we need to go."

He didn't notice anything, thank goodness, only grabbed her hand to draw her outside. His chatter blurred like birdsong. She sat with him and set the glider in motion, aware the entire time of Daniel standing in the doorway watching them, his hands in his pockets.

She could not—could not—look at him. Managed not to meet his eyes at all as she nudged Malcolm into thanking him for lunch, and steered them out the front door.

This despair was worse than the earlier ache of regret. Much worse.

I keep wondering…

Now she knew. It was the same. No, not the same; different. Better. She was more sensitized to his touch. She could shame herself so easily, wanting him as she had never, perhaps would never, want another man.

Did he have his answer? she wondered bitterly. Was it any more welcome than hers?

"Mom!" her son complained, tugging at her hand. "Slow down!"

From somewhere, she summoned a grin. "I'm sorry. I forget how short your legs are, munchkin."

"The car is right there anyhow, isn't it, Mom?"

"Yes, it is." She produced her keys from her purse. "And in you go, kiddo."

He was asleep before she'd gone a dozen blocks, leaving her to her bitter reflections.

DANIEL SPENT THE WEEK asking himself what he was playing at, anyway. No, he hadn't plotted in advance to kiss Rebecca. But he hadn't resisted the temptation very hard, either. From the minute she stepped in the front door, her gaze wary, he'd felt… God, he hardly knew. Intense satisfaction because she was back where she belonged? Yeah, he couldn't deny it. Pleasure that she and his son were *both* here? Sure.

He'd spent the previous week, after issuing the invitation, flooded with memories. Everywhere he looked in his house, he saw her. He'd brought women home only a couple of times after Rebecca left, and had been sorry both times. They didn't belong.

She did, although after she was gone he never let himself quite realize how much he missed her.

Now, every piece of furniture, every room, reminded him of her. The sofa where she would read, the kitchen table, the dining room where they'd entertained friends, the balcony where they'd sat, feet dangling, and lazily talked as the sun set...every inch of the house seemed permeated with her. He'd even kept that damn antique cherrywood rocking chair he'd bought when he was seeing her, though it was too small for him. It currently sat upstairs in his bedroom, completely useless, and yet...he hadn't been able to bring himself to get rid of it. He was glad she hadn't seen it still there.

She had kissed him back. The fire was still there, but she didn't seem very happy to discover that. She hadn't wanted to be here, and he was still shaken by her anger. Daniel couldn't blame her for it, either. He had driven her away, then brooded alone in this damn house for months before he even considered asking a woman to dinner. He hadn't been ready to marry Rebecca, but he hadn't wanted to let her go, either.

What he was finding was that he never *had* let her go, not entirely. She'd stayed at the edges of his thoughts, like an elusive scent. No other woman moved the way she did, with that dancer's grace; he was never as satisfied talking to anyone else, man or woman. He'd never felt the same passion for another woman.

It bothered him how much she'd changed. Becoming a mother was probably responsible for some of that, especially being a single parent; she could never relax her vigilance, never quite trust anyone else to take care of Malcolm as well as she did. He guessed there'd been a financial struggle, too, even though she claimed she'd been able to take care of both of them. What he did know was that she had become more serious and considerably more guarded. She didn't seem to laugh much anymore, at least around him. She wasn't the relaxed, warm, open woman she'd been.

Or at least, Daniel thought ruefully, she wasn't with him. He had seen her face light up often enough for Malcolm's benefit. He suspected she was serene, gentle and affectionate to her students, too.

Hell, maybe she hadn't changed at all. Maybe she just didn't like him.

Daniel grimaced. Why would she? He was demanding she hand over her son to him part of the time. He embodied her worst fears, of a father who would yank one way while she pulled the other, damaging Malcolm emotionally.

He wanted to kiss her—*had* kissed her—while she probably hated his guts.

Remembering Joe's question, Daniel gave a humorous laugh. She'd looked less than thrilled when he told her he would have married her once he found out she was pregnant. So marriage for Malcolm's sake wasn't an option she was willing to consider. He had wanted to believe that, like

him, she was giving it some thought now. It seemed...
logical. After her flare of anger today, though, he had to
guess she wasn't in favor.

He still panicked when he imagined being tied to this
woman and no other for the rest of his days, having a son,
maybe more kids. He wasn't sure she'd understood what
he was trying to say when he told her he wished he could
be what she needed, but that was still what scared him.
Would he let her and Malcolm down when they needed
him? He wasn't even that sure what his role would *be* as
a husband and father. How was he supposed to know, after
having virtually raised himself?

But he wasn't only panicked when he thought about
Rebecca as his wife. He also felt an emotion both insidi-
ous and potent. Longing. He was a kid with his nose
pressed to the glass, wanting the wonders inside, afraid
they weren't for him.

Thinking about Rebecca moved him to call Vern and ask
if he could stop by one evening. If he didn't ask his questions now, he might never get the chance. Vern Kane was
eighty-three, and he and his second wife had moved a
couple of years back to a seniors apartment complex in
Walnut Creek, inland from the city. Mable was develop-
ing dementia and Daniel knew they were planning for the
transition to assisted living. They'd be able to stay together
even as her condition worsened.

The complex was nice, the architecture Spanish and
the roof red tile. He'd only been here a couple of times,
but Vern had reminded him of the apartment number.

Mable let him in, kissed his cheek and led him into the
living room. "Vern, that nice young man is here."

Daniel realized she had no idea who he was.

Settled in his recliner, Vern started to lever himself up. Daniel waved him back. "No need to get up. Glad to see you, Dad." The word *Dad* stuck in his throat, but he'd forced it out. He hadn't decided yet how direct he was going be.

He accepted a soda, and Mable left them alone.

"Missed her soaps today," Vern said. "Lucky for her, I stuck a tape in."

He'd noticeably aged this past year. His hair had begun receding thirty-five years ago; now, only a wispy white tonsure remained. His hands were liver-spotted and arthritic, his neck crepey, but his faded blue eyes were still shrewd.

"She didn't know me," Daniel observed.

"You're not around often." He hesitated. "She didn't know Patty the last time she came by, either."

Patty was their oldest child. Since she lived nearby and had stayed close with her parents, Daniel suspected she was here often.

"She looks good otherwise."

"Her heart's stronger than mine. I had an angioplasty last fall. Did I tell you? Another of these damn blockages. But they keep reaming me out, and I keep going."

Daniel grinned. "You could be ten years younger."

"Don't care so much about myself. But leaving Mable, now... I don't like that idea. I can see when she's confused the way she looks for me..." Vern's brooding gaze settled on the doorway beyond which they could hear the TV. It took a moment before he gave himself a shake and focused on Daniel again. "This just social, or is there something you need to tell me?"

He decided not to waste any time.

"I've had Mom on my mind lately. Did she ever talk about Adam's father?"

His bushy white brows rose. "You mean, Billy?"

The restraint in Vern's voice answered one of Daniel's questions. "Uh…no."

"She didn't want you boys to know."

"About Robert Carson?"

"Was that his name? She never told me." He mulled that over. "All she said was that there had been a married man. Broke her heart."

"She had another baby. Did you know that?"

Vern pushed back in the recliner. "You don't mean after you?"

Daniel shook his head. "After Adam. A girl. She let Carson take her and raise her as his own."

"Jo did that?" He looked stunned. "How the heck did you find this out?"

Daniel told him then about the letter Sarah Carson had left to be opened after her death.

"So this woman knew all that time and put up with it?"

"Apparently she loved Jenny and it sounds as if they moved past Robert's infidelity."

Vern gazed toward his big-screen TV as if the past was playing on the dark screen.

"Your mother was a strange woman," he said at last. "Beautiful, of course."

Daniel guessed she was. By his earliest memories, she was in her midforties, her hair already threaded with gray. A slender woman in her twenties and maybe thirties, by her forties she was too thin. Brittle, he sometimes thought. But he had seen enough photos of her as a girl, a wartime bride and a young mother. She was a beauty, with that copper-bright hair and big gray eyes. The smile he'd seen so little of could have lit a room and must have made men flock to her.

"I couldn't believe she looked twice at me. Oh, I was successful enough by then, and maybe that was part of the appeal. Not having to struggle to pay the bills. But still, all she had to do was flash those eyes at a man, and he'd trip over his own feet to get to her."

"She was a flirt?"

"No-o. I'm not sure she meant to have that effect. With one more look, she could freeze a man between one step and the next, too. Did that more often than she summoned. I don't know what it was about her eyes. You could see she was hurting, but brave and making the best of it, too. Somehow I thought I could fix everything that was wrong for her."

When he fell silent, Daniel said quietly, "But you couldn't."

"No." Vern's mouth twisted into a near smile. "Didn't take me long to realize I was a stand-in. I even wondered…" He swallowed whatever he'd been going to say, his gaze sliding away from Daniel's.

He made a snap decision. "Whether I was really yours."

Vern's gaze swung back to his and his eyes narrowed. "This Mrs. Carson had something to say about that, too?"

"No. But I've been looking back and doing some wondering, myself. Why you and Mom didn't stay married any longer than you did, and why you always seemed ambivalent about me."

"Ah, well, I wouldn't say that." Vern cleared his throat. "You were a fine young boy. The problems your mother and I had…"

"Were directly related to whether you believed I was yours."

Vern harrumphed some more, but finally said, "You get to my age, your realize it's too late to make up for mistakes. I'll admit I've had some regrets. It wasn't as though you had any other father waiting to take over."

"And not much of a mother, either." Daniel rolled his shoulders, trying to ease his rigid muscles. "She admitted to me before she died that she didn't want to be a mother again at forty. I can't really blame her, I suppose. I think she was depressed when I was young. By the time she took over raising Adam's boy, Joe, she'd come out of it. She did fine by him. She tried to do better by me, too, but by then I wasn't having any of it."

Vern nodded. "Do you have some reason to think you aren't my son?"

"Yes." Daniel told him about the birthmark and the DNA test he was waiting on.

Vern reached for a mint from a candy dish, then unwrapped it so slowly, Daniel could tell he was buying time. "So I was right," he said finally.

His attempt to sound matter-of-fact didn't quite come off. Sure, he'd known in one way that Jo had either used him or betrayed him, but maybe a part of him had always wondered whether he'd been wrong.

"I'm afraid so," Daniel said.

"You'll let me know?"

"Sure."

"Not that it changes any of my regrets." The faded blue eyes met his squarely. "None of this was your fault. I could see that Jo was neglecting you, and I left anyway, too full of my own hurt to think about you. I've meant for years to say how sorry I am."

Was he asking for forgiveness? Examining his churning emotions, Daniel didn't know if he could give it, not and be honest. The pain of all those canceled visits should have left nothing but old scars, but they still wrenched when he moved wrong. A five-year-old boy, not much older than Malcolm, he'd thought his daddy was rejecting him.

But looking into those eyes that had become rheumy, he found he could say steadily, "I appreciate you saying it. I, uh, found out recently I'm a father, which is what got me thinking."

"A father?"

Of course he had to explain, and produce a studio photo of Malcolm taken last Christmas that Rebecca had given him.

"Looks just like you." Vern's disbelieving gaze kept going from the picture he held in one tremulous hand to Daniel's face and back again. "Isn't that something."

"He's a nice kid. Smart, confident. But he's wondered about why he doesn't have a father. Now that he does…" Daniel shrugged awkwardly. "I want to do it right."

"Sounds like you already are." Vern handed the photo back with seeming reluctance. "I can see Jo in him, too."

"It was a shock the first time I met him. Malcolm's got his mother's eyes, though."

"Then she must be pretty."

"She is. She was a dancer when she was young. Teaches elementary school now." His throat closed. "I was an idiot to let her go."

"Is there any going back?" Vern asked.

Daniel realized he was twitching. "I don't know. She'd say no right now. I don't think she likes me very much. But, uh, I'm trying to change that."

Vern reached out unexpectedly, and Daniel clasped the gnarled hand. It was stronger than he would have expected.

"Tell you what, son. You hurry up with that. Mable still likes to dance. I wouldn't mind dancing at your wedding."

Damned if he wasn't choked up enough that all he could do was nod. And when he said goodbye a few minutes later, he added, "Thanks for telling me this, Dad."

Funny how that one little word came out easier now than it had half an hour ago.

CHAPTER NINE

REBECCA HAD ALMOST MADE UP her mind that the time had come to tell Malcolm that Daniel was his father, whether Daniel pushed the issue or not. The visit to his house had done it. She couldn't go on this way. She just couldn't.

But still, somehow, the days passed, and she hadn't said anything. Cowardice. It wasn't so much that she was afraid to tell Malcolm; he was young enough to accept news like that without the sense of betrayal an older child would feel. No, she put off a necessary conversation because right now she still felt as if Mal was all hers. *He* thought he was. The moment he knew who his father was, she would have lost a part of him. Time spent with him, of course—the weekends and holidays he'd be with Daniel instead of her. But also his unrelieved loyalty and love and sense of belonging. He'd belong to Daniel, too.

And there she went, being petty again.

Rebecca sat in her classroom, free to think even as she kept an eye on her students who were writing laboriously in their journals. Most concentrated fiercely. Paper rustled and pencils scratched. Jacob shuffled to the pencil sharpener for the third time in the past half hour, while Rosalie and Summer whispered.

These past few weeks, it had occurred to Rebecca that

she might have left Daniel without telling him she was pregnant not only because she believed that he wouldn't want her and their baby, but also because part of her was unwilling to share. That part of her had *wanted* to be a single parent, free of all the complications and emotional stew sharing a child would involve, whether you were married or living separately.

No—she really *had* believed he wasn't ready for marriage and family, at least not with her. She still believed that. But she also suspected her own motivations had been much murkier than she'd thought. She hoped she never had to admit as much to him.

"Summer," she said, rousing herself, "please move to Joshua's desk for the rest of the day." Joshua had been absent all week.

"But, Ms. Ballard...!"

She raised her eyebrows.

Radiating indignation, skinny, dark-haired Summer took her pencil and journal and moved, dropping with an audible thump into the chair. Rosalie bent her head studiously and pretended *she* had nothing to do with any of this.

The bell for recess, thank goodness, rang. Rebecca made Jacob stay behind for five minutes while he sharpened all his pencils in preparation for the afternoon's work.

"Walk," she called after him, when he was done and bolted into the hall.

Perhaps tonight, she resolved, she would talk to Malcolm.

Of course she didn't.

Thursday night, Daniel called. Malcolm was already long since in bed. She had graded papers earlier and was curled up at one end of the sofa, reading a new novel by one of her favorite fantasy writers.

"I realized we hadn't made plans for this weekend," Daniel said.

Annoyed by his assumption that she would make time for him every single weekend, she wondered what he would say if she told him she and Malcolm already had plans.

Instead—yes, more cowardice!—she said only, "He has a birthday party Sunday. We've already bought the present."

"A toy bulldozer for Chace?"

Going back to her spot on the sofa, phone cradled between ear and shoulder, she was startled into a laugh. "No, the birthday girl is the preschool princess. All do her bidding. Malcolm doesn't actually like Noelle very well, but everyone else will be at the party, and it is at the roller rink—which is a terrible idea for kids their age, and I may never forgive Noelle's mother. But Malcolm is determined to go."

"Why won't you forgive Noelle's mother?" Amusement threaded Daniel's husky voice. "And why a terrible idea?"

"Because four- and five-year-olds can't roller-skate. And because Jamie—Noelle's mother—is counting on just about every parent staying at this wretched party. The rink is too crowded for her to keep an eye on the kids. Plus, the only way they can skate is to hang on to their parents for dear life. The last time I went to one of these, I had to hold two kids up, and eventually one of them tangled his feet with mine and I went down hard, on my tailbone. Which hurt for *weeks*."

"I see." Now he was laughing at her, she just knew he was. "So how about if I come?"

The offer made her feel as if she'd just gone down

again, so hard she'd had the wind knocked out of her. Was this going to be the first time she waved as Daniel took Malcolm away? Somehow, she managed to sound no more than inquiring. "You mean, take him for me?"

"Uh…I meant go with you." There was an obvious pause, followed by a reluctant, "But I suppose there's no reason I couldn't, if you need some time to yourself."

She was miserably conscious of relief even as anger squeezed her. Why did he keep wanting to play family?

No, wait—could it be that he was just nervous about taking Malcolm by himself? Was she just…well, a buffer for him on all these happy outings?

Maybe.

That thought was unaccountably depressing.

"No," she heard herself say, "I was planning to go. But you might as well find out what's in store for you."

"Do fathers go? Or is it mostly mothers?"

"On a weekend thing like this, it's about half and half. You won't be out of place."

"It wasn't that," he said stiffly. "I was just…curious."

"Even when I was a kid, a fair share of fathers—" Rebecca stopped. *Oh.* His father hadn't taken him to other kids' birthday parties. Maybe his single, working mother hadn't been able to or willing to, either. Or to afford the seemingly endless gifts. Knowing he'd hate it if he thought she felt pity, she said only, "Malcolm will enjoy having you there."

"Thanks." He was quiet for a minute. "I went to see my dad last night. I mean, Vern."

Made wary by the change of subject, she asked, "Did you tell him you suspect he's not your real father?"

"Yeah. We worked our way around to it. I asked him

about Mom. He talked about how beautiful she was, and how lucky he'd felt that she even looked at him. Sounds like it took him a few years to figure out that she'd used him to give me a name. But he knew she wasn't a happy woman. He thought he could change that."

"And he was wrong."

"Yeah." Daniel sounded weary. "What she did to him was contemptible."

"Unless," Rebecca said tentatively, "she really believed she could learn to love him."

"I don't know what to think." He fell silent again, for long enough that she wished she could see his face. "Or why I care."

Rebecca had to blink back tears. "Of course you care! For one thing, none of us wants to repeat our parents' mistakes."

He made a rough sound that might have been a laugh. "No. I don't want to do that."

"I still catch myself making excuses for my parents, even though I've never quit being mad at them, too. But I want them to have *meant* well. To have been acting out of love, however misguided. Because otherwise...otherwise..." Her throat closed.

"You have to admit they didn't give a damn," Daniel said in a monotone.

She swallowed. "I suppose."

"I've never tried to delude myself."

That was the saddest thing Rebecca had ever heard anyone say. What he meant was, he hadn't been *able* to delude himself, considering how glaring his parents' indifference and neglect had been.

"Did you tell him that he'd hurt you?" she demanded.

"Not in so many words." Daniel paused. "He volunteered an apology. Vern is eighty-three now, has had heart trouble. I guess you start thinking. He said the way he abandoned me was one of his regrets."

Her ire deflated. "Oh. I suppose that was nice of him."

Daniel laughed, as if her grudging concession had lightened his mood. "I did think it was nice of him. I had the sense that…uh…maybe he'd value a closer relationship."

She could picture him shifting, hunching his shoulders in that way he had when discomfited. Daniel might be pleased to learn that Vern Kane did care, at least a little, but he'd also be thrown for a loop. He wasn't accustomed to people caring. He might have no idea how to respond.

How could she have been dumb enough to fall in love with a man who might well be incapable of any kind of reciprocity?

"Will you go see him again? Now that you know— well, are reasonably sure—he isn't your father?"

After a moment he said, "I don't know." Then, "Maybe."

She vaguely recalled that Daniel had half sisters. Or had thought he had half sisters, although of course they weren't related to him after all. Heather and… She couldn't remember the other one's name.

"Does he need you?" she asked.

"Need me? No. Jen's in Chicago now, but Patty lives nearby."

Patty. That was it. She was the snotty older girl who had been painfully jealous when Daniel spent the occasional weekend with his father and his new family. The younger sister, Heather, had been more inclined to worship this big brother. Daniel had told Rebecca a few stories, when he had been especially relaxed. He hadn't, so far as she could tell, maintained any relationship at all with these half sisters. By the time he was a teenager, visits to his father's home had stopped altogether.

She still remembered the way he had shrugged. "The visits mostly ended by the time I was…heck, nine or ten. Vern still called occasionally. He took me to a couple of ball games, showed up a few times for my games when I was in high school. And he did arrange for a summer job on one of his construction sites. But it was pretty clear I wasn't part of his family."

His tone had been entirely impassive. She had ached for him nonetheless.

"Basically, he wants your forgiveness," she said now. "So he can forgive himself."

Daniel grunted, clearly amused. "Is that so bad?"

It took her longer than it should have to concede. "Probably not." She was shocked to find how much she wanted *someone* to suffer for Daniel's sad childhood. Vern Kane was the only one left who could.

"You don't believe in forgiveness?" he inquired.

Did she? Oh, she forgave friends for forgetting a luncheon engagement or her birthday, a fellow teacher for forgetting to pass on important information. But could she forgive either her mother or father, if they begged her on their deathbed?

"Yes," she said stiffly. "Of course I do." *Maybe.*

"Really forgiving someone, deep down…" He shrugged, his voice scratchy. "That might come hard."

Yes. It would. *Saying* you forgive someone might not be that hard. Giving them peace. But deep down, in your heart forgiving… Examining herself, Rebecca thought, *I've been angry so long, I'm corroded.* Maybe the best she would be able to do, if the time ever came, was to try.

As if reading her mind, Daniel said, "What about me? Will you ever be able to forgive me for letting you down?"

If he ever said the words, *I love you,* Rebecca was stunned to discover that she could forgive him almost anything. Her parents, no. Daniel, yes.

Oh, God.

Somehow, she crafted a tone of vague surprise. "Did you let me down? I thought we just…parted ways."

Immediately, his voice became guarded. "Is that what we did? Well, there's no going back, is there?"

But I want to, she thought with sharp longing. *I want to say to you, "I'm pregnant," and have you laugh with delight and swing me in a circle and beg me to marry you. And I want…I want…*

Such small words, and ones she couldn't imagine Daniel ever saying, not to her.

Crisply, she agreed, "No. There isn't."

"Sunday," he said, once again no more than a pleasant near stranger. "Does this party include lunch?"

"No, it's from ten to twelve."

"Shall we go out for lunch afterward?"

Of course he'd want at least that much time with Malcolm. "Sure."

Rebecca was filled with turmoil as she hung up and thought, *I'm as desperately in love as ever.*

She couldn't go on this way, pretending for Malcolm's sake that it was great fun going on outings with her buddy Daniel. She had to tell Malcolm the truth.

REBECCA WAITED UNTIL story time the next evening. She and Malcolm settled on the sofa, Mal having chosen several library books for her to read to him.

She took the first book from him, but left it closed on her lap. "I want to talk to you first."

Already in his pajamas, he swiveled on his butt so he could look up at her. "I can still go to Noelle's party, right? I bet I can really skate this time. 'Cept I don't want you to let go of my hand until I'm *sure*."

Rebecca laughed. "Yes, you can still go to Noelle's party, and no, I won't let go of your hand until you're sure. I promise."

He nodded. "Okay."

Such trust. Most of the time, she took it for granted, but occasionally, like tonight, she felt a clutch of awe and pleasure mixed with the fear that someday she'd let go too soon and fail him.

"This is about Daniel."

"He can't come?" Malcolm sounded disappointed. "I like it when he does stuff with us. I thought…it might be kinda like… Um. You know."

She knew. Kinda like having a dad.

"No, Daniel is still planning to come, too. The thing is, there's something about him I haven't told you." She took a deep breath. "Daniel *is* your father."

Her son stared at her, his brown eyes so like hers even as the face tilted up to her looked shockingly like Daniel's. "He's…my dad? I mean, *really* my dad?"

"How can you be a dad but not really?"

"You know. Like Kelsey's dad. He's a…a…"

"Stepfather," Rebecca supplied.

"Yeah, except he *acts* like her dad." Malcolm's face crinkled. "I don't know what happened to her other dad."

"I think he died." A car accident, if she remembered right.

Any hope that he would continue to be distracted by speculation about other kids' fathers was erased when Malcolm frowned. "You said my dad didn't 'specially want to have a family. Like us. Only, Daniel acts like he does. Right, Mom?"

Heart aching, she said, "Yes. He does. People change, honey." She closed her eyes. "Or maybe I was wrong then to think he wasn't ready to be a dad."

"Oh." Mal thought about it. "So he came to find us?"

"No, you remember that day at the restaurant, when we were with Aunt Naomi? And you came outside when I was talking to Daniel? He called me later and said he wanted to spend time with you."

"Does that mean you're gonna get married?" He grew more eager. "And he'll be here all the time? And maybe he wants *another* kid, too, 'cuz I'd like a baby sister. Or maybe a baby brother, but I think I'd like a baby sister better."

She laughed even though she felt like crying, and enveloped him in a hug. "I know you want a baby brother or sister! You keep saying so! But you're not going to get one anytime soon. And no, Daniel won't be here all the time. We aren't getting married. It's *you* he wants to spend time with, not me. Mostly you'll spend time with him without me. Eventually you'll go to his house some weekends. Like Polly, who can't come to Noelle's party, because she's going to her dad's house this weekend." Bad example, she realized immediately, seeing his expression. Hastily she added, "She's probably going to be doing fun stuff with him instead."

"But what if she really, really wanted to go to Noelle's party?"

"Then I'm betting her dad would have switched week-ends, so she could be home for the party. I know Daniel wouldn't want you to miss anything important."

"Oh." He hadn't made any attempt to pull back from her embrace. Instead, he kept sneaking looks up at her. "Do I have to go spend the night at his house? Because I like it when you're there."

She smiled at him, because she couldn't possibly let him know how terribly she hurt. "I think it'll be okay if we take this slowly. That's what we've been doing. I thought it would be better if you already knew Daniel before you found out he's your dad. You do like him, don't you?"

His head bobbed vigorously against her. "He's *real* nice. He's even got the same color hair as me, right, Mom?"

"Yes." She laid one cheek on his head, hoping to hide the hot tears that spilled over. "Your hair color is one of the things you got from him. *And* your freckles."

"And I like bulldozers, too. Like Daniel does." He snuggled against her in silence for a moment. "Do you think he's going to want me to call him Dad now?"

"Yes." She squeezed her eyes shut, trying to stop the flow of tears, but failing. "Yes, I think he'd like that."

Malcolm pulled away abruptly to stare at her in aston-ishment. "How come you're crying?"

She laughed and wiped her cheeks. "I guess I'm happy and sad both. Because I think Daniel will be a great dad for you, but…I liked it when it was just you and me, too."

He looked worried now. "I won't have to go with him lots, will I, Mom? 'Cuz I like being with *you.*"

"No. You won't go with him lots, and especially not when you don't want to. Daniel doesn't want you to be scared or sad."

"Okay." She could tell he wasn't entirely satisfied, but he said, "Can we read stories now, Mom?"

"You bet. After I go blow my nose."

As she headed for the bathroom, he said, "Maybe I'll call him Dad when he comes Sunday."

Oh, Lord, she thought. *I'd better warn Daniel that I've told him.*

BY THE TIME HE PULLED into Rebecca's driveway on Sunday, Daniel was as nervous as a pimply faced sixteen-year-old with a fresh driver's license picking up a girl for a first date. He'd been stunned when she phoned yesterday to tell him that Malcolm now knew Daniel was his father.

"Why now?" he'd asked hoarsely.

"I just…thought the time had come." She sounded evasive. "He was excited that you're coming tomorrow, he likes you, he's seen your house. He was ready."

More generosity. In the beginning, Daniel had agreed only reluctantly to this charade. That first day, when they went to the beach, he had realized she was right. Pretending he was just an old friend had taken pressure off both Malcolm and him. Truth be told, a couple of outings would probably have been enough; they were comfortable with each other by then.

Reasonably comfortable, he amended, ruthlessly honest with himself.

But he also hadn't felt ready to be solely in charge. He'd

never been alone with a preschooler. What if Malcolm cried? Or wanted something he couldn't provide?

And, damn it, he'd liked spending time with Rebecca, too.

Did this mean the three of them wouldn't do anything together in the future? he wondered, getting out of the car. Would they say no more than hello and goodbye when he picked Malcolm up and dropped him off?

The other night, it was her he'd wanted to talk to. He'd thought she would understand some of what he had felt when Vern said he was sorry, and when he still called him *son*. He hated the idea of losing even this pretense of friendship.

And although she'd insisted that Malcolm was happy that he would have a father now, Daniel was still nervous about facing him. What if she'd exaggerated and Malcolm was only grudgingly okay with the idea?

God! His palms were clammy as he formed a fist and knocked on the front door.

He heard a flurry of footfalls inside and the door was flung open. Malcolm grinned at him. "Mom says you're my dad!"

"Uh…yes. I am."

"I've always wanted to have a dad," the boy confided. "Can I tell everyone else you're mine?"

He was aware that Rebecca stood back, within earshot but letting them have this moment. He didn't look away from the bright, happy face of his son.

"You can tell anyone you want."

"And can I *call* you Dad?"

His throat seemed to have swelled closed. He nodded, swallowed, and managed to say, in a voice that didn't sound like his, "I'd like that."

"Okay, Dad," Malcolm declared. "Do you know how to roller-skate?"

Good God. Were his eyes getting misty?

"I, uh, think that's one of those things you don't forget how to do."

Predictably, Malcolm asked, "What other things don't you forget to do?"

His mother laughed and came forward. "We'd better go or we'll be late. Mal, where's Noelle's present?"

The boy made a face. "I think it's in my bedroom. It's a dumb present anyway."

Rebecca rolled her eyes. "Her mom didn't think she'd want a bulldozer."

Daniel choked back a laugh. Malcolm raced off to grab the girlie gift, whatever it was.

"It's a Bratz doll. She's an ice-skater. There didn't seem to be a roller-skating one."

"A brat?" he echoed.

She kindly spelled out the name. "They're popular with the girls right now. They're sort of Barbie-like. Noelle likes both, her mother says, but once I dragged Mal away from the heavy equipment aisle at the toy store, he chose this one. He was quite decisive, mainly to avoid lingering. He probably didn't want to be seen in the overwhelmingly pink aisle."

Daniel's laugh was genuine, but oddly, it hurt, as if he'd had a bad cold and had a sore throat and chest. "He really is okay with this." He indicated himself with an abortive gesture.

"I told you." Rebecca's smile twisted. "He was thrilled."

He was luckier than he deserved. One hell of a lot luckier. Daniel had a flash in which he wondered again how he would have reacted if she'd told him back then that she was pregnant. His shock would undoubtedly have showed. He hoped he wouldn't have said something cutting, like, "Did you decide it was time to move our relationship forward?" Maybe it was just as well neither of them would ever know.

Malcolm tore back out, triumphantly bearing a package wrapped in sparkly paper with a shiny bow. "I found it! Can we go now?"

Laughing, Rebecca said, "We can go. See?" She held up her hands. "I didn't even bring my purse. So I don't have to worry about it while we roller-skate."

The rink, it developed, was brand-new, thus explaining its popularity as a venue for birthday parties.

"The high school has a roller hockey rink, you see," Rebecca said. "They share it with the Boys & Girls Club. That stirred interest, I guess. Now everyone wants to skate. The Skate Inn opened just two months ago."

New or not, inside the place looked about like the roller-skating rink Daniel vaguely remembered from his own childhood. One of those mirrored balls rotated above the rink, and the place was crowded with kids and adults both circling all in the same direction to the beat of tinny music. More stood in line to rent skates or sat putting on their own Rollerblade skates. A concession bar sold the usual burgers, fries, hot dogs, licorice ropes and ice cream. A few glass-fronted rooms with long tables were presumably designed for parties.

"There's Chace." Malcolm jumped up and down and waved his hand.

The other boy and his mother stopped.

"This is my dad," Malcolm told them, pride ringing in his voice.

Rebecca laid a hand on his shoulder. "Daniel, this is Chace and Judy Dunhill."

"Daniel Kane," he said, shaking the mother's hand.

Her glance was speculative—she evidently knew Malcolm had never before had a father anywhere to be seen—but her bruiser of a son was completely uninterested. "I want to get skates. Can we do that now?"

"Yeah!" Malcolm agreed. "Can we?"

"No," Rebecca said. "We're going to go wish Noelle a happy birthday first, and leave the present in the room. We'll find out whether cake and present opening comes first, or whether there's time to skate now."

The boys, groaning, conceded. There had to be fifteen kids in the room designated for Noelle's birthday party, at least as many adults, and a table heaped with gifts. Skating, Rebecca learned after a brief parental conclave, was to come first. Each child was given a certificate for a free rental.

Daniel and Rebecca opted for roller skates rather than blades. Malcolm wasn't given a choice. They sat down in a row and laced up, Daniel hoping he remembered how to do this. Falling on his butt would probably sink his status irreparably in Malcolm's eyes.

Turned out he was initially awkward but stable. Rebecca moved with ease. Malcolm clunked along, trying to walk, hanging on to his mother with one hand and Daniel with the other.

They'd made one round when the birthday girl's mother waylaid them. "Any chance you could help Lydia skate, too?" she asked apologetically. "Her mom couldn't stay, and I need to be in the room."

Rebecca smiled at the girl clutching the railing. "Are

your skates all laced up? Oh, good." She held out a hand. "Here we go."

"I didn't fall down even once," Malcolm assured her. "It's easy."

Daniel coughed to disguise his laugh. Rebecca shot him a glance, her eyes dancing with amusement.

"Tell you what," she suggested. "Why don't I skate with Lydia, and Mal with you, Daniel? If we try to go four abreast, no one will be able to pass us."

"And some of the kids go *fast*," Malcolm said. He let his mother's hand go, gripping Daniel's even harder. "I wish I could go faster."

"Hey, no sport is easy when you first take it up," Daniel told him. "Give yourself a couple of years and you'll be tearing around."

"Yeah!"

Ahead, Lydia wobbled and lurched. Rebecca kept them moving forward. Half listening to Malcolm's chatter, Daniel watched her smile gentle encouragement at the little girl. Her neck, bared by the ponytail, was long and elegant. She skated the same way she walked, with effortless grace. His body tightened as he remembered nuzzling her nape below the heavy fall of hair, kissing his way down her throat. Wrapping his hands around her slender waist. He kept seeing her naked, her dancer's body pale, her smile luminous. The next second, Malcolm's chatter would register, and he'd realize they were at a birthday party, that she'd given birth to their son since he'd seen her lying on his bed, waiting for him to plant a knee between her thighs and bend to suckle her small breasts. That their son, like the birthday girl, would be five years old this summer.

And then she slowed and stopped by the boards. Her

glowing smile, so much like the one he remembered, touched first Malcolm and then him. "Are you having fun?" she asked.

"Yeah!" Malcolm said. "I'm getting better. Right, Dad?"

His son's irrepressible optimism and Rebecca's smiling approval worked some kind of bizarre spell. All Daniel knew was that he felt…different. Lighter.

"You're doing great. And we are definitely having fun," he agreed, and damned if he didn't mean it.

He couldn't remember that many times in his life when he had realized he was actively, genuinely happy. Not just triumphant, because he'd rammed through permits he wanted or gotten a sweet deal on a chunk of acreage. Not just sexually satisfied, not amused at a turn of conversation. Happy. Big grin trying to break free. Wanting this moment to go on and on. The whole shebang.

All brought to him by a particular boy and his mom, the woman he'd been idiot enough to let get away.

CHAPTER TEN

DANIEL CAME HOME TIRED and irritable after an inspection found shoddy electrical work on houses he was building in the East Bay. He'd walked through them with the electrical subcontractor, who had nothing but excuses. Daniel despised people who didn't take pride in quality workmanship, and he wouldn't tolerate any black mark against Kane Construction. He fired the guy on the spot and had to call in another electrical firm. Too little, too late. The development would now be delayed.

He grabbed his mail on the way in the door and tossed it on the kitchen table. What would be quick to make for dinner? He was too hungry to be patient. Daniel had gotten as far as opening the refrigerator door before the return address on one of the envelopes fanned across the table registered. MarTech Labs. The company running the DNA test.

He swung back and stared at the envelope. After a long moment of not reaching for it, he grimaced. What? Was he afraid if he opened it a lethal white powder would spill out?

No. Just confirmation that he wasn't who he had always believed himself to be: a Kane, construction in his blood.

So which answer would he prefer? To find out he'd

been fathered by a man who never acknowledged him? Or that he was the son of a man who'd given him his name, his profession and not a hell of a lot else?

He swore, the sound of his own voice startling in the quiet of the kitchen. Open the damn envelope. Yea or nay, neither result changed anything meaningful.

Daniel grabbed it and tore it open. He skimmed, glad he'd read up on DNA testing enough to more or less understand the report. The conclusion was clear enough, though; he and Isabelle Carson were indeed related. Robert Carson had to be his father.

He'd expected this result. So why did he feel as if he'd just taken a fist to his gut?

He stood there, reading the report over and over until the words jumbled incomprehensibly. The pages fluttered from his hand back to the table, and he gripped the back of a chair.

Apparently, he thought with grim humor, it didn't require a near-death experience for your life to flash before your eyes. Because that's what was happening to him right now. Calling, "Daddy, Daddy!" and seeing a look on his father's face so remote, it might have been dislike. Sitting at the dinner table with Vern and his new wife and knowing he didn't belong. Waiting for the phone to ring when Dad had *promised*. The conversation with Mom when she'd expressed regret for her failings as a mother, but never said, "I panicked and married a man I didn't love because your real father, who I do love, is married and not willing to leave his wife."

Anger scalding him, he couldn't understand why she hadn't told him. Why take that secret to her grave? Didn't he have a *right* to know who his father was?

Well, now he did, no thanks to her. No thanks to anything but the merest chance—Belle Carson bending to pick up the earring.

If not for that, Daniel was unlikely to have spent much time with her in the future. To see her in a bikini, say. Maybe Joe would have; it was possible Joe would have noticed the birthmark and thought, *Wait a minute, isn't that like…?* But maybe not; he hadn't seen Daniel's in years.

Still in turmoil, Daniel flipped through the rest of the mail, then went back to the refrigerator. He still had half a jar of salsa and decided to make quesadillas. They didn't take long to cook, and despite his turmoil he was hungry.

It was a couple of hours before he'd fully wrapped his mind around the news. Daniel tried to work, gave up and tried to read. Couldn't concentrate on anything.

He was tempted to call Rebecca. He didn't even know why. Would she listen only to be polite? Even assuming she gave a damn, what could she say that would help?

Finally he glanced at the clock and decided to call Belle. She was the one of the new relatives who seemed to care the most, even though the news would hardly be earth-shattering to her. *She* knew who she was, had grown up the secure and likely pampered granddaughter of Robert Carson.

He scrounged in his wallet to find the slip of paper with her phone number, then dialed. She answered after just a couple of rings. "Hello?"

"Belle, this is Daniel. Uh, Daniel Kane."

"Oh!" She sounded breathless. "You finally heard?"

"Got the results today. Probably not a surprise. It would appear you can start calling me Uncle Daniel."

She laughed with apparent delight. "I'm so glad!" There was a pause. "Except…"

"Except?" he prompted.

"You must have terribly mixed feelings."

He hesitated, unsure if he wanted to talk about those feelings with this young woman, a near stranger. And yet, she'd clearly given some thought to how this would affect him, and he remembered that strange moment when they'd looked at each other after comparing birthmarks. Something had…clicked. He'd already found out that Sue Bookman was his niece, and felt nothing special. This relationship wasn't any closer, but those matching birthmarks had inextricably tied them together.

"You could say that," he admitted. "I thought I was prepared for this. What other reasonable explanation was there for our having identical birthmarks, especially such oddly shaped ones? But when I opened that damn thing tonight, I was still stunned and—" he pinched the bridge of his nose "—angry. How did my mother screw up her life so badly, and so many other people's along with hers?"

"I suppose love makes us reckless."

"You mean, stupid and heedless of consequences?" he said harshly.

"Foolish, maybe. If Matt had already been married…" She stopped. "I hope I would have had the sense not to let myself fall in love. Or not to act on it. But it's hard to be sure."

He only grunted.

"And Grandad deserves as much or more blame! Think about it. Wasn't he taking advantage of your mom right after the war? I mean, there she was, a new widow and vulnerable. He was supposed to be taking care of her, and what did he do but sleep with her!" Indignation rang in her voice. "And it wasn't as if they were swept away, that it was one crazy moment with unintended consequences.

Oh, no. Instead of…well, helping her get on with her life, he kept her as his mistress. If he ever intended to leave Grandma, he decided not to after she got pregnant with my dad. But he wanted to have his cake and to eat it, too. I think what he did is nearly unforgivable. I mean, it doesn't sound as if he even provided financial support."

"I don't know," Daniel said thoughtfully. "Once I paid her outstanding bills and probate was over, I dumped Mom's papers in cardboard cartons and haven't looked through any of it. It's possible he did, at least in the early years."

"What about after you were born?"

There was the question. Had his mother married Vern Kane because she couldn't bear the stares and whispers of a less tolerant era, and the stigma of illegitimacy that would follow him? Because she'd already been dating Vern and knew him to be a thoughtful, steady man who would make a fine husband if only she could bring herself to love him? Because Robert Carson *hadn't* offered financial support and she was desperate?

Or because she was equally desperate to keep him from ever knowing that she had become pregnant after one tempestuous night?

God. He hoped one night. He hoped like hell the two of them hadn't continued an on-again, off-again affair over decades. He wanted to think better of his mother than that.

"I might do some research," he said, realizing the idea had been in the back of his mind for a while. "All this might settle better if I had some answers."

"I think all of us will be better off to know more. I suppose Sue and Joe and I are one step removed. It's got to be more traumatic when it's your mother and father, not your grandparents. The funny thing is, Aunt Jenny has taken all this in stride." She gave a little laugh. "Well, I guess it's not funny—it's her. She's nothing like Sue. I doubt she agonizes." She sighed. "The one who has taken it hardest is Dad."

"So I gather. What I've never understood is why. He's the only one of us who *didn't* get any surprises."

"I think he grew up arrogant. Jenny was adopted, he was the oldest kid. Maybe Grandma and Grandad made too much of him being the Carson. Or maybe it was all in his head." She paused. "Do you know he and Mom are separated now? He's… Well, a difficult man. I've spent too much of my life rebelling. That stupid diamond necklace has become a huge symbol to him."

The Carson family necklace, a treasured heirloom that Sam Carson had assumed would be his after his mother died, threatened to tear the family apart. Sarah Carson had left it to Jenny instead—recompense, maybe, for all the lies. The way Daniel understood it, Sam had lost the last round in his lawsuit to reclaim possession, but nobody believed he'd given up.

"He's brooding" was how Joe had put it.

Pip, part of that conversation, had scrunched up her nose. "Sulking, you mean."

Daniel had seen that Sam could be charming. He didn't know him well enough to venture an opinion on his current state of mind.

Belle, too, was still thinking about her father. She said, "Dad hated that he wasn't the oldest son, that Adam was. Finding that out seemed to diminish him. Which is silly."

"Has he heard about our birthmarks?"

"I'm hardly speaking to him at the moment. But I

will tell him about you. That…wow. He has yet another brother."

"News that will thrill him." Daniel found he was grateful that Belle and Sue *were* glad to welcome him to the family. He hadn't needed family, God knows, but it would have been worse to learn none of these new relatives wanted anything to do with him.

Sure, he mocked himself. *Say that again with conviction when you're stuck at a huge Thanksgiving get-together with kids running around screaming and the men faking camaraderie while they watch football in the living room.*

Yeah, but he *did* like Joe. And Pip. With that soft New Zealand accent, she was starting to feel like someone he could relax with. Trust to make Joe happy. And Belle and Sue were okay, so maybe he would like their husbands, too, once he knew them better. Hey, he and Joe, along with Sue, would be the first to bring children to family gatherings. So he couldn't complain much. He did like the thought that he had some family to offer to Malcolm, especially since Rebecca was estranged from her parents.

"Who cares what Dad thinks?" Belle said cavalierly. "*I* think it's very cool that you're my uncle Daniel, and so does Sue. And you're young and hot, which makes it even better."

He was surprised into a laugh. "Not so young. I'm thirty-eight."

"Yes, but Dad is fifty-eight. So you're closer in age to us than to our parents. And you can't tell me women don't fling themselves at you wherever you go."

Damn it, now he was embarrassed. "Not that many women on construction sites."

"Really? I thought lots were going into the trades these days. You must employ some, don't you?"

"Mostly in the office. I did contract a female electrician today. So, yeah. They're around."

"Good," she said. "I'm sure, in your position, Dad wouldn't."

"He doesn't sound arrogant so much as insecure."

"That may be, but either way I'm tired of it." There was a note of finality in her voice. "I'm proud of Mom for leaving him."

"We are a screwed-up family."

"Do you know," she said, "the funny thing is that I'd have sworn Grandad and Grandma loved each other. That she missed him terribly after he was gone. I felt…safe with them, if that makes sense. Maybe they had a bad patch when Dad was just a little kid and that's when he became insecure about how important he was. And maybe when Grandad first brought Jenny home he thought he might be the only one who'd love her, so he paid her too much attention right when Dad was feeling like his place in the family was shaky. Kids do, when a new baby comes along."

Yeah, Daniel supposed so, although by the time his mother had taken in Joe, Daniel hadn't felt threatened. He'd closed himself off already. He hadn't been jealous of how much Mom had been able to give Joe.

One thing to his credit.

"You've given a lot of thought to this."

"Well, of course I have. After all, we've been untangling this for ages now, ever since Grandma's attorney read us that letter."

"Yeah, I understand that. Adam was…stunned. He'd believed all his life that his father was this war hero who would have been the dad-of-the-year if only he hadn't died.

But no, it turns out Robert just chose not to acknowledge him. As for me… Well, the part I've struggled with is discovering that Mom had another baby. A baby she gave away."

He sensed that she was nodding. "I got off easy, didn't I?" She sounded almost rueful. "It blew Sue away. She and Joe were such close friends in high school. I think maybe Joe was in love with her. And now to find out they're first cousins!"

"First cousins have married before. But, yeah, it would have been weird," he conceded. "Joe told me that Sue was the one to end things, not him."

"Now she thinks maybe she sensed something. He *does* look an awful lot like Grandad, in pictures from when he was young. So maybe that was it."

They talked longer, but didn't say anything important. Some of Daniel's restlessness had subsided by the time he hung up, though. He guessed he'd just needed to talk to *someone.* Maybe anyone would have done. Then again, maybe not; he felt at ease with Belle like he did with Joe. They seemed to be sliding into friendship, which he guessed was what most of this conversation had really been about. That, and introducing him to the intricacies of this new family.

Her parents had separated, for example. He didn't really care; the couple of times he'd met Sam Carson, Daniel hadn't liked him. He'd been enraged when he heard that Sam had talked Adam into selling him Billy Fraser's Medal of Honor. That medal had meant a hell of a lot to Adam, representing all he had of the man he'd believed was his father. Yeah, the medical bills were steep, but some things shouldn't have a price.

And then, damn it, Sam had given it back at the funeral, letting Adam take it with him to his final rest. That was a surprisingly decent thing to do. And…Sam was Daniel's brother. Half brother. A connection by blood that was real, whether or not either of them welcomed it.

So maybe it would be interesting to find out why he tended to be such a jackass, given that he'd been his father's only acknowledged son.

Daniel was better acquainted with Emily Carson, since she'd visited Adam regularly in the hospital. She had thought her husband was wrong in refusing to accept that they were brothers, and she had been determined to make up for his rejection. She was a pretty, gentle, gracious woman. Belle, he thought, had taken the best from both her parents.

Sleep didn't come easily to Daniel that night. *What a goddamn mess!* he kept thinking. Was it really possible for a man to love two women? Or had it been nothing but arrogance and lust?

Had it occurred to anyone to wonder whether Robert Carson had had other women? Other children?

If so, his wife hadn't known about them. She *had* known about Jo Fraser, and had evidently forgiven him for that transgression. So maybe she'd believed it truly was love he felt. Which, Daniel wondered, would hurt worse? To find out your husband enjoyed other women on the side without necessarily feeling any deep emotion, or to find out he had been close to leaving you for a woman he did love and—apparently—never was able to forget?

Not the kind of thing Daniel usually wasted any thought on. Why would he, when he'd not only never been married, he'd never been in love? But he remembered when he insisted on coming to Rebecca's house and it occurred to him that she might have a husband and even other children. He'd felt gut-churning rage. He hadn't seen her in five years, and yet he had violently disliked the idea of her with anyone else.

He disliked the idea even more now. What if she started dating some guy? What if she got *married?* He'd be relegated to being Malcolm's father, whose schedule had to be considered when the family made plans.

Over my dead body, Daniel thought grimly, staring at the streetlight leaking around the curtains. Rebecca was *his.* He couldn't figure out how else to articulate the emotion that made his chest feel hollow.

Would it be so bad to get married? To forsake all others?

For the first time, he considered the idea without feeling any panic and concluded that no, it wouldn't be bad at all.

Something to think about.

Something else guaranteed to hold sleep at bay.

DANIEL CALLED REBECCA'S house the next evening, hoping she'd answer rather than Malcolm, just so he could hear her voice. Judge whether he was exaggerating his attraction to her.

But Malcolm answered, saying hello and then, without covering the phone, yelling, "It's Daniel, Mom! I mean, Dad!"

Wincing, Daniel pulled the phone a few inches back too late to save his eardrum.

"I had a great day," Malcolm told him. "Guess what?" He didn't wait for any response. "I get to spend tomorrow night with Chace. I don't think I'll get scared this time. I've never stayed all night at anyone's house before, except

Aunt Nomi's. But Mom said maybe I should practice. For when I stay at your house. And Chace and I are real good friends. Most of the time," he added judiciously. "When he isn't all braggy."

"About his dad's truck."

"Uh-huh. But now I can say so what, because my dad has a bulldozer. And that's better."

Daniel laughed. "I'm glad to be useful."

"I'd like you even if you didn't have a bulldozer," his son told him earnestly. "But I'm glad you do."

Should he tell the boy that he had more than one bulldozer? And a lot of other heavy equipment? Yeah, but maybe he'd need to pull them out of the hat later, when Malcolm had become less impressed by only one measly piece of earthmoving equipment.

"I'm glad you're practicing for staying with me," he said. "But I hope you don't get scared when you do. You liked my house, didn't you?"

"Yes, but I 'specially like it when Mom's there, too."

You and me both, kid.

"But I'm getting bigger all the time," Malcolm continued. "It won't be that long until I'm five, like Noelle. I can't remember how long Mom said it would be. And then I'll go to kindergarten. 'Cept I can already read. I mean, not whole books. But *some*. Like *'bat'*. And *'hat'*. Mom says I'm real smart, when I haven't started school yet."

Daniel thought he was, too. He felt a ridiculous swell of pride.

Malcolm rattled on. All Daniel had to do was ask an occasional question. Here he'd worried about making conversation with a four-year-old over the phone! This one had the art of conversation down pat.

"What's your mom going to do without you home?" Daniel managed to ask casually. "Go party with your Aunt Nomi?"

Malcolm thought that was hysterical. His mom didn't party! And Aunt Nomi had a friend. A *boy* friend.

"She goes somewhere with him every Friday. And then she calls in the morning so she can tell Mom all about it. I don't know why she does that," he confides. "Once I picked up the phone, and she talked and talked, and it was really boring. But Mom said you have to listen when your friends want to talk. So that's what she was doing."

"I see," Daniel said gravely, pleased at his information-gathering strategy. Should he ask to talk to Rebecca? Invite her out?

Or should he just drop by tomorrow night and hope she was having a peaceful evening at home? Was she listening to Malcolm's side of the conversation? Maybe he could pretend to have forgotten Malcolm was away for the night.

Or maybe he should just say, "I wanted to catch you home alone." Wasn't honesty the best policy?

Unless she slammed the door in his face.

Somehow, he thought she wouldn't do that. On the other hand, he suspected that if he asked her out, she'd say no.

He was smiling when he ended the call *without* asking to speak to Malcolm's mom.

REBECCA FELT...RESTLESS. Which was really dumb. She had often thought how nice it would be once Malcolm was old enough to occasionally spend the night with a friend. In four and a half years, she'd had barely a handful of evenings to herself. She went out sometimes—it wasn't as though she didn't hire a babysitter occasionally, or leave

Mal with Naomi for a few hours. And he had spent the night at Naomi's a couple of times, but always when Rebecca had to be away. Otherwise—she just wasn't used to him not being here.

So no wonder she felt a bit unsettled. Plus, she wouldn't be at all surprised if she had to go pick him up at some point this evening, or even late tonight. A first sleepover for a boy his age could be scary.

Still, she should be doing something more extravagant than cooking a dinner she knew he wouldn't like and planning to read one of the books she'd picked out at the library yesterday. *She* should be going out with a man. Naomi told her often enough that it was past time.

Rebecca had told herself she just hadn't met anyone who appealed enough to her. Of course, it was hard to be attracted to another man when you were still in love with the last one.

She turned the burner on to heat as she sliced beef into thin strips, then browned them and cut up an onion into slices thin enough to be near-translucent. All the while, she kept…oh, expecting the phone to ring, she supposed.

Malcolm wouldn't cry, of course. She smiled, imagining how brisk and reasonable he would be.

Mom, I think I want to practice spending the night some other time. Tonight's not a good night. I'd like it better if you were tucking me in tonight, instead of Chace's mom.

She measured burgundy and water, adding them to the sizzling strips of beef, then reached for the jar of bay leaves. Already it smelled wonderful. She'd have her burgundy beef on brown rice, Rebecca decided, another food her incredibly picky son was quite sure he didn't like.

She had just put the lid on the pan and turned the heat to low when the doorbell rang. Her hand jerked. Who on earth…?

But she knew, even before she opened the front door a cautious crack and saw Daniel Kane on her doorstep.

CHAPTER ELEVEN

REBECCA THOUGHT SHE'D become used to his presence, able to—almost—turn off her powerful awareness of his body. But this time Malcolm wasn't here. If she let Daniel in, they'd be alone. That changed everything.

Of course, he was as imposing as ever. In jeans and a brown-and-russet plaid shirt in some nubby fabric open over a brown T-shirt, he was the sexiest man she'd ever seen. His face was craggy and pure male, his mouth tight to disguise whatever he felt.

"Daniel," she said warily.

"I hope you don't mind me showing up like this."

"What if I told you I had company?"

A shutter seemed to close over his expression. "Do you?"

A flutter of excitement told her even before she opened her mouth that she was about to be reckless. She made a face at him. "No. But I wish I did, just to teach you to call first."

"If I'd called, you would have made an excuse."

"Probably." She hesitated, then finally opened the door wide and stepped back. "Fine. Come in."

Choosing not to comment on her ungracious invitation, he walked in, so close to her she had trouble breathing. *Damn him.* And yet, she reminded herself, he'd been civil when she asked him to meet her for lunch that day in the city. She owed him for that.

She closed the door, then faced him. "Daniel, why are you here?"

He was silent for a moment, and she saw some struggle on his face. "I've been thinking about you this week." His voice sounded slightly hoarse. "Wanting to talk to you."

"About Malcolm?"

"No." He cleared his throat. "Actually, uh, about me."

About *him?* She studied him, noticing belatedly the way his hands were shoved in his pockets, his shoulders hunched. New lines drawn on his face.

Understanding dawned, along with compassion. "You got the DNA results back."

His mouth twisted. "Yeah."

"Oh, dear," she said involuntarily.

He frowned. "Why do you say that?"

"Because I doubt either answer would be a relief." She touched his arm. "Come on back to the kitchen. Let me check on my dinner."

Following her, he said to her back, "I was going to offer to take you out."

"I'm making burgundy beef, and there's enough for two." She smiled over her shoulder. "Although the leftovers would have made a great lunch."

Daniel paused in the kitchen doorway, his broad shoulders filling it, the gravel back in his voice when he said, "I was presuming a hell of a lot, showing up here like this."

"Yes, you were, but I'd like to hear what you learned."

"I'm related to Belle Carson," he said. "Robert was my father."

"Oh." She gave her dinner a perfunctory stir, but studied him the whole time. "How do you feel about it?"

He gave a grunt that was probably supposed to be a laugh. "How do you think? Pissed. Relieved. Illuminated. Hell, confused, shocked, indifferent. Ask me in five minutes and who knows what I'd say?"

Rebecca picked one word out of this string. "Why illuminated?"

He stayed in the doorway, watching her. "Because it explains a lot."

"Why your dad walked away."

He nodded.

"What did you think before? That it was because he was so mad at your mom?"

"No." He shrugged as if it didn't matter. "I thought it was me."

"You?" she echoed, appalled. "You were a child!"

"What else was I supposed to think?"

What else would he think, a five-year-old boy whose father hardly bothered to call after he left? Rebecca imagined Malcolm, if she suddenly lost interest, and felt tears sting her eyes for this man, who had believed his entire life that he was somehow lacking.

"I'm not sure it's an improvement to find out my real father was even less interested." He sounded…detached. As if they were talking about somebody else.

And yet he'd come here tonight to talk about this. He'd admitted to confusion and shock, too. Even to anger. Which meant the indifference he projected was a big fat lie.

"You said yourself that he might have assumed you were Vern's son," she reminded him. "And that's if he and your mother maintained any kind of contact. What if she told him not to call again? That she couldn't bear to see him? It might be that he never knew about you."

He shook his head. "I don't believe it. He had sex with her. You can't tell me he wouldn't have kept an ear to the ground, wanting to be sure there weren't consequences."

Consequences. He said the word drily, reducing himself to a mere nuisance.

"I played sports," he continued. "Later on, he'd have seen my name in the newspaper. No. He had to know about me."

"Could your mother have flat-out lied? Told him you were Vern's?"

He gave another of those shrugs that broke her heart. "Sure. If you'd been Robert, would you have believed her?"

She didn't say anything, but he could probably read her answer on her face. No, of course she wouldn't. She would have insisted on the truth. She would never have turned her back on a child of hers.

Any more, she thought, than he was willing to do. Raised with so little love, how had Daniel Kane turned into the kind of man who was incapable of abandoning his son, even though he hadn't planned for him, hadn't wanted him? She couldn't imagine.

Her chest burned. How could she hold on to any resentment at having to share Malcolm? If ever anyone needed someone to love, it was Daniel.

"Well, he was an idiot," she declared, bending to clatter pans in the cupboard while furiously blinking away tears. She thought she'd subdued them by the time she straightened with a saucepan in her hand. "To be so careless in the first place. And then to have two sons that somebody else raised. I'm glad he's dead. I wouldn't want Malcolm to have to pretend to love him."

"I wouldn't have asked that of Malcolm," Daniel said in a mild voice. "Not when I sure as hell wouldn't have been willing to pretend."

Rebecca made herself revert to her original point. "But…it might not have been all his fault."

"No. Some of it was Mom's."

There it was again, that utterly flat, expressionless voice that hid…something. A great deal of hurt, was Rebecca's best guess.

"What was she like?" she asked curiously.

He was silent long enough she wasn't sure he'd respond, but eventually he did start talking about his mother while Rebecca put water on to boil for the rice, cut up broccoli and found a pan for it, and made a salad.

He had never known his grandparents, which made his mother harder to put into perspective. Very young, she'd married a man who immediately went off to war. He survived the fighting only to die shortly after coming home. Robert and her husband had served together, and he had evidently felt a responsibility toward her. One that had quickly become more.

"Apparently Mom managed to pass Adam off as her husband's child, although he was born a month too late. She built Billy Fraser up to be this big war hero and fabulous guy." He shrugged. "Maybe he was. They looked happy in their wedding picture."

He talked about the job his mother had held in the county assessor's office, about her fondness for baking even though she worried about her weight and made everyone else eat the fruits of her labors.

"Which wasn't a problem when any of us lived at home. Wait'll Malcolm starts shooting up. I could put food away, and Mom always swore Joe could push back from the table, stuffed, then be back foraging in the refrigerator an hour later."

His mother had been a big reader, one reason he was, as well. They'd visited the library once a week, religiously. She couldn't afford to buy many books, although she often had a bag of paperbacks from the secondhand bookstore, too.

"When I picture her," he said in an odd tone, "I always see her in the living room, the lamp making a pool of light in the darkness, her head bent over her book. She'd be lost in it. I could tell when she looked up that she'd forgotten there was a here and now."

He didn't have to say, *She'd forgotten she had a son.* That memory made Rebecca sad, the idea that Daniel hadn't had a place in that living room, or else it would have been better lit in his memories.

The last thing he said before she served dinner was, "Funny how little I really did know Mom."

Rebecca shook her head. "I simply can't imagine." And she couldn't. Daniel must have been so much like Malcolm: smart, cute, eager. Had Jo Fraser not loved him because she thought he was Vern Kane's son and not Robert Carson's? But even then—he was *her* son. Shouldn't that have been what mattered most?

As they sat and began to dish up, Rebecca said, "I'm amazed the phone hasn't rung yet."

"Malcolm?" A grin tugged at Daniel's mouth. "He did tell me he thought he wouldn't be scared this time. Because after all, he's almost five. Although he couldn't remember how far away his birthday actually was."

She laughed. "Yeah, the passage of time is still a puzzle to him."

"It's relative to all of us. Depending on whether we want something to happen, or we dread it."

"True enough," she said lightly. She felt…odd. As if some champagne had joined the blood flowing through her body. She seemed to *fizz*. What was going to happen? Did she *want* it to happen?

Did she even have to ask herself that question?

Rebecca closed her eyes. *Oh, I'm as big a fool as Jo Fraser was, taking back the man I love, over and over again!*

She grabbed for something, anything, to say. "I don't suppose you plan to change your last name."

He raised his eyebrows. "Carson Construction doesn't have the same ring to it."

"No-o… But you wouldn't have to change the name of the business, since it's so well established."

He was shaking his head. "No. I have no desire to take on his name. A name is a gift. He didn't give me his."

And Vern Kane had, whatever his other failures as a father. Rebecca nodded.

"Most of these new relatives aren't Carsons, either. Sam will be the only one once his daughter Belle is married. Jenny took her husband's name, too."

"No boys to carry it on."

He looked at her. Of course there had been boys. Adam and he both ought to have been Carsons, which would have made Joe a Carson, too.

"Do names matter anyway?"

"I think they might," Daniel said thoughtfully. "They have power. Kids get ridiculed for the wrong name. Actors choose names that express… God knows."

"Magic. Charisma."

"Anything but the ordinary," he agreed. "A business rises and falls in part because of the name the founder chooses. We judge people by their names."

"Kane is a good one," Rebecca decided.

"You sound like Malcolm."

Oh, Lord, so she did. She remembered how awful she'd felt when he had announced that Kane was a *good* name, and she couldn't help thinking it should have been his.

"Well, it's true."

Daniel watched her, his eyes dark and intense. "I missed you. Talking to you."

Please don't do this to me, she begged silently, but said only, "You must have other friends."

He shrugged, his gaze not leaving her face. "Joe."

She set down her fork. "You have other friends!"

"People I entertain. Maybe enjoy. Nobody else I could talk to about this." He frowned. "Sam Carson's daughter, Belle. We've talked."

What an idiotic time to feel jealous! And hadn't he said she was getting married?

"She's the one with the birthmark that looks like mine. She was trying to tell me about family the other day."

"Do they know about Malcolm? I mean, besides Joe?"

He shook his head. "Hasn't come up."

It seemed they had safely left behind dangerous territory. *I missed you.* She rose. "I'm afraid I don't have any dessert to offer. And my coffee is instant, but if you'd like a cup…"

She knew what a coffee snob he was. He shook his head, but in an automatic way, not as if he cared whether she was offering powder from a jar or fresh-ground Bolivian dark roasted. He wasn't thinking about coffee.

He was thinking about her.

"Rebecca."

She froze.

"What if I'd come after you? What if I hadn't accepted the note as goodbye?"

Her legs failed her. She sank back into the chair. "I don't know." Her voice came out husky, barely above a whisper. "I suppose...I would have had to tell you."

"The note didn't sound as if you minded parting ways. Did you?" He made a gesture. "Malcolm aside."

She couldn't look away from him. Lying would be the best tactic. *I thought we'd taken the relationship as far as we could. Sound...blithe. Surprised he'd ask now.*

"Yes, of course I minded." She glared at him. "I thought you were tired of me. That hurt. And then, when I found out I was pregnant..." Her throat clogged.

"You should have told me."

"Why?" That old pain pressed at her rib cage. "It wouldn't have made you love me when you didn't. Or want to get married. Or even be a father. You'd made it plain your answer would have been none of the above."

A muscle in his jaw spasmed. "I was scared."

His voice was so soft, she wasn't sure she'd heard right. She *couldn't* have heard right.

"What?"

"Conversation with a woman is usually, uh, a means to an end."

"That's...that's an awful thing to say."

His shoulders moved. "But true. I'm not saying I haven't enjoyed talking to women I've been involved with. But that wasn't the point. I didn't...count on it." Lines creased his forehead again, as if he'd disconcerted even himself.

He took a moment before he finished, "It was different with you."

She tried to comprehend. "You liked talking to me. And that *scared* you?"

"Needing someone else doesn't come naturally to me."

That almost made her cry. Of course it came naturally to him, as it did to every helpless newborn! But Daniel, while never truly neglected or abused, had been taught that no one else cared all that much about him. He had to be sufficient unto himself. And whatever he had come to feel for her had threatened that self-sufficiency.

"You can't tell me you didn't find another girlfriend right away." *Please, please tell me you didn't.*

He shook his head. "It was a while. Six months, maybe. And even then…" He moved restlessly in his chair. "No other woman has ever stayed the night at my house."

No one had taken her place at the breakfast table, even if they had in his bed. Longing and hope dug their claws into her.

"What are you saying?" she whispered.

"Like I said. I missed you." He shoved back the chair and stood. Suddenly his voice was hoarse. "Every god-damn day."

Rebecca let out a sob. She wanted to hear other words, but these…these were a miracle all their own. She stood, too, and they met at the foot of the table.

No chance for second thoughts. He yanked her against him so hard, their bodies slammed together. His fingers tangled in her hair and tipped her head back so his mouth could claim hers. No tenderness, only raw hunger. The clutch of desire was so much more vicious than she remembered it.

One of her arms was painfully bent between them. She freed it and flung both around his neck, on tiptoe to press herself closer yet. Her mind blurred; Daniel was holding her, kissing her, as if he'd spent years dreaming about this kiss.

Her legs sagged; he backed her against the wall with a thump hard enough to rattle the china cabinet. Her shirt fell to the floor first, his on top of it. The hooks of her bra defeated him, and he swore and lifted his head long enough to deal with them. The next thing she knew, he hoisted her high enough to allow him to suckle her breast. With a squeak, she wrapped her legs around his waist and pressed against his erection as he took her other breast into his mouth.

Oh, now she wanted his T-shirt off even more. She pushed it up, even knowing she couldn't succeed without him letting her go. And she didn't want him to let her go.

"Beautiful," he said, in an unrecognizable voice. His face was taut, almost savage. He kneaded her butt, rocked her against him.

Would they make it to the bedroom? If they'd gotten their pants off, he could take her against this wall. Except...

"I'm not on birth control," she gasped.

He went still, then swore. "I think I have a condom in my wallet."

If he didn't have one... She almost didn't care. Some risks were worth taking.

His mouth closed over hers once again, his tongue sliding along hers in a primitive rhythm that made her belly cramp. She peeled his tee off; he kept kissing her, even as he pulled the wallet out of his back pocket and opened it.

They pulled apart long enough for him to open the wallet and extract a slim packet.

I won't think about why he carries one.

"I want you on a bed."

She managed a nod. Self-control was good. Comfort was good. Not essential, but how would she feed Malcolm peanut butter sandwiches at this table with the memory of rutting on the floor beside it?

They bumped walls and corners. Rebecca left her shoes in the living room, her jeans in the hall. She had his unbuttoned, and his breath rasped as they staggered into her small bedroom. Daniel lifted her and dropped her on the cloud-soft duvet, stripped off his jeans and followed her down.

His hand was between her legs. She moaned his name, arched. "Please."

Daniel rose above her. His hands were shaking as he tore open the packet and rolled the condom on. Seconds later, he nudged at her entrance even as he kissed her as if his life depended on this connection between them.

For a second it hurt, having him press into her. She was ready—oh, so ready—but this felt new again. It had been so long; she'd had a child in between. Daniel must have felt her stiffen; he lifted his head and watched her face as he pushed deeper, deeper, going so slowly she could see the strain on his face. And then he was buried to the hilt, filling her utterly.

"Okay?" he asked.

"Yes." An inner tremor shook her, a hint of something sweeter, wilder. "Yes."

He eased back as carefully, then pushed inch by inch, his eyes never leaving hers. This time, as he retreated, she lifted her hips to hold him, to welcome him, and his control snapped. He thrust, again and again, his lips drawn back from his teeth, his eyes molten. Rebecca clutched at his shoulders with desperate hands and wrapped her legs around him so he couldn't escape, not now, not this time. Never again. And her body simply…imploded. Some strange sound escaped her, maybe his name again, she couldn't have said, as pleasure flooded her the way hot lava flowed sizzling into the sea.

She'd drawn Daniel with her. He jerked and groaned, his face buried in her hair. His weight sagged onto her, but she didn't care. This must be what it felt like in the aftermath of a tornado, she thought, dazed, the silence absolute and shocking, the walls around them probably no longer standing. She would open her eyes any minute and find out.

The phone on her bedside stand rang.

Rebecca whimpered. Daniel mumbled an obscenity and pushed up on his elbows.

"You don't have to answer."

"I won't. Unless it's Malcolm."

"Do you have caller ID?"

She nodded.

The mechanical voice from the answering machine in the kitchen announced, "Dunhill, Mark."

Rebecca squeezed her eyes shut for a moment, then fumbled for the phone. "It's him. Or maybe Judy."

Daniel flipped off her to lie sprawled on his back.

She picked up the phone. "Hello?"

"Mom?" Malcolm sounded terribly young. "I know I said I'd try to stay, but I'd really like to come home."

"Aren't you having fun?" she asked, marveling at her ability to sound so much like usual.

Daniel groaned and laid his forearm over his eyes.

"Yeah! We had lots of fun, and I liked Mrs. Dunhill's spaghetti almost as much as yours. But now it's time to go to bed, and…and I want to go to bed at home. Maybe *next* time I can stay all night."

"Yes. All right. You tell Chace's mom I'll be there in a few minutes. Okay?"

"Okay!" He sounded jubilant. "Bye, Mom!"

"Bye, sweetie." She hung up and let the phone drop onto the bed.

Daniel lifted his arm enough to roll his eyes her way. "You couldn't say, 'Tough, kid, you'll survive'?"

"He's four. And not so tough. Besides, do you have another condom?"

"Crap. No."

"Well then."

"God," he said, and pulled her on top of his big body so that he could kiss her, a leisurely, sensuous exploration of her mouth while his hands kneaded her back.

Maybe Malcolm *could* spend the night….

Daniel slapped her butt. "No condom."

Flushed, she scrambled off him with scant dignity. "Right. I need a shower."

He didn't follow her into the bathroom, thank heavens. No condom, she remembered. No birth control. He hadn't wanted the first child, and wouldn't want another surprise.

That hurt.

She'd kept her hair from getting wet by bundling it up on her head. As she got dressed, Rebecca couldn't help wondering what he *did* want. Besides…well, what he'd already gotten.

I missed you every single goddamn day. What did that mean? *I love you?* Or *We had something good, let's recapture some of it?* Surely he must see that things were different now. How would she explain to her young son that the time she spent with his father didn't mean anything, that they were just having fun for old times' sake?

Should she ask? Let matters unfold? Admitting to as much vulnerability as he had must have been hard for Daniel. He didn't like acknowledging that he had frail human emotions at all. Maybe it was unreasonable of her to expect more right away.

But, she didn't think she could survive having him again, and losing him. If she'd been devastated the first time, what would it be when a few months from now, a year from now, he moved on, but she had to keep seeing him because he was Malcolm's father?

Just like that, she was fighting for breath. *I shouldn't have done this.*

Eventually she regained enough control to leave the bathroom with a semblance of poise. Daniel was already dressed and had laid her strewn clothing on her bed. Was he gone? But no, he waited in the living room, standing beside the sofa, his laser-sharp gaze going straight to her face when she appeared.

But he said only, "I'll drive."

"You don't have to stay."

"I'd like to see Malcolm."

"Oh." *Breathe.* "Yes. Okay. Then let's go."

Chace lived less than ten minutes away, thank goodness. Rebecca didn't even try to make conversation on the way. Daniel drove in preoccupied silence.

He waited in the car while she collected their son, who

was delighted that Dad was here to get him, too. He started to fall asleep during the ride home, though, short as it was, and Daniel had to carry him in.

"Did you brush your teeth?" Rebecca asked.

He blinked at her over his dad's shoulder. "Uh-huh. Chace's mom made us. But I didn't like Chace's toothpaste. I wished I had our kind."

Their house had only the one small bathroom, so they shared toothpaste. Maybe if she'd sent it with him, he would have stayed the night.

Yes, but maybe this was better. Her foolishness had had a time limit.

Daniel didn't make any move to leave. Once she'd helped Mal into his pajamas and pulled his covers up to his chin, Daniel bent and gave him a clumsy kiss that seemed to be an imitation of her more practiced one.

"Good night, buddy."

"'Night, Mom. 'Night, Dad," Malcolm murmured sleepily. His eyes were shut by the time she turned off the light and pulled his door half-closed.

Daniel followed Rebecca to the living room.

"He has amazing self-possession," he said, surprising her. "Is he ever shy? Or unsure of himself?"

She couldn't help a small laugh. "No, I don't think so. I swear, he was born with that ability to engage with people."

"He didn't get it from me," Daniel muttered.

"I don't know. Maybe you *were* like that. Before…" She stopped, then said apologetically, "He looks so much like you. I can't help seeing you as a child and wondering in what ways you were like him."

He ignored that, only watched her for a moment with

eyes that had darkened and looked somber. Then he dropped his bombshell.

"This probably isn't the time or place, but… Rebecca, will you marry me?"

CHAPTER TWELVE

HE'D ASKED HER to marry him?

Assailed by dizziness, Rebecca held on to the back of the sofa as she gaped at Daniel. After a moment, she found enough voice to whisper, "You're serious?"

"No, I joke about things like that all the time." He hunched his shoulders, a frown knitting his brows. "Of course I'm serious!"

Then why was he all the way across her living room, his expression brooding? Why hadn't he pulled her into his arms? Why wasn't he kissing her, coaxing her, romancing her?

Because this wasn't about romance.

"Um… Why are you asking?" She had to lay her fears on the table. "Because of Malcolm? Because it would be convenient if we were married?"

"I want you and Malcolm both in my house. But it's more than that. I told you. I missed you."

With some asperity, Rebecca said, "I miss having my sister as an ally. That doesn't mean I want to spend my life with her."

"What we just had was…amazing."

Sex. He was talking about sex. He couldn't spit out the words, *Making love*. No, the best he could do was *What we just had*. That chilled her.

"Yes, it was. So marrying me would be convenient *and* you'd get great sex."

"Damn it!" He scowled at her. "What do you want me to say?"

Oh, God. She had to ask.

Rebecca swallowed and said, in a voice that was just a little tremulous, "I can think of only one reason to get married. Do you love me, Daniel?"

His face didn't change expression. And yet, as surely as if she'd been touching him, she felt his entire body tighten and...retreat. "That's...not a word I make a habit of using."

"I know," she whispered.

"I could lie to you."

"Don't. Please don't."

"I like you. I want to talk to you. Being inside you is...like going to heaven." His voice became scratchier. "I need you."

"But you don't love me."

"I don't know!" He broke away to pace toward the kitchen, then swung back to face her. "Why does the word mean so much?"

He'd just confirmed her worst fears about him. She kept her voice level.

"It's not the word that matters so much. It's what lies behind it." How sad, it occurred to her, that she had to explain love as a concept, as if he were an immigrant who didn't grasp some uniquely American custom. "*Liking* doesn't hold up the same way real love does. Friends drift away from each other. It's love that makes someone family. Worth fighting for, even when things get hard."

He grunted. "You can say that, even after watching your parents in action?"

"Their…love turned out to be destructive." Yes, it had been love. "But, you see, they kept fighting because they didn't want to let go. If they'd just liked each other, enjoyed sex, they'd have split up at the first hint of trouble."

"And you *want* that?"

"Yes." She lifted her chin. "Yes, I do. I want a man to love me enough that he's never willing to let go." *Unlike you.*

He stared at her for the longest time. "I…don't know how to give you that. How to be sure."

She would not cry in front of him. She hadn't the last time; she wouldn't this time.

Rebecca nodded. Her voice emerged as barely better than a whisper. "I know."

"Damn it, Rebecca…!" His face twisting, he took a step toward her.

"No." She backed up until she bumped against the wall. "You need to leave now, Daniel."

"We could be happy," he said, with something that sounded very like desperation. Desolation.

"Would we? The need to be loved would eat at me, and you… You'd keep wondering how you'd let yourself get tied down. And Malcolm would be happy, until we broke up, when he'd be devastated. No." She shook her head and kept shaking it, as though she'd forgotten how to stop. "Please go, Daniel."

"If you think you're getting rid of me that easily…" he growled.

It was all she could do not to crumple. "I know you want to keep seeing Malcolm. But…we need to find a better way for you to do it. You're his father. We're not a family. We shouldn't be lying to him."

He swore and swiped his hand over his face. Could he, too, be near tears? But he seemed to have scrubbed away the emotion.

Still, he sounded hoarse. "We weren't lying. I wasn't."

"Daniel—" Her voice broke.

"I'm going." He passed by her close enough to touch. Opened the door. Paused, his back to her. She stood still, waiting, but he walked out and closed the door without saying another word.

She stood there until headlights bounced off the front window, and his car backed out of the driveway, then accelerated on the street. Only when she could no longer hear the engine did her knees give way. Rebecca slid down the wall, wrapped her arms around herself for comfort, and cried.

THAT WEEK WAS ONE OF THE bleakest of Daniel's life. He replayed the conversation so many times the spool would have broken if it had been film. He could think of a thousand alternatives to what he'd said.

Maybe what I'm feeling is *love.*

Maybe. Yeah, way to sweep a woman off her feet.

And was it true? He didn't know.

I won't let you go. Ever.

That, he thought, could be truth. Was. Now that he'd had her back in his life, he couldn't imagine *not* having her.

But those weren't the words she wanted to hear.

Somewhere along the way, he got to wondering. She'd asked whether he loved her. But she had never said, "I can't marry you because I don't love you." Which meant… God. He had to believe it meant she did love him.

Agony could intertwine with happiness like cancer in-

filtrating healthy cells. Inseparable. Incurable, without cutting out the entire mass. How could he, a man who didn't
know the meaning of the word *love,* feel such inexplicable
pleasure at the idea of one woman loving him?

His mother must have loved Robert Carson the way
Rebecca wanted to be loved. Nothing, including unhappiness and the loss of her only daughter, had shaken that
love. What had the bastard ever done to deserve that kind
of devotion? Nothing! Impregnated her three times. Stolen
her baby girl while abandoning her to raise the boys alone.
But he never really left her, not long enough for her to heal,
for her to let go.

*I want a man to love me enough that he's never will-
ing to let go.*

The only love Daniel had known was hurtful, darkness
that shadowed lives, stripped the joy out of them. Because
of it, his mother couldn't let go. Did that make it triumphant?

He didn't get it.

He called her midweek. Coolly, she agreed that he could
take Malcolm Sunday. To the zoo? Excellent idea.

He'd see her at least. That was something. Maybe.

This was a really lousy time to hear from his newly discovered sister, Jenny. But she called nonetheless, told him
she and her husband were out here visiting Sue, and asked
if she could come see him. She didn't want to say why, and
he had no choice but to agree.

She arrived at the promised seven o'clock on Thursday
evening. When Daniel opened his front door, he found her
on the doorstep with her husband

Jenny was now fifty-six. Adam would have barely been
out of diapers when she was born, which was why he

hadn't remembered the existence of another baby. She was damn near a foot shorter than Daniel, maybe five foot three, if that, dark-haired, dark-eyed and stylish.

"Daniel!" She beamed at him as if they were best friends. Before he could retreat, she reached out and gave him a quick hug. Then she said, "Of course, you know Luke."

The two men shook hands. Luke Bookman wasn't quite Daniel's height, but close. Sue was their only child, getting her blond hair from her dad and her brown eyes from her mother.

"Come on in. Coffee?"

They ended up following him to the kitchen, with Jenny oohing over his house. "It's absolutely gorgeous! Did you restore it yourself?" She wanted to hear about everything he'd done, then said, "Please tell me you'll host our next family gathering. Everyone is going to want to see this place. Why didn't Joe ever say where you lived?"

Not until the coffee was poured, sugar and creamer provided, did she settle back and study him. "We don't look much alike."

"No, although given how dark Joe's hair is... Your coloring might have come from our mother's side of the family."

"Yes." She became pensive. "Joe looks extraordinarily like Dad, you know. I'm surprised nobody ever noticed."

"Sue was the only one who'd known him long." Daniel hesitated. "Do you have any pictures?"

"Haven't you seen one?" she said.

"Joe showed me a couple. I was, uh, wondering more about Sarah." He didn't know why, but he'd been thinking about her lately.

"Oh." She bent to pull her wallet out of her purse.

"Big mistake to ask," Luke said with mild amusement. "Jenny *always* has pictures. Lots of them."

He was right. She unfolded a regular accordion of clear plastic sleeves. A plump-cheeked baby, school pictures of a bright-faced blonde, the same girl grown, all whipped by as she searched. Finally she laid out two.

The first was obviously a wedding photo of Sarah and Robert Carson gazing into each other's eyes. Sarah was a pretty woman made beautiful by happiness.

Happiness, Daniel thought, that had been transitory.

The second photo had been taken years later. Both were white-haired. Once again, though, he had that sense of connection between the two of them, of gentle affection at the very least.

A lump in his throat, he pushed them back to her. Jenny studied his face for a moment, then folded up the pictures and stowed her wallet away.

"Joe tells me you've never been married?"

He compressed his mouth, shook his head, then said, "I do have a son."

Of course she wanted to hear all about Malcolm. He told her, within reason. She listened with apparent delight, asking all the right questions.

Funny thing, because once, as she leaned forward, lips parted, he saw his mother in her. Just a flicker, but distinct. That same expression, open, curious, the same curve of the mouth.

"You look like her," he said abruptly. "Not coloring, but… Your face."

"Really?" Vulnerability made her seem almost childlike. "Joe wasn't so sure."

"I just had one of those moments. As if she was sitting here." Daniel shook his head to clear it. "She wasn't a happy woman. You appear to be."

"Yes." She smiled at her husband, who took her hand. "I am." Her smile died and her forehead puckered. "I wish I could have known her."

"Even though she gave you up?" he asked brutally.

"She must have thought she was doing the right thing for me. It's not like she gave me away to a stranger."

"No." And Jenny likely *had* been better off, even if she'd grown up believing a lie—that she was adopted rather than being as much her father's child as Sam was.

Maybe, Daniel thought wryly, what he ought to regret was that his mother hadn't given him away, too.

"And Dad... I wish he'd told me himself, but at least I always knew he loved me." Her face clouded. "What I can't understand is how he could have given me every-thing, and you and Adam nothing."

There was a question.

Daniel heard himself say, "I'm not sure he knew I was his son. I don't think even Mom knew who my father was."

"Still, Adam..."

She sounded so woeful, Luke let go of her hand to wrap an arm around her and give her a squeeze. She flashed him a grateful smile, the tenderness between them palpable, enough to make Daniel shift uncomfortably and transfer his gaze to his nearly untouched coffee cup.

"You must wonder why I asked to see you," she said.

He met her eyes again. "I did."

"Well, you see, I have something for you." She turned again to her husband, who reached into the pocket of his jacket and handed her a jeweler's box.

What in hell…?

"We've talked. All of us in the family. You were the most left out. Well, and Adam, but he's gone now. And we decided we want you to have this. To say, you're a Carson, too. And…you're entitled." She pushed the small velvet jewelry box across the table to him.

Daniel felt…distant. As if he was looking down on this tableau. Down, even, on himself. He saw his hand reach out and take the box. There was a pause before he snapped the lid open and stared at the extraordinary diamond necklace nestled inside.

He'd heard about the Carson family heart-shaped diamond, passed down from eldest son to eldest son, supposedly a gift to an early Carson from his love, the daughter of a rich man. They would never be allowed to marry, and she'd given it to him so that he could afford to pay his passage to America. He'd worked his way instead, and kept the necklace. The necklace was worn only occasionally because it was so valuable. Somebody had, in all seriousness, called it the "heart of the family." The diamond itself had to be several karats—it was certainly one of the biggest stones Daniel had ever seen and the most unusual shape— and the setting was old and lovely, crusted with sapphires. He imagined giving it to Rebecca, seeing it lying against the creamy skin at the base of her throat. He rarely felt lust for objects, but at that moment he did.

In the next moment, he snapped the box shut and pushed it back across the table. "I can't take this."

Jenny gazed at him. "Of course you can. Why shouldn't you have it?"

"He didn't acknowledge me. I don't want anything that was his."

"Joe was sure you'd say that." She made no move to take back the velvet box. "I told him I'd persuade you."

He still felt as if he was having an out-of-body experience. "How do you plan to do that?"

"Repeat that we all want you to have it." She took a deep breath. "Mom left it to me, you know."

"I heard," he said neutrally. What he'd heard was that Sam had thrown a monumental tantrum.

"Sam wasn't happy."

"Uh-huh."

"He always manages to push me around. I made Sue take it, because she's much better at ignoring him."

Daniel frowned. "If it means so damn much to him…"

Her back straightened and she squared her shoulders. "Sam has always had his own way. The one thing we're all agreed on is that this time he won't get it, not after how he's been acting. *Especially* after the way he's treated Emily. As big a crud as he's capable of being, who knows whether he'd even leave it to Belle?"

"Then give it to her," he suggested.

She smiled even as she shook her head. "She doesn't want it, either. Lately it's become…oh…like a toy a bunch of children are squabbling over! By passing into your hands, it becomes a symbol of family pride again. Because *you're* family, and you deserved to be a part of it much sooner."

God help him, he was going to be stuck with it. Daniel stared at it with all the enthusiasm he'd feel for a pet tarantula someone had entrusted to him. He detested the idea of accepting a family heirloom Robert Carson had prized. He knew damn well Adam hadn't wanted it, either, any more than Joe did. Hell. Was he the third or fourth person she'd tried to bestow it on?

He tried again. "It must be worth a small fortune. For God's sake, sell it! Split the money. Get something positive out of it."

"Oh, no." She gazed at him wide-eyed. "It has to stay in the family. Anyway, none of us need the money."

He muttered an obscenity. Jenny looked shocked, her husband amused. Why, Daniel wondered, was he getting the feeling she was nowhere near as innocent as she looked? She had him hooked, flopping on the dock, gasping for breath.

"Leave it to your son. Oh, I can hardly wait to meet him! I love the idea of there being a next generation, don't you?"

He stared helplessly at her, outmaneuvered.

"We'd better go now. We're on our way to an airport hotel. Our flight out is in the morning."

Daniel recalled that they lived in Florida but visited often. Jenny had timed this perfectly—hand off the diamond to him, then flee to the other side of the country before he could react.

"I'll put it in the safe," he conceded. "But this discussion isn't over."

She only smiled.

Damn, he thought with incredulity. She was his sister. If she'd known… If they'd both known… Somehow he suspected Jenny wasn't the kind to have let him slip between her fingers. She and Luke had all but smothered Sue with love, from what Daniel had heard. He wondered how different his life would have been if he'd had a fiercely protective big sister when he needed her.

He let her hug him again on the way out the door and even kissed her cheek, still disorientated but definitely back in his body. When they were gone, he returned to the kitchen and opened the velvet box again to study the Carson family heirloom. "Crap!" Finally he took it upstairs to the safe that was in his bedroom. He wanted it out of sight as soon as possible. Out of mind.

He should be so lucky.

SATURDAY, REBECCA HAD the boy ready to go out the door when he arrived, gave him a vague smile without quite meeting his eyes, and pretty much shoved Malcolm out after a quick kiss and a, "You two have fun." The door closed in their faces.

The four-year-old gazed at it in perplexity. "I wish Mom was coming," he said, with a wistful note.

"She said she had things to do today," Daniel lied. *Like avoid me.*

Malcolm trudged to the car, waited while Daniel put the booster seat in, then accepted help buckling. "But Mom *likes* the zoo," he said, once Daniel got in, too, and shut the door.

"Do you two go often?"

He shook his head. "Only on field trips. Mom always goes on field trips. Practically always," he added, scrupulously.

"Well, I'm betting we'll have fun going by ourselves. I haven't been in years. In fact, I can't remember the last time I went to the zoo."

"Really?" Malcolm gazed at him in amazement. "But you live real close."

"I don't go to the beach very often, either. Or to Fisherman's Wharf. And they're both close."

Malcolm talked most of the way. He told Daniel about his friends, about the goats at his preschool, about Aunt Noni's Friday-night date.

"I heard her tell Mom they had a big fight and she's not so sure she likes him anymore."

She and Rebecca had probably spent the morning consoling each other, Daniel thought with a twist of his mouth.

Once they arrived at the zoo, Daniel grabbed a map and set out, assuming they'd see the entire zoo. It didn't take ten minutes to disabuse him of that notion. Malcolm was easily distracted, and slow. If an animal was sleeping and not visible, he wanted to wait, not move on. He would get tired long before they made the circle. For a while, Daniel hoisted him onto his shoulders so he could speed up the pace, but Malcolm had no problem expressing his dissatisfaction.

A sign pointing to the Children's Zoo caught Daniel's eye, and he steered them that way. There, they hit pay dirt. The Insect Zoo enthralled Malcolm, offering a goliath tarantula that could get up to ten inches across and which was able to regrow a leg if it lost one. Malcolm loved that idea and started hopping on one leg saying, "See? Look! My leg's growing and growing and…" Triumphantly he planted it on the ground. "And now I've got two legs again!"

He liked the Giant African millipede, too, which was long enough to give Daniel nightmares. The Children's Zoo was home to the meerkats and prairie dogs, both of which entranced Malcolm, and he was happily at home in the family farm, where he could roam at will, petting goats, donkeys, pigs and calves. They admired the American Cream draft horse, a huge, dignified creature with patient, kindly eyes. As enamored as he was of earthmoving equipment, Malcolm liked making the acquaintance of the nineteenth-century version.

He also liked the lunch of hot dog, soda and snow cone, far less nutritious than Mom generally encouraged. By the time they finished eating, he was flagging. Daniel swung him onto his shoulders again and carried him to the car.

"Did you have fun?" he asked, helping buckle the boy in.

"Yeah!" Malcolm's smile dimmed when he added, "But it might have been even more fun if Mom had come. Huh?"

Yeah. It might have been. But, damn it, the possibility was real that they'd never all go anyplace together again. How were they going to explain it to Malcolm?

That was Rebecca's job, Daniel decided grimly. Her choice. She had to justify it to her son.

Their son.

Of course Malcolm was asleep long before they reached Half Moon Bay. Rebecca had to let him in when she opened the door to find him carrying a limp, seemingly boneless child.

"Why don't you get the booster seat out of my car?" he suggested.

She gave a choppy nod and let him pass. In the boy's bedroom, Daniel took off Malcolm's shoes, then pulled the covers over him. After a moment, he bent down and gave him a kiss that felt no more natural than the first time. And yet, as he backed out of the room, he felt a tenderness and a near-painful twinge he guessed might be love.

When he returned to the living room, Rebecca had already set the booster seat on the sofa and was waiting by the open front door. She looked so damn beautiful, glossy hair up in a bun, chin high.

"Did it go all right?" she asked.

"Yeah. He was especially taken with a tarantula."

She shuddered. "Great."

"He said Mom didn't want to go in the Insect Zoo the last time you were there."

"He was right. Mom didn't." She stared uncompromisingly at him. "Daniel, I'm not going to ask you to stay."

His jaw tightened. He walked past her and out onto the porch, taking with him the scent that was only hers. Stopping, not looking at her, he said, "We'd have both enjoyed the day more if you'd been with us."

"You two need to have a relationship separate from me," she said with finality. "Goodbye, Daniel." She closed the door. The click of the lock might have been in his imagination.

As he walked to the car, he wondered whether it would hurt this much every time.

STANDING INSIDE, WELL BACK from the window, Rebecca watched Daniel get in his car, sit there for a minute with his head bent, then finally start it, back out and drive away.

Dry-eyed, hands pressed to her chest, she wondered whether she could survive this every other weekend, month after month, year after year. Was this what her parents had experienced? Had they tried at first? Been polite? Shared news of the girls' accomplishments? She didn't remember, only imagined anguish slowly blinding them to their daughter's needs. Driving them to find a way to make the other person feel something, even if it was rage.

Once again, Daniel was gone. *I could have had him. I could have said yes, and hidden my hurt, and pretended I didn't mind the lack of a few words.* Knowing she could have had almost everything that mattered made it so much worse.

For the hundredth time this week, she asked herself if this was really better. "No," she whispered, closing her eyes. "No."

But she, who had tried so hard as a child to bandage the rifts in her family, to make the best of each displacement both for herself and her sister, also knew what it would do to her to pretend that *almost* was good enough.

Her hands flew up to cover her face and hot tears dripped from between her fingers.

CHAPTER THIRTEEN

NARROW STEPS LED TO the basement, lit only by a single, bare bulb. Daniel rarely came down here. He was claustrophobic enough not to enjoy the dark, windowless space.

He had piled boxes from his mother's house in a corner years ago. Out of sight, out of mind. Making decisions about her stuff should have been Adam's job, of course, but as usual Adam hadn't been around. Thank God Joe had been.

Most of the furniture and household goods, they'd divided up or sold. Clothes and costume jewelry, they'd boxed and given to The Salvation Army. Which left quite a bit they hadn't been able to deal with quickly. Jewelry that might have had sentimental value to her, or was particularly nice. Photographs. They'd stored some decorative pieces that felt like part of their pasts, too—vases, figurines, a moustache cup, a few knickknacks she had cherished from her childhood.

Daniel had seen to it that outstanding bills were paid. Otherwise paperwork went into cartons, too. He'd meant to go through it all someday; most could probably be tossed or recycled. She had carefully kept tax returns and credit card and bank statements, for example, years worth of them. Letters, too, including a packet written to her during the war by her first husband. It was the letters and personal mementoes that were Daniel's current focus, but he supposed he might as well be systematic about this and not cherry-pick the few boxes of papers that might be most interesting.

He made a number of trips up and down, starting with eight boxes. He piled them beside the kitchen table, where he could spread out paperwork and where the lighting was better.

This was probably an exercise in futility, he thought impatiently. God knows what he expected to find. To the best of his knowledge, she'd never kept a journal, which was what he really wanted: her voice from beyond the grave, explaining every decision she'd ever made. Tax returns were no substitute. But baring her soul for posterity wasn't Jo Fraser's way. Chances were, she'd kept her secrets to the end.

Bank statements didn't go back long enough to tell him whether she'd received any unexplained payments. Daniel did spot the regular deposits she'd received for child support from Vern. The money wasn't much, but Vern had never stopped paying it, whatever doubts he'd had.

Daniel started by shredding the statements, even though the account numbers were no longer valid. He felt better reducing them to a pile of confetti. She had wanted her body cremated, not buried, and she wouldn't want her private affairs lying visible for anyone to see in a recycling bin somewhere.

The second box was filled entirely with credit card statements going back to when he was ten years old. Out of curiosity, he dug down and flipped through the early statements.

She always had been careful with money. It turned out,

she'd rarely used credit. Most of these charges were at places like Sears and JC Penney department stores. School clothes or shoes for him, he guessed, bought when she didn't have the cash. He'd grown like a weed during those years, and his mother had had too much pride to shop at thrift stores. Welfare or even food stamps were out of the question.

"We just bought those!" he could remember his mother saying too many times as he outgrew yet another pair of jeans. He would stare down to see his ankles in white sweat socks below the hems of the jeans. He went through shoes even faster.

They always went shopping as soon as she noticed he'd shot up another two inches. He didn't recall ever being embarrassed by what he wore, and he realized that had mattered to her. Whatever else she was, Josephine Fraser was proud.

Troubled to realize that he'd taken for granted all those new clothes for a growing boy, Daniel wished he'd just once acknowledged the sacrifices she must have made.

Or did her pride demand that he never know those new clothes were more than just a nuisance?

He shredded these statements, too, bundle by faded bundle.

The next box held a quilt that had been on her bed as long as he could remember. It was obviously handmade and old, faded from too many washings. He thought it had been a wedding present when she married William Fraser, but he didn't know who it was from. He wished he'd paid more attention. Maybe somewhere he'd find a note about it.

Nestled in the quilt was her jewelry box, which held trinkets that Joe and he had guessed were meaningful to her. Her wedding rings were in here, too. Since he'd already looked through it, Daniel set the jewelry box aside for last.

He'd intended to give just a couple of hours to this probably fruitless search for some meaning in his mother's life, then turn on his laptop and do some real work. But once he started, he couldn't tear himself away.

No, it was more than that. He has this gnawing sense of urgency. It was as if he *had* to find something that would...hell, he didn't know. Free him? Convince him that love, if it existed at all, wasn't always cruel? That he was capable of committing a lifetime to one woman?

Whatever it was he sought, he needed it soon. Before Rebecca gave up on him. If she hadn't already.

Daniel found loose photos that hadn't gone into any of the albums. His mother hadn't been able to afford to have pictures developed very often, so the boys took big jumps in ages, from gap-toothed kindergartners to lanky teenagers in basketball uniforms. There was, he saw now, more familial resemblance between him and Adam than he'd thought existed. Believing as he had that they had different fathers, he'd seen what he expected to see. Looking now at photos of them at the same ages, lying side by side, he couldn't imagine their mother couldn't have told they were both Robert Carson's sons. Their builds, their cheekbones, the way their ears lay against their heads, grins that lifted higher on one side than the other... Yeah, they were brothers, all right, even if one was dark-haired, the other a freckle-faced redhead.

Josephine Fraser was indeed an extraordinarily lovely woman. She glowed in the wedding photo that had always hung in an oval frame in the living room. A second, studio portrait of her as a young woman, beautiful and dreamy-eyed, had been displayed below it. She never looked as happy again in the few photos they had of her, including the one taken of her and Vern at their wedding over twenty years later. In that picture, she was composed, serene, and yet…detached.

Rather, Daniel thought, staring at the photo, the way he felt most of the time. Had the ability to hold a big part of himself back been learned from her, a woman who had been deeply wounded when she had loved unreservedly?

He had memories of happy times, fleeting impressions of tenderness: a kiss, a smile that held such pride his chest had swelled. But they were few. The mother he mostly remembered had been stern, tired, distant.

She had admitted, during that talk they'd had only six weeks before she died, to having been dismayed to find herself pregnant when she was almost forty years old.

"I didn't have the energy I had when your brother was born," she said. "Or the patience. Everything seemed harder. It didn't help when things weren't going well with your father. We fought, and you were there big eyed and scared…" She'd paused, regret in her eyes. "Then later, I went through menopause, and I think I went a little crazy for a few years. If there's any part of my life I wish I could do over, it's being your mother. You were such a good child, but you got quieter and quieter and quit turning to me at all."

"Being a single mother had to be hard," he had said stiffly, the closest he had come to offering forgiveness.

He didn't remember her ever seeing a doctor during those years. He didn't suppose she'd gone on hormones to treat the symptoms of menopause. She'd had health insurance through her job, but how adequate it was Daniel didn't know. Struggling to raise him, she might not have been able to handle co-payments and prescription costs.

He dropped the photo back in the box and squeezed his eyes shut. He didn't remember ever saying to her, "I love you, Mom," not even there at the end, when they both knew she was dying. Joe was more her son than he was, he'd figured. Daniel had wanted to believe he didn't love her, although now he knew better.

She had let him down in some ways. In others, she'd never failed him. He hadn't wanted for anything but hugs and her approval. She had gone to parent-teacher meetings, hung his report cards on the refrigerator, made sure he had the basketball shoes he needed. He even remembered a hideous mother-son talk about responsible sex and birth control, about the time he turned fifteen. She had been grim but determined.

Had *any* of her three pregnancies been planned? Not the one that resulted in him, for sure. But maybe she had wanted Adam, or at least been careless on purpose. Had she felt so empty after Billy's death, she needed to have someone to hold on to? Had she truly fallen in love with Billy's friend Robert yet, or was he just a comfort to her? Did she want a baby she could almost believe in her heart was Billy's after all?

The second pregnancy, though. That was something else again.

Daniel shook his head and opened another box. China figurines, a couple of vases she'd often filled with flowers from her garden. Some of these he repacked, a few he left out to use. He'd ask Joe if he wanted a few more mementos.

More financial records, none from early enough to tell him whether Carson had ever paid child support. Daniel kept the shredder running, flattened the now-empty cardboard boxes. He went down to the basement for more, and this time the first he opened revealed the letters she'd kept as carefully as she had her financial records.

She must have been a prolific letter writer. He wished he had *her* letters, not just the responses to them, but hope quickened in him. If he were to learn any of her secrets, it would be here.

Batches were bundled with rubber bands or tied with ribbons. On top were letters from a childhood friend. It appeared they'd continued to correspond into their seventies, even though to his knowledge Jo never went back East where she'd grown up, and he doubted her friend had made it all the way out to California, either. He read the last letter written in Mary Culligan's spidery scrawl first.

I'm afraid the cancer is winning. I've asked to stay at home until the end, and Kate has arranged for hospice care and is here often herself. Truthfully, Jo, I don't fear death. I feel sure Edgar is waiting for me, and I'm eager to see him again.

She finished,

Since I may not be able to write again, I did want, just once, to say how grateful I am for having one person—you—with whom I could always be honest. Why is it easier to confide in a piece of paper and the memory of a young friend than it is to the people you see every day? I don't know, only that it is so. I pray I will know your face when we meet again.

Most letters were still in their original envelopes. He flipped through and laid them out by postmark date, the earliest at the top.

Daniel got up and poured himself a cup of coffee, then reached for Mary's first letter, written in 1941. He quickly became immersed.

Jo and Mary had been best friends in high school. Both got married young, Mary to her school sweetheart, Jo to a young soldier who had caught her eye and her heart. Jo came west to live with Billy Fraser's mother, who apparently was not altogether happy with the marriage, but perhaps came to love her son's young bride. She died herself of breast cancer before the end of the war; Jo had written him with the news, but didn't know whether he'd get it before he came home, as he was already in transit.

Mary sent her condolences when Billy in turn was killed in an automobile accident.

"How kind his friend is!" she marveled.

You must feel so alone. Have you considered coming home? Even with your parents gone, you do have old friends here. But perhaps you've made so many there, you feel secure.

She congratulated Jo on her pregnancy, nothing in that letter or later ones suggesting she knew the baby wasn't Billy Fraser's. When she wrote about the next pregnancy, however, it was clear she'd been told about Robert.

Oh, Jo! How can you love a man who is already married? Are you so certain he loves you? And how will you *explain* this child?

Explain was underlined three times.
The next letter was dated six months later.

My heart is breaking for you. My miscarriage was terrible enough, and I never even held the child. I cannot imagine what it must have cost you to give up your baby. I won't ask whether you're certain you did the right thing. You would have thought and thought and thought, without ever considering yourself. As you say, her father can give her so much more. If only you are positive love is part of what he will give her.

Daniel reached for his coffee, took a sip. It was cold. Already reaching for the next letter, he set the mug down.
    Mary had had another miscarriage. She was beginning to believe she would never bear another child, and worried her husband was disappointed not to have a son.

Perhaps we both love Kate all the more because we now know how precious she is! I hope your heart is undivided, and you are able to give it all to Adam. Better yet, I wish you would meet a man you could love, someone who would make you forget Robert. He didn't deserve you.

No. The son of a bitch hadn't deserved her. Daniel rubbed burning eyes.

When had his mother changed from the starry-eyed young woman Mary recalled to the stern, relentlessly frugal, unhappy mother he remembered? Had Billy's death done it, after she had given herself entirely to a future with him, traveling across the country and leaving behind everything and everyone she knew, enduring his mother's critical company for the wartime years? Raising Adam alone? Or was it when she gave away her baby girl to what she prayed was a better life?

Daniel thought he knew the answer.

He read on, learning how much his mother had worried about him and eventually been hurt by his coldness. Yet she had never tried to raise a bridge, never explained herself to him.

Until that one conversation, when he should have listened harder than he had.

He found precious few other answers in the remainder of the letters. Billy's, written on battlefields and in bouts of utter tedium, were touching and boyish. Hers, likely sent by return mail, had to have been saccharine if the tone of his was anything to go by. Believing that Josephine Fraser, even a very young Josephine Fraser, had written fulsome love letters strained Daniel's imagination. Maybe Joe would believe more easily; although he knew better than anyone how stubborn she could be, he had also seen a more affectionate, playful side to the woman he'd called Nana Jo.

Finally, Daniel opened the jewelry box and reexamined his mother's few, treasured pieces. Her first wedding ring was plain gold, inscribed With All My Love, Billy. Daniel had never seen it on her finger. In his memory, she'd worn the other, slightly more elaborate ring without

an inscription, and a diamond engagement ring, too, given
to her by Vern. She'd kept wearing them after the divorce,
asking for the respect given to a married woman even
though she went back to the last name Fraser.

No other rings. Robert Carson wouldn't have given her
one. Rings implied a promise.

Daniel fingered these three, wondering what they should
do with them. None were hugely valuable. Engagement
rings were sometimes handed down in families, but given
the history of Josephine and Vernon Kane's wedding, he
for one would rather start afresh if Rebecca changed her
mind.

Looking at the other pieces of jewelry, he decided to ask
Joe what he thought. His own inclination would be to sell
the lot, except perhaps for that first wedding ring. He
thought she'd loved Billy Fraser. She'd treasured this ring
and his war medal. It seemed…indecent to let it be melted
down for gold.

Daniel felt a rush of anger, thinking about that diamond
pendant upstairs in his wall safe, comparing it to these bits
that were all his mother had ever owned. Sarah Carson had
worn that glorious necklace to local society events, while
Jo was putting Daniel's new jeans and T-shirts on a credit
card and paying them off five dollars at a time because her
salary didn't stretch far enough to afford them. Where was
the justice in that?

Daniel was about to close the box when he saw the yel-
lowing envelope on the bottom. He'd missed it the last
time, when he and Joe had hastily gone through Mom's
things. Was this a letter she'd kept near, where she could
take it out to look at easily?

But there was no address on the envelope, no postmark.

And inside was a photograph rather than a letter. A snapshot of his young mother with Robert Carson. They were at the Presidio; the Golden Gate Bridge rose in the background. Having a carefree day away from anyone who would recognize and condemn them?

She was laughing, radiant as she looked up at the tall man who gazed down at her with an expression that sent goose bumps down Daniel's arms.

Love. Goddamn it, it had to be love.

Sarah Carson had believed he intended to leave her, until he found out that she, too, was pregnant. Was this photo taken during the brief period when Josephine Fraser thought she would soon be marrying this man she had so unexpectedly come to love?

Daniel touched his mother's face with the tip of a finger, the merest brush. He let out a ragged sound and was shocked to realize his face was wet.

These were his parents.

Glowing with happiness, while Sarah Carson sat at home, probably not yet suspecting that her husband's heart had been given elsewhere.

Daniel remembered the photos Jenny had showed him of Robert and Sarah, including the one of their wedding, when they gazed at each other with quiet joy. *Could* a man love two women? Sarah wasn't the beauty Josephine had been. Had Robert felt lust for his mistress, tenderness for his wife? And yet, Daniel remembered Joe telling him about the man he'd talked to at Josephine Fraser's funeral, the man he had later realized was Robert Carson. He'd brought roses to lay on her casket, pale lilac, smelling like the perfume she wore when she dressed up. He wouldn't have come to the funeral if he hadn't kept her in his heart, would he? And yet, hadn't there been love in the way he looked at his wife in that second photo Jenny showed him, the one taken when they were white-haired and their children raised and grown long ago?

Their children. One of whom was Jo's baby, given away to find a better life, or maybe as a gift to the man she'd loved so deeply.

God. Daniel roughly wiped his cheeks. Answers? There weren't any.

"YOU OKAY?" NAOMI ASKED quietly. Mal had run ahead of them into the fish-and-chips joint. "You haven't been yourself lately."

"Who could I be but myself?"

Her friend leveled a look at her. "You know what I mean."

Rebecca hesitated. She'd kept functioning by pretending everything was fine. Finally she said, "I haven't heard from Daniel in almost two weeks."

"You said no."

Naomi was the only person in the world Rebecca had told about his proposal. The only person she would tell. And even then she hadn't confessed how many hundreds of times she'd questioned her decision. He couldn't say the words, but did that necessarily mean he *didn't* love her? He said, *I missed you. Every goddamn day.* Wasn't that love?

To her friend, she said unhappily, "I know."

Sounding tentative, her friend suggested, "You might be better off if he loses interest in seeing Malcolm."

"But Malcolm wouldn't."

They were joining her son in line at the counter. Naomi

lowered her voice, so that her words were just for Rebecca's ears. "Now, there's a change. You were so convinced you and Malcolm were a team. Weren't you wishing, not that long ago, that you'd run off to the wilds of Montana or some such place?"

Rebecca rolled her eyes.

"Can I have clam chowder, Mom?" Malcolm asked, tugging at her hand. "And lots of crackers? You can ask them for extras, right?"

"I'll ask them for extras," she agreed. He liked the chowder but not the clams, so mostly he dipped the crackers in and ate them.

Malcolm dominated the conversation at the table. He was in his element; Aunt Nomi was one of his favorite people in the world, and she was hanging on his every word.

She didn't mention Daniel again to Rebecca, even obliquely, until she was dropping them off at home. Then her last words were, "When you want to talk, I'm here."

Rebecca nodded, trying to smile but failing abysmally. *Don't cry. I can't cry. How could I ever explain to Mal?*

"What did Aunt Nomi mean?" he asked loudly as she unlocked the front door. "What would you want to talk about? We talked lots today."

This smile was steady enough to fool an undiscerning four-year-old. "We did, didn't we? She just meant girl talk. Like after her Friday-night dates."

"Oh." *Those* didn't interest him. "Do I gotta take a nap?"

"Yes, you have to lie down. If you don't fall asleep, that's okay. You can look at a book."

She said that almost every day. And almost every day he dropped off to sleep the minute his head hit the pillow.

Not for long; Malcolm's naps were getting shorter and she guessed would soon be history, appropriately enough since he'd be in kindergarten come fall. She planned to register him for full-day classes, one of several options, to match her schedule.

She was trying so very hard these days to calmly focus on the life she'd laid out, on the plans she made on her own. For days and days after Daniel left that night, some part of her had clung to the ridiculous hope that he would be back. That he would be able to say, "I love you."

But the hope had withered, until all that was left was a tiny, hard kernel that had lodged in her chest. It felt like the husk left when a seed had blown away, still solid even after its vital purpose was finished.

When a week went by and then another without even a phone call from him, and Malcolm started asking questions, Rebecca had to wonder whether Daniel had ever been the man she'd slowly, reluctantly begun to believe in. Out of anger at her, would he really disappoint the boy who had begun to trust him? She didn't want to think he could be so cruel, but wasn't that the trouble with Daniel? He was so hard to know. So…opaque.

She was just about to call him that evening and give him a piece of her mind when the phone rang.

Malcolm jumped off the stool where he'd been helping butter French bread. "Can I get it, Mom? Can I get it?"

Her heartbeat sped up for no reason. "Do I have a choice?"

He grinned at her and fumbled the phone. "Hello?" Then, joyously, "Dad! You haven't called in a really long time! Mom said prob'ly you were just busy, but you come see us *every* weekend. Why didn't you?"

It was agony hearing only one side of the conversation. She could make out Daniel's deep rumble, but no words.

"Okay," Mal said finally. "Mom, we aren't doing anything Sunday, are we?"

She shook her head. *We?* Or was Malcolm the one who wanted to include her in any outings?

"Here's Mom," her son said, and thrust the phone at her.

Rebecca wiped off her hands and took it. "Daniel?"

"Hey," he said. "Sorry for the silence."

Very evenly, she said, "I assumed you were busy."

"No, it's been…more complicated than that."

"Complicated?" she echoed.

"Yeah. I'm hoping to see you without Malcolm. Talk to you."

"Didn't we say everything already?" She went still. "Or is this about something else?"

He wouldn't offer to give up his parental rights altogether, would he? Now, after Malcolm had gotten to know him and accepted him as Dad?

How could the idea seem so appalling, when only a few short months ago her greatest dread had been that Daniel would discover he had a son?

"I have things I'd rather not say over the phone." His voice could be maddeningly uninflected when he chose. This was one of those times. "Will you give me a hearing, Rebecca?"

What could she say but, "Yes, of course. When did you have in mind?"

"Saturday? Day or evening, whatever's better for you."

They might as well have been discussing when to hand off Malcolm for their next father-son outing. Something that would soon be routine.

"Malcolm has another birthday party Saturday. This time, thank goodness, at the birthday boy's house. I'm dropping him off at eleven."

"I'll be at your place right after eleven, then," he said, voice deepening but still constrained.

"All right," she agreed. "I'll see you then."

When she set the phone back in the cradle, her hand was shaking.

And I thought the past two weeks were hard.

This one would be agony. What was important enough for him to say that he had so formally scheduled a time with her? Why, oh, why, couldn't he have just dropped by, surprising her, and gotten it over with?

Would he still want her if she said, "I was wrong?"

CHAPTER FOURTEEN

DANIEL FLEXED HIS FINGERS on the steering wheel as he drove. He focused briefly on his hands and they went still. A minute later, he realized he was doing it again. One more in a line of nervous tics he seemed to have developed these past weeks.

Yesterday, at the office, his personal assistant had suddenly said, "What the hell's with you, Daniel? You're making *me* nervous!"

"What…?" He had looked down to see that his fingers were rat-tat-tatting on the desktop in time to some inner anxiety. "Sorry," he'd said, and stopped.

At home, he'd gotten out the soft juggling balls he'd had since his college years and taken to juggling again. He could think better, with those damn balls flying, than he could staring into space.

It was the solitude that was getting to him, he had decided. Which was a strange thing for a loner like him to be thinking. But getting back together with Rebecca—making love with her again—had showed him one thing: he was living a sort of half life. Engaged at work, satisfied there, but in stasis the rest of the time. He *had* no personal life. Had convinced himself he didn't need one.

Now he knew he was wrong.

Knew his mother had been wrong. She had sacrificed too much for Robert Carson. Maybe what he'd felt for her, he had called love, too; Daniel couldn't be sure. But the reality was, Robert had put another woman first. Had loved her more, when it got right down to it. And rather than giving her heart to another man, Jo Fraser had stubbornly clung to her loneliness. Her determination to suffer in the name of love hadn't been healthy for either Adam or Daniel.

Yeah, she'd loved Adam, but maybe more because he was Robert's son than because he was Adam. And whatever love she'd been able to give Daniel had been a washed-out version of the real thing, too insubstantial for even a child to trust. His suspicion was that she really had thought he was Vernon Kane's son, not Robert's. For whatever reason, she hadn't seen Robert in his face, and so she couldn't give him the real deal. By that time, seeing herself in him wasn't enough. Maybe *she* felt unlovable.

Fingers rhythmically gripping the steering wheel again as the highway descended toward Montara, Daniel gave a harsh laugh. God, did he know that feeling.

He wished he had the slightest idea what Rebecca would say today. Three weeks ago, he'd convinced himself that all she wanted were romantic words. Figure out whether he could say them with feeling, and he was home free.

It wasn't until he was lying sleepless one night, staring at the city light seeping around his curtains, that he'd realized the real problem. He'd balked at saying "I love you" to Rebecca, but was confident he could promise forever and a day without a qualm—and keep the promise. Why would he ever want another woman, when he had her?

If you really *have her,* whispered a voice in his head.

He'd moved restlessly, irritably in bed. What did that mean? *If?* Once his ring was on her finger, she was installed in his house, mother of his child, maybe pregnant with another baby…

He felt cold inside. His mother had given him all the trappings, too. Never let him go without. Never missed a parent-teacher meeting, chauffeured him to the activities that mattered to him. Seemed pleased with good grades, had talks with him about bad ones. But distance had opened inexorably between them anyway, starting before he could even remember. Because she didn't really love him.

What was it Rebecca had said?

It's not the word that matters so much. It's what lies behind it.

She had grappled for an explanation. He couldn't remember how she'd put it exactly, but it was all about how, without love that went bone deep, people drifted away from each other. Mere liking, sexual attraction, a sense of obligation, none of these made for the same level of commitment.

That was what he'd really been looking for in his mother's papers and photos, he thought, lying there in the dark. Some evidence that, contrary to what he'd always believed, she really had loved him.

What he'd come up with was a big, *I don't know.* Or maybe it was, *Yeah, probably, but not enough.* She'd given too much to Robert Carson to have anything left over for her second son, because he wasn't Robert's.

How disappointed had she been? he wondered rather clinically. When he was born with red hair instead of Robert's blond or Vern's brown hair. When she saw no sign to tell her whose child he was. Had she felt relief, because his face wouldn't torment her with what she'd lost, as Adam's very existence must have? Disappointment? Regret?

All of the above?

It didn't matter now. What did matter was how Rebecca felt. Because what he'd realized, drifting through that half life, was that he needed the damn words, too. "Sure, I like you, Malcolm gives us something important in common and, oh, yeah, the sex is great," was not what he needed to hear from her. It wasn't enough. He felt incredibly dense to have thought it was all she needed to hear from him.

Today, where Highway 101 curved treacherously along Devil's Slide, he'd stolen a look over the crumbling cliff to the ocean hammering the rocks far below and recognized the abyss he had been envisioning in front of him. If she didn't love him, nothing could save him from that gaping, dangerous emptiness.

And what made him think she did? That she could, when no one else ever had?

Damn, was he scared.

He realized he had passed El Granada without even glancing to his left at Cabrillo Heights. Open, fallow fields lay to each side of the highway. He could see Half Moon Bay ahead.

If she said no today, how could he come back tomorrow to pick up Malcolm, seeing the emptiness that his life would be spreading before him?

By God, he thought grimly, he'd be here anyway. No matter what, his son wouldn't grow up with the slightest doubt about whether his father cared.

Don't think about it.

Heart hammering, he made the last few turns. Her car wasn't in her driveway yet. He parked at the curb, turned off the engine and set the emergency brake, then sat there.

Nothing in his life had ever mattered as much as this did. And he'd never been so out of his element.

He waited for a very long five minutes before he saw her car coming in his rearview mirror and got out as she pulled into the driveway.

She climbed out and shut her car door, facing him as he came up the driveway toward her. She looked...good. Better than good. Her legs were long and slender in black leggings or thick tights of some kind. Over them, she wore a fluffy, deep red sweater that came down to midthigh and had a rolled collar that bared her collarbone and throat. Her hair was up in that ballet bun she so often wore, long dangling earrings sparkling with gold and ruby red, too. Her expression was utterly composed, but also wary.

"I hope you didn't wait long."

He shook his head.

"Come on in." She led the way.

He felt as though he had to say something. "You must spend a fortune on birthday presents," was what came out.

Rebecca gave him a wry smile over her shoulder as she unlocked the front door. "You're not kidding. At this age, kids mostly invite all their classmates to their parties. Mustn't hurt anyone's feelings, you know. Malcolm likes to pick out the presents for his best friends, but otherwise I keep an eye out for sales and usually have a couple of toys on hand." She continued toward the kitchen, letting him shut the door. "Coffee?"

"Uh…"

But she'd already disappeared into the kitchen. He followed her there, too.

The coffeemaker on the countertop was burbling. She must have set the timer before she left. She poured two cups, pushed one toward him, stirred sugar into hers without offering him any, and then looked at him.

"What's this about, Daniel?"

I love you. Marry me.

Too abrupt.

He leaned one hip against the counter edge. "I meant what I said, about not giving up."

She watched him, her face unreadable.

"I went through my mother's stuff last week. She'd kept a box of letters. Some from her first husband, from old friends."

There was a discernible pause. Was she interested at all? But finally, as if she couldn't help herself, she asked, "Did you learn anything?"

"Not as much as I hoped," he admitted. "I wish I had the letters she wrote."

Had her expression softened, or was it his imagination?

"Some mysteries might be better left unsolved," she suggested, cradling her coffee cup in her hands. Steam rose, and she dipped her head to breathe it in.

"Maybe."

"Did you hope to find out why she gave your sister up? And whether she knew who your father was?"

He grimaced. "A little of both." Okay, deep breath. "I realized the other day that what I wanted to find out most was whether she'd actually loved me."

Rebecca blinked, then set down her cup. "You said she wasn't especially maternal, but surely…?"

"She said 'I love you' sometimes? She signed notes 'Love, Mom.' Does that count?" God, did that sound pathetic. He made an impatient gesture. "Before she died, she told me she loved me. I just didn't believe her."

After a shocked moment, Rebecca asked, "And now?"

"And now I think she did, but not the way she would have if she'd known I was Robert Carson's son."

"That's…awful."

He shook his head. "I'm just trying to explain why love is a hard concept for me. I had a pretty screwed-up childhood."

She didn't have to say that hers hadn't been a piece of cake, either. And there was the irony: thanks to parents with broken hearts and blinders on, they were both wary people more inclined to assume love didn't exist, or if it did it was a problem, than to believe in happily-ever-after.

"When you got pregnant," he said, "why *didn't* you tell me?"

Her gaze slid from his. "We've already gone through this."

"Didn't you wonder why, if I was losing interest in you, I also made love with you like…" He half laughed, without humor. "Like I couldn't live without you? Wouldn't be able to get up in the morning if I didn't have you that night?"

Now she was looking at him, but maybe not at the him in the here and now. "Yes," she whispered. "Yes."

"But…?"

"I was scared." Her eyes, huge and dark, gradually focused on him. "And you weren't calling as often." She gave an odd shrug. "I suppose I expected the worst."

"That I'd be your father reincarnated?"

She gave a pitiful excuse for a laugh. "Oh, even worse. That I'd be my mother reincarnated."

He took that in. "So let me ask you something else."

She worried her lower lip with her teeth, but she nodded.

"Did you think you were in love with me? Back then?"

He lost the ability to breathe as she stared at him, seemingly stricken.

"I...yes." She bowed her head, concentrating fiercely on her coffee. "Of course I did. I have never had casual sexual relationships."

"But you weren't a virgin when we met."

"No, but I'd gone to bed with only two men before. One was my college boyfriend, one not long after. I was serious about both of them at the time."

"You thought you were in love with them, too." His voice was hard.

"Yes." Her chin rose at last, her neck seeming longer in her defiance. "But I knew the difference later, when..."

He took a step closer to her. "When?"

"When I met you."

"You're the one who said love meant holding on. Not giving up." He let a silence open. "Why did you give up on me, Rebecca?"

"I told you!" Tears shimmered in her eyes. "I was scared!"

He reached out and gripped her upper arms, his hands kneading gently. "Scared for Malcolm? Or for yourself?"

She sniffed, the sound forlorn and almost childish. "Both, I suppose." She wiped her cheeks. "Daniel, what are you saying? That I'm a lousy one to talk about love, when I'm obviously not capable of it?"

"No." His chest burned. "I'm trying to ask whether you do love me. Whether you can."

She went completely still for a long moment, then

searched his eyes, her own revealing... God. He couldn't tell. Only that the gold flecks in her eyes shimmered. "What do you mean, *can?*"

Truth time. He sucked in a ragged breath. "I mean, somewhere along the way these past three weeks, while I, uh, did some self-examination, I got to wondering whether my real problem was being afraid to love someone, or whether the bigger issue was that I didn't believe anyone could love me."

She gaped at him. Then her mouth snapped shut and her eyes blazed with pity, or love or indignation. Maybe with all three. She lifted her hands to cradle his face. In a voice that shook, Rebecca said, "How can you even wonder? Growing up the way you did, and you're still a strong, confident, successful man! I did think I loved you, back then. And maybe I did, but it was nothing compared to what I felt when I realized how determined you were to make sure Malcolm had a father. And when I saw you with him, that first day when we went to the beach. You were somehow exactly what he needed, even though you never had a role model. You wanted something different for him than what you had, and somehow you knew how to give it."

God help him, his cheeks were wet. He turned his head, pressing his mouth against her palm, letting tears drip onto her hand.

"I never forgot you," she told him in a broken voice. "But it was that day when I fell painfully, irrevocably the rest of the way in love with you. And knew I couldn't bear it if you didn't love me."

She was the one to wrap her arms around him and hold him as close as she could. He gripped her convulsively, face buried in the curve of her neck. His mouth worked as he tried to get a grip on himself.

They just stood there in the damn kitchen, rocking slightly, holding each other. Daniel felt light-headed, stunned. She loved him. Despite his idiocy, despite his fears, despite everything he'd put her through, she loved him.

He finally loosened his grip enough to look down at her. "A couple of months ago, I'd have said I didn't cry."

Rebecca rose on tiptoe and kissed his wet cheek. "You do love me, don't you?"

"Oh, yeah."

"You know, I had just about decided to call and accept your offer. To…gamble that you could learn. Or maybe to trade the chance to have a few years with you for the heartbreak I expected later. I'm not sure."

"No heartbreak." He kissed her forehead, nuzzled his nose against hers. "I couldn't stand it if you ever left me. These last weeks…" He had to stop and clear his throat. "Without you…"

"Were the absolute worst of my life," she finished for him. Her brown eyes were the color of melted chocolate dusted with gold. Tears sparkled like diamonds on her lashes. Tears that were a hell of a lot more precious to him than the supposed heart of the Carson family.

He thought again how beautiful that pendant would look against her smooth skin, and knew she would never wear it. There was apparently no denying that he was Robert Carson's son; maybe he and these disparate relatives would all find a way to feel like family. But he'd never be wholeheartedly a Carson, and neither he nor Rebecca were the ones to guard the family's heritage.

In that moment, looking down at the face of the woman he loved, he knew who that person was. Decided he'd happily hand it over.

He kissed Rebecca, not with passion, although he felt that, too. But this was about love. Their lips brushed, clung, tasted. He pulled back a couple of times just to see her face again.

She loved him. Incredible.

Believe it.

Finally he straightened and reached in his pocket. "Maybe I should wait, but I'm not a patient man."

She laughed at him. Then she saw what lay in his palm, and gasped.

"Will you marry me?" he asked again, newly afraid he was assuming too much.

"Yes!" Fresh tears filled her eyes and spilled over. "Oh, yes!" She flung herself back in his arms, pressed her mouth to his.

This time, raw hunger roared through him. He needed her, in the most elemental way possible. Groaning, Daniel strained her against him and devoured her mouth.

At last he ripped away from her long enough to say, "I want you."

"I want you, too."

She glowed, the most beautiful woman he'd ever seen. His. No *if* this time.

Seal the deal.

He barely had the self-restraint to reach for her left hand and slide the ring on it. When it fit perfectly, Daniel felt triumph. He'd studied the fingers of every woman who came in the jewelry store to come up with a size. They'd all smiled and indulged him. He didn't like the idea of the symbolism if the damn thing had been too big and fallen off, or wouldn't go on in the first place.

She looked down, too, at the fire refracting from the solitaire oval-cut diamond set in gold. "It's exquisite."

"We can get a different ring if you'd like."

Rebecca lifted her head, her smile tremulous. "Daniel, this ring is every woman's dream. You're not getting it off my finger now."

"Good." The word was barely a growl. He lifted her in his arms and headed for her bedroom.

If she said yes today, he had meant to make love to her so slowly, so tenderly, she couldn't help but feel cherished. But they hadn't even reached the bedroom before she was shoving his shirt off and nipping his neck. He dropped her on the bed and went down on top of her, one knee braced between her thighs. They broke apart only long enough to shed clothes and toss them like confetti. She was wet and ready, and he had to be inside her.

But he groaned as he nudged her. "I meant to go slow."

Her legs wrapped him, tightening, pulling him in. "Please, please, don't. I want you *now.*"

He plunged. Heaven, wrapped in one woman. How had he ever doubted?

"I love you," he said hoarsely, and gave himself over to her.

REBECCA LAY IN A STATE of bliss. She couldn't breathe, but who cared? It was Daniel's weight bearing down on her, Daniel rubbing his cheek against her tangled hair, Daniel still whispering words of love in her ear.

What if she hadn't run from him five years ago? Would he have been ready to recognize that he was in love? Or would he have grudgingly married her, and strained against the chains that bound him? He had changed in those years, she thought, but then so had she. So maybe, after all, this had been perfect timing.

He made a ragged sound and rolled to the side, his arms still tight around her. She laid her head on his shoulder and splayed her hand on his powerful chest. She found herself gazing at the ring he'd put on her finger.

It had to be the biggest diamond Rebecca had ever seen. She might have protested, except she suspected it mattered to him to be able to afford to give her something so extraordinary. She found it astonishing that, given his self-doubt, he had still become the man he was.

"I can hardly wait to tell Malcolm," she murmured.

The large, calloused hand that had been kneading her hip paused. "How long until you have to pick him up?"

"Um…" She turned her head to see the clock. "One hour. Well, I should go in fifty minutes."

"We shouldn't waste the time."

Rebecca giggled. She hadn't felt so young and carefree in what seemed a lifetime. "We're cuddling. Is that wasting time?"

"No." He shifted again, this time onto his side so he could kiss her. "No time with you is wasted," he said against her lips. "I don't want to be without you anymore, Rebecca."

Caressing his hard cheek, she said, "I do have to finish out the school year."

"I assumed so." He studied her. "Will you want to keep teaching?"

"Yes, for now." Rebecca hesitated, unsure for the first time. "You haven't said… But if we decide…"

"To have another kid?"

She nodded.

"Oh, I want another one. Or two. I missed so much. This time I'll be there every step of the way."

Guilt assailed her. "I'm sorry."

"No." Daniel shook his head. "Who is to say we'd have made it five years ago. We go on from here with me thanking God every day that I found you again."

"Yes." Her eyes filled with tears, blurring that craggy face reshaped in lines of tenderness she didn't remember. "It was the luckiest day of my life."

With one thumb, he gently wiped away the tears as they fell. "Why don't we commute for now between our houses? Part of the week in San Francisco, part down here. Make it fair." He hesitated. "Or maybe you want to stay down here long-term."

"No. Oh, no!" Rebecca pressed a kiss to his mouth. "I love your house! And Half Moon Bay…well, this is where I made a home, but not where I really wanted to be. That was always with you."

"Malcolm will miss his friends."

"He'll make new ones," she said firmly. "And personally…" She lowered her voice. "I can't stand Chace."

She'd surprised a rumble from him.

"He looked like a whiner."

She wrinkled her nose. "He is a whiner. *Our* son can do better."

He kissed her again, lingeringly, nipping at her bottom lip. "Malcolm is heading toward five."

"Uh-huh." Now her thoughts were blurring. She touched her tongue to his.

His voice got rougher. "Pregnancy takes nine months."

"Hmm."

"Unless we want a huge gap between children," he kissed her deeply, pulled back to look down into her eyes, "we might want to get on with it."

She felt a surge of desire.

"Pregnancy?" she said breathlessly. "Or getting married?"

He pulled back just enough to watch her for a reaction. "Both."

He was still afraid, she realized. Maybe they both would be for a long time. But the idea of making love with the intention of creating a baby, of carrying his child, of seeing him holding his infant son or daughter, filled her with a rush of desire and joy all swirled together.

"Yes. I love you," she said simply.

Growling something under his breath, he dragged her on top of him and kissed her with ravenous hunger. "I swear," he said, before or after he'd buried himself in her, "someday we'll take our time."

But not today.

EPILOGUE

FEELING IT WAS HIS DUTY and obligation, Daniel made some effort to get to know Sam Carson. Part of him rebelled; Adam was his brother, not this stranger. The only brother he wanted.

But facts were facts. They shared a father, they shared blood.

Losing his wife seemed to have chastened Sam some.

"Isabelle told me," he said, that first time Daniel phoned. After a minute, he added, "I suppose there's no chance this blood test is wrong."

Since his voice held resignation rather than real doubt or rage, Daniel was amused. "Men are convicted of murder based on those same blood tests. Police departments all over the country would be surprised to find out DNA testing is unreliable."

"Then I suppose you are my brother," Sam said grudgingly. "I keep thinking there can't be any more surprises, and then there are."

Daniel understood that thinking. "My guess is, we're out of surprises. Unless..." He stopped himself.

But Sam read his mind. "Dad had yet another woman on the side?"

Made sense the thought had occurred to him of all people, given that Sam was known, during the course of his marriage, to have had a number of women on the side himself.

But he went on, as if he were shaking his head even as he spoke, "I don't think so. Years ago, he gave me hell…" He stopped himself, likely remembering that Daniel might not be privy to all the family dirty linen. "He was strait-laced in most ways. And he and Mom… No. I wouldn't believe it."

"And yet."

"And yet," he agreed, with a sigh.

Sam didn't say, *Welcome to the family,* but he didn't outright reject Daniel the way he had Adam, either. And Daniel kept remembering Billy Fraser's war medal Sam had paid quite a bit of money to buy from Adam, then laid in Adam's coffin. He must have softened, started thinking about family. What other explanation was there for him giving the medal back, letting Adam take it in death?

Sam called Daniel not two weeks after that first con-versation and suggested lunch at his club. Daniel smiled and agreed.

They met the following day, shook hands, eyed each other warily and made small talk after glancing at menus and placing their orders. Finally Daniel said, "I like Belle. She has amazing confidence for her age."

A fleeting emotion crossed Sam's face. Sadness, maybe? "That may be more due to her mother than me. Isabelle and I have always butted heads."

Daniel raised his brows as though he was unaware of their troubles, and let Sam talk about his pride and his regrets. Good to hear he had some.

"Belle doesn't want to hear anything I have to say," he concluded. "But Emily keeps me updated."

"Oh? Didn't Belle say you were separated?"

"She doesn't know everything she thinks she does," he blustered. "Her mother and I have had a few problems, that's all." After a long pause, face flushed, he said, "We're talking."

"I've met Emily," Daniel said noncommittally. "She's a lovely woman who was very kind to Adam."

"She's my wife, and she'll be staying my wife." He glared at Daniel, as if he'd challenged Sam's sense of himself.

In all fairness, Daniel reflected, he had. Unwittingly, but the discovery that Adam and Daniel existed at all and that his adopted sister, Jenny, was really his half sister had indeed jarred Sam Carson's world from its axis. Maybe, in the end, that would be healthy for him, since he'd already been well on the path to alienating his wife and only child. But it was too soon to tell whether he'd be able to reconcile himself to these assaults on his status as the only legitimate Carson heir.

Daniel still didn't like Sam. Suspected he never would. But if anyone could understand this older brother's struggle, he could. In their own ways, they had both felt the same shaky sense of insecurity at their places in their families. Maybe it had come out in different ways, but they had this in common, as well as blood.

Daniel reached in his pocket and pulled out a jewelry box. "I have something that belongs to you," he said, sliding it across the table.

"THANKS FOR COMING." Daniel shook hands with Matt Malone, then held out his arms when Belle flung herself at him for a hug. Beside him, receiving guests, Rebecca was smiling and talking to Jenny and her husband, Luke.

They'd decided to keep their wedding small, family and closest friends only, and to hold the reception at his house. Daniel was still dazed from the wedding.

Side by side, Malcolm and Kaitlin had come down the aisle first. Kaitlin was less solemn than she'd been at her father's wedding, more pleased with herself. She found familiar faces in the pews and flashed smiles. Malcolm wore a suit and tie, his hair slicked flat. He sneaked glances at his cousin, the experienced flower girl, although where she scattered petals evenly he tended to release them in gobs. Reaching Daniel's side, he said in a piercing whisper, "I did that real good, didn't I, Dad?"

Amusement stirred the audience.

But except for placing a hand on his shoulder and squeezing, Dad ignored him. He couldn't look away from Rebecca as she walked down the aisle in a cream-colored suit sewn with tiny pearls. She smiled at him the entire way, her eyes never leaving his. When she stopped in front of the minister and turned to Daniel, he saw the gold flecks dancing in those eyes.

Once, he'd thought he could look into her eyes forever. He couldn't even remember why the idea had scared him.

"I do" hadn't been hard to say at all. And the words *"I declare you husband and wife"* hadn't scared him.

No, facing his fears had freed him of them. He only hoped Sam was as lucky.

Almost everyone was here at the house now, he thought.

"Mom and Dad were in the back at the church, weren't they?" Belle asked. "Did they beat me here?"

He shook his head. "Haven't seen them yet."

He and Rebecca began circulating, accepting more hugs and congratulations. How the hell had he gone from having two—count 'em, *two*—close relatives to having enough to pack his house? But, except for Sam and Emily, they were all here.

Jenny and Luke, warm and accepting beyond Daniel's understanding.

A noticeably pregnant Sue with her husband, Rick, who didn't seem to want to take his gaze and hands off her, as if she were a miracle he still couldn't believe. She had no other babies right now, Daniel was told; she thought for once in her life she'd concentrate on only two. They had left Rick's niece and now Sue's adoptive daughter, Carrie, with her grandmother, figuring a wedding wasn't the occasion for a one-year-old.

Joe, Kaitlin and Pip, whose gait was beginning to resemble a waddle and who hastily found the sofa and sank onto it with noticeable relief. Daniel was amused by Joe's pride. He stood behind the sofa, his hand on her shoulder. While Daniel was watching, she lifted a slender hand and laid it over her husband's much larger one.

Belle, springy gold curls escaping her attempts to confine them, looked only slightly worried about her missing parents. Matt Malone, the CEO of Diamonte Pizza and her fiancé, was sticking as close to Belle as Rick did to his wife.

His wasn't the only family here. Rebecca, after much waffling, had invited both of her parents and their current, respective spouses, as well as her sister. Astonishingly, all of them had showed and were behaving very well. Lea looked less frail than Daniel remembered her, and he saw that she was currently talking to her mother with obvious restraint, but talking.

Daniel squeezed Rebecca's arm and nodded their way.

She raised her brows and murmured, "You know, we may yet have a knock-down, drag-out scene today."

"Over my dead body."

Out of the corner of his eye, Daniel saw Malcolm march up to Kaitlin and say, "You want to come see my bedroom? I can show you the balcony, too. Except that's not my room, and I can't open the window. Dad says I have to be with him to go out on it."

"Um, sure."

Her dad nodded, and the two kids headed upstairs. They were too far apart in age to have much in common, but Kaitlin was mature for her age. She wouldn't mind playing a game or two with Mal.

Daniel caught sight of Naomi Tuttle, who of course had been maid of honor, flirting with Eric Stannard, the contractor in charge of the Cabrillo Heights subdivision. They'd met a couple of times already.

"Are they dating?" he asked his wife in a low voice.

She flashed a grin at him. "Yep. Didn't I tell you what she said Saturday morning?"

Daniel groaned. "I don't think I want to know. Not if it has to do with his sexual prowess."

Rebecca made that tiny, choked sound that told him she was suppressing a laugh. "Oh, well, then…"

He had to kiss her, a brush of the lips that ended up being more and resulted in a round of applause from their nearby family members. Rebecca was blushing when they surfaced, and he couldn't swear he wasn't, too.

The sound of the doorbell ringing didn't come as any surprise. Rebecca beside him, he opened the door to find Sam and Emily Carson on the doorstep. Her hand was tucked in his arm, and she looked beautiful in a blue suit.

Touching the pendant at her throat, she said, "I feel overdressed. But Sam said…"

Daniel kissed her cheek. "I asked him to tell you to wear it. It seemed…fitting today."

Her husband was congratulating Rebecca.

Emily gazed gravely at Daniel. "Giving it to him was an extraordinary gesture, Daniel. I thank you from the bottom of my heart." She tried for a smile. "Not for myself…"

"I understand." He gripped her hand and squeezed, glancing over his shoulder to see that Sam was occupied greeting his daughter and son-in-law. "Because he needed it, and none of the rest of us did."

"Yes. I think…it made a difference."

Belle had said that Sam was taking classes in anger management at Emily's insistence.

"You know," Belle had said bemusedly when telling Daniel about it, "if Santa squeezes his bulk and his bag of goodies down my skinny little chimney this year and twinkles at me, I won't be more than slightly surprised. I now believe anything can happen."

Laughter seemed to come more easily to Daniel these days. And why not, he thought now, turning his head to enjoy the sight of his wife exchanging pleasantries with his family. The reminder of the Christmas season past, and the ones to come, gave him a mellow feeling. A tree, sparkling with lights, would fit nicely in front of the bay window. He liked the idea of Malcolm excitedly bouncing on the bed Christmas morning to awaken his parents.

Family, he thought, made a difference.

Jenny knew Daniel had given the necklace to Sam. Despite what she'd told Daniel the day she foisted it on him, she'd always thought that was the right solution. She moved swiftly to hug Emily when she saw her, and even to greet her brother, who hadn't always been decent to her. But, changed or not, he was being genial today.

Neither Belle nor Sue had known the ultimate fate of the Carson diamond. Neither looked put out.

He'd made the right decision, Daniel thought, watching Sam escort his gracious wife the length of the narrow living room. Here were all the Carsons, together for the first time, and the extraordinary diamond that was the heart of the family was where it belonged. Sam cared; Sam would keep a flame burning that the others might forget to fan. And Sam, if Daniel was any judge, was at peace now.

As was Daniel.

"We've done our part," he said in Rebecca's ear. "Can we leave now?"

His wife just laughed at him. "Not a chance. We have family and friends to entertain first." She tucked her hand into his. "Shall we?"

"We can do that," he agreed, and looked at the mantel, where the portrait photograph of his mother was displayed in an inlaid oval frame. A beautiful young woman, she smiled gloriously at the camera, certain life would be magical. Regret that her life had instead been hard and that grief had ultimately tamped out her joy momentarily shadowed the day for Daniel, but then he saw that Jenny was looking toward the photograph, too, her face pensive.

We're all together, Mom. All but Adam, and even he had a chance to meet his sister before he died. We're all one family, the way you would have wanted it.

The thanksgiving he cast silently was to Sarah Carson, a woman whose generosity had given them all this chance.

Perhaps, Daniel thought, Robert had made the only choice he could, given the mistakes that had come before.

One more look at his mother's face, one more at his sister's, and Daniel smiled down at his wife. "Did I mention that I love you?"

Her smile was soft and beautiful. "It so happens you did."

* * * * *

* * *

'THIS EVENING I'm flying to New York for two weeks,'
Jasim imparted with a casualness that made her heart sink
like a stone. 'That's why I had you brought here. I own this
apartment and you'll be comfortable here while I'm abroad.'

'I can afford my own accommodation although I may not
need it for long. I'll have another job by the time you
get back—'

Jasim released a slightly harsh laugh. 'There's no need for
you to look for another position. How would I ever see you?
Don't you understand what I'm offering you?'

Elinor stood very still. 'No, I must be incredibly thick
because I haven't quite worked out yet what you're offering
me....'

His charismatic smile slashed his lean dark visage.
'Naturally, I want to take care of you....'

'No, thanks.' Elinor forced a smile and mentally willed him not to demean her with some sordid proposition. 'The only man who will ever take *care* of me with my agreement will be my husband. I'm willing to wait for you to come back but I'm not willing to be kept by you. I'm a very independent woman and what I give, I give freely.'

Jasim frowned. 'You make it all sound so serious.'

'What happened between us last night left pure chaos in its wake. Right now, I don't know whether I'm on my head or my heels. I'll stay for a while because I have nowhere else to go in the short term. So maybe it's good that you'll be away for a while.'

Jasim pulled out his wallet to extract a card. 'My private number,' he told her, presenting her with it as though it was a precious gift, which indeed it was. Many women would have done just about anything to gain access to that direct hotline to him, but his staff guarded his privacy with scrupulous care.

Before he could close the wallet, his blood ran cold in his veins. How could he have made such a serious oversight? What if he had got her pregnant? He knew that an unplanned pregnancy would engulf his life like an avalanche, crush his freedom and suffocate him. He barely stilled a shudder at the threat of such an outcome and thought how ironic it was that what his older brother had longed and prayed for to secure the line to the throne should strike Jasim as an absolute disaster....

* * *

What will proud Prince Jasim do if Elinor is expecting his royal baby? Perhaps an arranged marriage is the only solution! But will Elinor agree? Find out in DESERT PRINCE, BRIDE OF INNOCENCE by Lynne Graham [#2884], available from Harlequin Presents® in January 2010.

HPEX0110B

HARLEQUIN *Presents*

Bestselling Harlequin Presents author

Lynne Graham

brings you an exciting new miniseries:

PREGNANT BRIDES

Inexperienced and expecting, they're forced to marry

Collect them all:

DESERT PRINCE, BRIDE OF INNOCENCE

January 2010

RUTHLESS MAGNATE, CONVENIENT WIFE

February 2010

GREEK TYCOON, INEXPERIENCED MISTRESS

March 2010

www.eHarlequin.com

REQUEST YOUR FREE BOOKS!

2 FREE NOVELS PLUS 2 FREE GIFTS!

HARLEQUIN®

Super Romance®

Exciting, emotional, unexpected!

YES! Please send me 2 FREE Harlequin® Superromance® novels and my 2 FREE gifts (gifts are worth about $10). After receiving them, if I don't wish to receive any more books, I can return the shipping statement marked "cancel." If I don't cancel, I will receive 6 brand-new novels every month and be billed just $4.69 per book in the U.S. or $5.24 per book in Canada. That's a savings of close to 15% off the cover price! It's quite a bargain! Shipping and handling is just 50¢ per book*. I understand that accepting the 2 free books and gifts places me under no obligation to buy anything. I can always return a shipment and cancel at any time. Even if I never buy another book from Harlequin, the two free books and gifts are mine to keep forever.

135 HDN EYLG   336 HDN EYLS

Name	(PLEASE PRINT)	
Address		Apt. #
City	State/Prov.	Zip/Postal Code

Signature (if under 18, a parent or guardian must sign)

Mail to the **Harlequin Reader Service:**
IN U.S.A.: P.O. Box 1867, Buffalo, NY 14240-1867
IN CANADA: P.O. Box 609, Fort Erie, Ontario L2A 5X3

Not valid to current subscribers of Harlequin Superromance books.

**Are you a current subscriber of Harlequin Superromance books
and want to receive the larger-print edition?
Call 1-800-873-8635 today!**

* Terms and prices subject to change without notice. Prices do not include applicable taxes. Sales tax applicable in N.Y. Canadian residents will be charged applicable provincial taxes and GST. Offer not valid in Quebec. This offer is limited to one order per household. All orders subject to approval. Credit or debit balances in a customer's account(s) may be offset by any other outstanding balance owed by or to the customer. Please allow 4 to 6 weeks for delivery. Offer available while quantities last.

Your Privacy: Harlequin is committed to protecting your privacy. Our Privacy Policy is available online at www.eHarlequin.com or upon request from the Reader Service. From time to time we make our lists of customers available to reputable third parties who may have a product or service of interest to you. If you would prefer we not share your name and address, please check here. ☐

HSR09R

New Year, New Man!

*For the perfect New Year's punch,
blend the following:*

- *One woman determined to find her inner vixen*
- *A notorious—and notoriously hot!—playboy*
- *A provocative New Year's Eve bash*
- *An impulsive kiss that leads to a night of
  explosive passion!*

When the clock hits midnight Claire Daniels
kisses the guy standing closest to her, but
the kiss doesn't end after the bells stop ringing....

Look for

Moonstruck

by *USA TODAY* bestselling author

JULIE KENNER

Available January

---

red-hot reads

www.eHarlequin.com

HB79518

HARLEQUIN® Super Romance®

COMING NEXT MONTH

Available January 12, 2010

#1608 AN UNLIKELY SETUP • Margaret Watson
Going Back
Maddie swore she'd never return to Otter's Tail...except she *has* to, to sell the pub bequeathed her, and pay off her debt. Over his dead body, Quinn Murphy tells her. Sigh. If only the sexy ex-cop *would* roll over and play dead.

#1609 HER SURPRISE HERO • Abby Gaines
Those Merritt Girls
They say the cure for a nervous breakdown is a dose of small-town justice. But peaceful quiet is not what temp judge Cynthia Merritt gets when the townspeople of Stonewall Hollow—led by single-dad rancher Ethan Granger—overrule her!

#1610 SKYLAR'S OUTLAW • Linda Warren
The Belles of Texas
Skylar Belle doesn't want Cooper Yates around her daughter. She knows about her ranch foreman's prison record—and treats him like the outlaw he is. Yet when Skylar's child is in danger, she discovers Cooper is the only man she can trust.

#1611 PERFECT PARTNERS? • C.J. Carmichael
The Fox & Fisher Detective Agency
Disillusioned with police work, Lindsay Fox left the NYPD to start her own detective agency. Now business is so good, she needs to hire another investigator. Unfortunately, the only qualified applicant is the one man she can't work with— her ex-partner, Nathan Fisher.

#1612 THE FATHER FOR HER SON • Cindi Myers
Suddenly a Parent
Last time Marlee Britton saw Troy Denton, they were planning their wedding. Then he vanished, leaving her abandoned and pregnant. Now he's returned...and he wants to see his son. Letting Troy back in her life might be the hardest thing she's done.

#1613 FALLING FOR THE TEACHER • Tracy Kelleher
When was Ben Brown last in a classroom? Now his son has enrolled them in a course, so he's giving it his all, encouraged by their instructor, Katarina Zemanova. Love and trust don't come easily, but the lessons yield top marks, especially when they include falling for her!

HSRCNMBPA1209